BECOME

SKYE MALONE

PRONUNCIATION GUIDE

Aveluria (av-eh-LUR-ee-uh)

Coriana (cor-ee-AHN-uh)

Dehaian (deh-HYE-an)

Driecara (dree-eh-CAR-uh)

Egan (EE-gan)

Greliaran (greh-lee-AR-an)

Ina (EE-na)

Inasaria (ee-na-SAH-ree-uh)

Jirral (jur-AHL)

Kreyus (KRAY-us)

Lisalia (lis-ALL-ee-uh)

Lycera (ly-SER-uh)

Neiphiandine (ney-fee-AN-deen)

Niall (nee-AHL)

Nialloran (nee-ah-LOR-en)

Nyciena (ny-SEE-en-uh)

Ociras (oh-SHE-rahs)

Prijoran (prih-JOR-an)

Renekialen (ren-eh-kee-AHL-en)

Sieranchine (see-EHR-an-cheen)

Sylphaen (sil-FAY-en)

Teariad (tee-AR-ee-ad)

Tiberion (ty-BEE-ree-un)

Torvias (TOR-vee-ahs)

Venika (ven-EE-kuh)

Yvaria (ih-VAR-ee-uh)

Zekerian (zeh-KEHR-ee-en)

1

CHLOE

The crystalline vial glistened in my hand, the black liquid within viscous and utterly opaque. I shivered just to be holding the slim glass, and at what could change about me once I drank the magical concoction inside.

"Chloe?"

I glanced to Baylie. Standing next to me in the shopping mall parking lot, she had a worried expression on her face while she eyed the vial.

"Are you going to take it?" she asked.

I swallowed down the tightness in my throat. I knew I should. The only way to stop the thing my ancestors had created – the Beast which had attacked us only a few hours before – was to become either one half of my heritage or the other, even if I wouldn't have a choice of which I'd be.

The thought of becoming a landwalker terrified me. After living as a dehaian for even this short time, spending the rest of my life unable to come anywhere near the ocean felt like a prison sentence.

Though that wasn't the only thing.

My gaze twitched toward Noah. On the other side of Baylie's car, he watched the parking lot and the others with us equally. It wasn't Ellie who bothered him; still sniffling occasionally, the poor girl seemed like she scarcely noticed anything around her at all. Hovering near her with concern on his face, Aaron was likewise okay – maybe. I wasn't sure what to feel about him. But his uncle, the police chief, on the other hand…

I grimaced. Chief Reynolds wouldn't do anything. He had yet to even leave his brown sedan. He looked like something had broken inside him, and the entire time we'd been here, he'd never glanced our way.

But meanwhile, Noah could hear us. A car-length of distance was nothing to a greliaran, no matter how quietly Baylie had spoken, and even as he tugged his buzzing phone from his pocket, I saw his gaze flick toward us.

I didn't know how to sort out what I felt for him and Zeke. I wanted to have the chance, though, and if this went wrong – *my* version of wrong – I probably never would. Greliarans didn't need to be close to the ocean in the same way as dehaians, but they also didn't like to be far from it for very long. Proximity to the water felt better, from what Noah had said, and with the strange hybridization of dehaian magic inside them, that made sense.

And if I was a landwalker…

I drew a steadying breath. I had to stop that creature, though. That hideous, sentient storm monster that had come close to killing us earlier today. I was endangering countless people by doing otherwise.

My fingers trembled when I pulled the cork from the vial.

"Joseph said I'd be out for a while," I told Baylie, working to hide my nervousness. "While this… does its thing."

She didn't respond for a moment, her eyes on the vial and the black gunk inside. "And if he screwed up?" she asked in a tiny voice.

"Baylie." It was difficult to keep the begging from my tone. I didn't need that worry on top of everything else right now.

"I-I know. I'm sorry. I just…" She exhaled sharply, forcing the fear from her expression. "Back of the car, then. You lie down there, and we'll just stay put till you wake up and we're, you know, certain which direction we need to drive."

I nodded. "Yeah."

Trying to keep from shaking, I lifted the vial to my lips.

"Chloe."

I glanced back at the sound of Noah's voice. He was covering his phone with his hand.

"Diane wants to talk to you."

My brow furrowed. His stepmom was calling for me?

He shrugged, reading my expression.

I returned the cork to its place and then handed the vial to Baylie. Circling the car to Noah's side, I took the cell from him.

"Hello?"

"Chloe, honey," Diane replied. "It's good to hear your voice. Listen, there's a girl here. She says she needs to speak with you. She won't tell us why, but she says it's an emergency."

Alarm moved through me. "Um, okay…"

I heard rustling on the other end of the line.

"Chloe? Are you—" More rustling. "Dammit, these phone things are awkward."

My heart began to pound. "Ina? What are you doing—"

"Zeke told me where you were staying a couple weeks back. Seemed a good place to start. Look, I—" The sound became muffled and I heard her say, "I'll just be a sec, alright?"

A heartbeat passed. I wanted to yell at her to just start talking.

"Okay," she continued while a door closed somewhere in the background. "Zeke's why I'm here. Things are… they're bad right now. You need to stay away from the ocean. Ren's got soldiers everywhere and…" She trailed off and then muttered something angry. It didn't sound like English. "Point is, if they catch you, they're planning to take you to the capital so Ren can put you on trial and then most likely execute you for Dad's death."

Ice shot through me. "*What?*" I shook my head, the words too ridiculous and insane to process. "Ina, where's Zeke?"

She hesitated. "He's been arrested. Granddad too. Ren's people found us. Niall was with them. I got away but—" She growled another incomprehensible curse. "Doesn't matter. Just stay away from the ocean. Get back inland. I'll figure this out, but Zeke… he'd want to know you're not anywhere they can find you. So just go. I can—"

"No!" I protested.

"Chloe, you have to."

I ran a hand through my hair, ignoring her. I couldn't leave Zeke. I wouldn't. Niall was there. That meant other Sylphaen probably were too. They'd *killed* people the last time they'd tried to get their hands on me, both here and in Nyciena. But I couldn't go to help Zeke either. Joseph had thought I could hide what I was and avoid the Beast's notice – as long as the thing wasn't close, anyway – but that didn't change the other dangers. Capture by the Sylphaen. Arrest by Ren.

Execution by either of them…

I swallowed hard. "Okay, um, listen. Are there any Sylphaen near the house? Anyone you've seen watching the place or who might know you're there?"

"What?"

"Sylphaen. Near the house."

She paused. "Yes. I mean, sort of. There were a few guys, but I got around them. I don't think they know I'm here."

I could hear the worry in her voice and I trembled. It made sense that they'd watch the house if they were still looking for me. I just hoped she was right that they'd missed her.

And that they'd miss me too.

"Okay," I pressed on. "Then just keep away from the windows so they don't see you and stay put, alright? I'm coming to you."

"Chloe, I need to get back to—"

"Just stay there!" I cried.

I exhaled, my heart racing. I could almost feel her shock through the phone. I doubted anyone *ever* shouted at the princess of Yvaria.

"Please, Ina," I finished more quietly. "I… I want to help. I'll be there soon."

She paused. "Alright."

"Thank you."

I hung up. My hand shaking, I lowered the phone.

"Chloe…"

I glanced to Noah, and from the tension on his face, I could tell he'd overheard everything on the other end of the phone call.

"What happened?" Baylie asked.

"They want to *execute* you?" Noah pressed.

"Who wants to do *what*?" Baylie demanded.

"Are these people more of that cult?" Noah continued.

I hesitated. I hadn't told them about Zeke. About how he was royalty back where he came from. It'd just seemed like an awkward conversation.

And now it was worse.

"They're not Sylphaen," I answered tightly. "Not… not all of them, anyway."

Noah exhaled, looking incredulous. "Okay, well, you have to run. This time, *please*. You *have* to run."

I didn't respond. I couldn't do that. I knew he was probably right. I had no way of fighting them and I needed to hide from the Beast regardless. But I couldn't. I just *couldn't.* Even if I didn't stand a chance and I didn't have a thing on Earth to negotiate with, I—

My gaze dropped to the vial in Baylie's hand. A shiver ran through me.

I glanced back up at Noah.

His brow drew down warily. "What?"

I wasn't sure what to say. Noah wouldn't agree, and possibly with good reason. This was madness.

But it was the closest thing I had to a plan.

And I wasn't going to leave Zeke to his brothers and the Sylphaen.

"Take me back to your dad's house," I said. "Please. I'll tell you when we get there."

ZEKE

Darkness vanished into a bright glare when the hood was ripped from my head.

The throne room presented itself in a rush, filled with alcoves and ornaments and dehaians for a hundred yards around. I was on the marble floor, kneeled there after the guards had shoved me down. My hands were still bound with shackles.

And Ren was seated on the throne ahead of me. An audience of hundreds surrounded us, held back by stanchions and soldiers alike. My gaze slid to them, catching on faces I recognized. The Deiliora sisters and their father. Count Velior and his mother. Friends of mine from around the castle as well, though none of them would meet my eyes.

But I got the message. Ren's, anyway. He'd made me wait for hours, blindfolded and chained to other dehaians while hovering goodness knew where, but it'd been for this. He wanted the spectacle. For the court to see me kneeled before him. He wanted to make sure no one would support me or help me, because my status in the king's eyes was more than clear.

Criminal. Traitor.

Maybe worse.

I looked up at him. With the enormous royal seal of Yvaria on the wall behind him, he sat high above all the other occupants of the room on the golden throne our father had used. A dozen guards floated in the water below him, wearing more armor and weapons than I'd ever seen anyone have around Dad.

But again, it was a message. Yvaria was threatened.

Too bad he didn't understand by whom.

"Your highness," Tiberion intoned, hovering next to me without ever looking my way. "I give you Prince Zekerian, lately found near the hills where we captured a contingent of Vetorian mercenaries."

"Was the girl with them?"

"No, your highness."

Ren looked down at me. "Where is she?" he asked coldly. "The girl who conspired to murder King Torvias?"

I stayed quiet, though my teeth clenched with the urge to tell him just how much of an idiot he was being. I wasn't going around with Vetorians – I'd been *avoiding* them, for pity's sake. And Chloe had no more conspired to kill our father than I had.

But I also knew it wouldn't matter. Ren wouldn't care.

His eyes narrowed at my silence. "Have you found any sign of her?" he demanded of Tiberion.

"No."

I looked back sharply at the response from behind me.

Niall swam through the aisle.

And he wasn't alone.

My blood went cold. Wisdom Kirzan drifted through the water behind Niall, his silver hair and scales shimmering in the brilliant light. His dark eyes were lowered, but around his mouth, a hint of a smile hovered, as if he perceived a joke but was keeping it private for the time being.

But he was here. In Nyciena. In my *home*.

"Ren," I tried, unable to stop myself. "What is this guy—"

"That's 'your highness', brother," Niall cut in smoothly. "Show respect to your king. And Ambassador Kirzan is our guest. Representative of the nonaligned tribes in the Prijoran Zone. He has come seeking our assistance regarding the threat of the mercenaries."

"You *cannot* be serious," I snapped.

"Are you claiming to know more about the activities of the Vetorians than someone from their region?" Ren asked.

I stared up at him, my heart pounding. "I'm saying he's Sylphaen. He's the one who—"

A disgusted noise escaped Ren. "*Sylphaen*. A dead cult a hundred years gone. Yet you're *still* clinging to that girl's story."

"Ren, damn you, *listen* to me! This man is not—"

"Enough!" Ren snapped. "Prince Zekerian, your words condemn you and make the necessity of the court's judgment clear. Do not compound your stupidity. For aiding in the death of King Torvias and for treason against orders of the crown alone, you should already be sentenced to die."

I froze.

"However," Ren continued, "as you are also of royal blood, I am inclined to show you mercies that your conspirators will not be allowed to enjoy, in the hope that someday you will see fit to repent of the damage you have caused our family. Thus, you are forthwith to be removed to the northern border, where you will spend the rest of your days under house arrest in the custody of the guard. Should you reconsider your protests of that traitorous spy's innocence and assist us in capturing her and any allies of which you are aware, I may be inclined to reduce your sentence."

I stared while he looked to Tiberion. "Take him to his apartment," Ren ordered. "Confine him there till transport can be arranged."

"Yes, your highness," Tiberion replied, bowing.

The soldiers grabbed my arms, hauling me up from the ground. I moved to shrug them off, and then froze when Tiberion put a hand to the shock fob on his belt.

"If you would come with us?" he asked quietly, the implication clear.

Shaking with anger, I swam with them while they pulled me away. By the throne room door, other guards surrounded a row of chained dehaians, most of them still blindfolded. But at the head of the line, Jirral hovered, shackles on his forearms and a look on his face like he was just waiting for the soldiers' attention to wander.

He glanced to me when the guards brought me closer. "Stay ready, boy. I'll get us out of this."

One of the guards tapped the shock fob at his belt. Jirral flinched, but didn't make a sound. He watched while the guards tugged me past, his expression unchanged.

And I couldn't imagine what he planned to do.

The guards continued onward, beyond a line of dehaians I could only assume were Vetorians. The marks on their fins still showed evidence of where blades had been clipped, and there wasn't a one of them that didn't have scars of some kind. Most had blindfolds over their heads, while others twisted their wrists inside shackles that stood no chance of breaking.

And then we were out in the hall again. Servants stared while we passed, something about their posture making them seem torn on whether or not to bow. Guards were everywhere, keeping watch by each hallway and alcove, and they only became more numerous the higher in the palace we swam. Swords and stone guns hung from the soldiers' belts, while knives crossed their chests on straps branded with the Yvarian crest.

I grimaced. I remembered this. The days after Miri had been taken looked just the same.

Tiberion paused when we finally reached my apartment. "I want half of you surrounding the outside and half of you in there," he ordered the guards. "And keep the chains on him. I don't want a repeat of last time."

He gave me a dark look and then swam off, leaving the guards to escort me into the room.

It was hard not to try to break their hold again, even if it would just get me shocked and not achieve much else.

Scowling, I headed through the fejeria leaves into my apartment. The soldiers moved immediately to seal the windows and door.

I sank onto the windowsill, ignoring them. I didn't know what Jirral thought he could accomplish, but it didn't matter. I'd find a way out of this.

Before my brother locked me up for the rest of my life.

Anger rose at the thought, even while my stomach twisted with nausea. Exile. I'd known it was a possibility. I'd known what helping Chloe could mean. I was lucky, all things considered, that he hadn't stripped me of my titles and sent me straight to prison – a former prince with the criminals my father had put there; oh yeah, that would've gone well – or else just ordered me killed on the spot.

But this…

Spending the *rest* of my *life* under house arrest on the northern border…

And Chloe wouldn't even get that. Not with that idiot already hanging a death sentence over her head.

I glanced to the guards, my heart pounding. It wouldn't happen. I didn't care what I had to do, I wasn't going into exile, I wasn't going to let him hurt her, and I *damn* well wasn't going to let that bastard Kirzan have the run of my home in the meantime.

I'd fix this… somehow.

CHLOE

A breath left me as Baylie pulled her car to a stop in the driveway of the Delaneys' white, mission-style mansion on the Santa Lucina coast. It'd only been a few days, really, since last I'd seen this place.

It felt like a lifetime.

Midnight was long since gone and, beyond the private driveway, every other house on the street was dark. Several lights still shone in the windows of the Delaneys' mansion, however; testament to the fact Diane and Peter were probably still awake despite the late hour. I hoped Ina was around too. My plan wouldn't work nearly as well if she'd grown impatient and taken off.

We pushed open the doors and got out of the car while, behind us, Chief Reynolds' brown sedan came to a stop. I'd helped him by taking away the pain of the ocean before we left the mall parking lot, but I still wished he wasn't here. I could tell I wasn't the only one who felt that way either. From the corner of his eye, Noah watched the chief as if trying to figure out how to make the man stay as far from his home as possible while simultaneously not letting the guy out of his sight.

I didn't blame him. Being repeatedly shot by someone would do that to a person.

We climbed the steps to the porch. The door opened before we reached it.

"Hey," Peter said, his tone tight and only barely welcoming.

He moved aside to let us come in. Beyond him, Diane waited by the archway to the front room, and relief showed on her face when she saw us. She hurried forward as we walked inside, putting her arms around Noah and Baylie in turn, while behind us, Peter locked the door.

"You doing okay, honey?" Diane asked me.

I nodded, even though it was only marginally true. I didn't have Sylphaen drugs in my system anymore. I knew I wouldn't die from changing into a dehaian like I'd feared last time I'd seen her.

But as for everything else...

"Thank you for staying up to let us in," I tried.

"Of course," Diane replied.

Peter didn't respond.

My brow drew down. They looked edgy and drained, like this wasn't the first time recently that they'd been up this late.

"Well," Diane continued, glancing back to the house with a tense expression. "Your friend is—"

She cut off as Ina strode around the corner from the kitchen. A dress of blue lace covered the girl, the flowing fabric setting off her brilliant sapphire eyes and revealing more of her scale bikini than it concealed. After only the barest pretense of a smile to the others, she locked her gaze on me, and I could see the anger in her eyes.

Leaving Noah to introduce Aaron, Ellie, and the chief, I headed down the hall toward her.

"It's been *hours*," she hissed.

"I'm sorry. We drove here as fast as we could."

She grimaced. "What did you want me to wait for?"

"I—"

I paused when Baylie came up behind me, Noah on her heels. By the door, Peter was speaking with Chief Reynolds and the others, while Diane cast glances toward us every few seconds.

Noah tossed a dark look to the chief. "Come on," he said to us, nodding toward the rest of the house.

We followed him to the kitchen. A sunroom made up half the space, while curtains I'd never noticed before were pulled over its windows to block the view of the sea. The strip lights above the counters and cupboards were dimmed, while to my left, the sunken living room was dark and curtained as well. On the kitchen island, I could see a trio of mugs – evidence, perhaps, that Diane and Peter had been trying to keep Ina occupied.

I doubted they'd had much luck. When we reached the kitchen, the girl could barely stand still. With her gaze twitching to the curtains, Ina seemed to be fighting the urge to pace, or else run out the door that moment and head back home.

"So?" she demanded.

I tried not to scowl at her tone. She wasn't the only one worried about Zeke.

"Are there any of those rock communication things near here?" I asked her. "Those boulders you guys use to call home?"

She shrugged. "Sure."

"Good. I want you to contact Niall."

Ina stared at me.

I drew the vial from my pocket. "You see this stuff? It's going to change me. Make me either totally like you and Zeke, or a landwalker. The Sylphaen won't want that. They want to kill me because they think that'll let them become like I am now. But if that stands a chance of going away…"

I left the rest of the statement unsaid.

"They let Zeke and Jirral go," I continued. "Or I take this. They lose any chance of getting their hands on what I am."

Ina's gaze slid to the vial. "Looks… gross," she managed.

I tucked the thing back into my pocket, not wanting to think about it.

"And if these guys listen?" Noah asked quietly. "What's in it for them? You let them take you?"

I shivered. "Then we run."

"Chloe…" Baylie tried. "This isn't—"

"You have a better option?" I glanced between her and Noah, my heart pounding. Neither of them spoke, and Noah's jaw muscles jumped while he looked away.

"Just go," I told Ina. "Say we'll meet them at Mariposa Beach. It's public enough that they'll have a harder time trying anything."

Ina hesitated. "Ren's the one holding them, though. I mean…"

She took a breath, tinges of worry and fear seeping past the confidence she was working to portray. And despite how every second felt like it was slipping through my fingers, I couldn't help but pity her.

Her family was tearing itself apart.

Ina seemed to steady herself. "Ren won't hurt them. I know he won't. But Niall won't be able to reach Zeke or Granddad past all of Ren's—"

"They got to me."

The resolve in her eyes flickered. She looked away.

"Niall said Ren was easy to manipulate," I continued, trying to be gentle despite the way the words made me shiver. "He told us that's why they let him live. He'll find a way around Ren's guards. He even controls some of them." I drew a breath. "Just go tell him what I said, Ina. Please."

She gave a small nod. "The relay is a ways from here. I'll be back in an hour or so."

"Thank you."

Ina didn't respond, watching me. Something pained touched her eyes.

"He'd tell you this wasn't your fault, you know," she said.

My brow furrowed.

Her expression tightened, as though she was deciding whether to say more, and then she just turned and snagged her bag from a chair. Quickly, she headed for the back door, leaving the implication hanging in the air.

Zeke would say that.

But the rest of them…

A shaky breath left me when the door closed.

"Who was that?"

I glanced back to see Baylie watching me. I fought to keep from grimacing. She hadn't been there when Ina and Jirral had showed up at Noah's cousin's place.

Though that wouldn't have made telling her the other details feel any less ridiculous.

"Ina," I said. "Zeke's twin sister."

Baylie paused. "And this Ren guy?"

I drew another breath. "His brother. The oldest one. He's, um… he's sort of the king now, back where they come from."

Her eyebrows climbed.

"Niall's their brother too," I continued. "The second oldest. He joined the Sylphaen though. The cult that wants me dead. He helped them murder his dad."

Silence greeted the words.

"So then, Zeke's…" Noah trailed off, but I could hear the rest of the sentence. Royalty. A prince.

"Yeah."

Noah paused, and then a tiny scoff escaped him. He looked away, his jaw working while his brow rose and fell.

I turned to the windows and the thick curtains blocking the view of the sea. I wanted to go over there, to check about storms on the horizon or see if there was any sign of the Beast at all. It was dangerous for me to be so close to the coast. There was no telling what could happen if that thing picked up on the fact I was here.

Taking a slow breath, I tried to concentrate on restraining the magic coming from me. I didn't know if it helped; I still felt jittery after the blast we'd taken while escaping from the Beast last time, and I had no idea how to control the signal Zeke and the other dehaians said they could feel coming off me in the water besides. But it was the best I could do. Leaving wasn't an option. Not for a while, anyway. Not till we heard back from Niall, or until Zeke and Jirral were safe.

Which, as strategies went, just had to work. Ina contacting Niall, all of us fooling the Sylphaen, everything. It just *had* to work.

I didn't have any other plans to fall back on.

Footsteps sounded behind us. I glanced over my shoulder to see Diane come into the room. At the sight of just the three of us, her brow drew down.

"Ina left," I explained.

Diane gave a nod. "Okay," she allowed, "well, I've got the others set. Ellie's taking the trundle in the room with you girls, and Mr. Reynolds and his nephew have the other guest room. Is there anything you kids need before you get to bed too?"

I hesitated, not sure what to say. I wasn't going to sleep. Not with Ina returning in only an hour or so.

"We're good, thanks," Noah answered.

Diane smiled, though from her expression, I could tell she didn't quite believe him. "Alright, then. Goodnight."

She returned to the hallway. A moment later, I heard her climbing the stairs.

"You want to get some sleep?" Baylie asked me. "Before she comes back, I mean?"

I shook my head. "No, it's fine. I'll just—"

"You've been up for days, Chloe," Noah interrupted quietly.

I hesitated, hearing the concern in his voice. I didn't look his way.

"I'll keep an eye out," he continued. "Let you know when she gets here."

"Come on," Baylie urged. "Please."

I grimaced. I wouldn't be able to sleep. Not with everything going on.

But I also didn't feel like arguing with them.

"Okay," I relented.

Leaving Noah to find a place in the living room, we headed for the stairs.

4

ZEKE

The guards in Nyciena were incredibly well trained, and until now, that fact had never bothered me.

But it was making escaping this place difficult as hell.

I glanced to the half dozen guards hovering just inside the window and the others waiting by the door. They hadn't twitched for hours. They watched my every move.

Clearly, my escape a few weeks ago had left an impression.

And then there were the shackles. There wasn't a way to break the locks. The signal on the things only reached so far, however. If I could get past the windows and get enough distance from the soldiers, I'd probably surpass their ability to shock me.

I just needed to figure out a way to distract them for a moment.

The leaves on the door rustled. My gaze snapped toward the sound. Niall came in.

And Kirzan was right behind him.

"Leave," Niall said to the soldiers. "We're here to collect him for transport."

"But highness, Captain Tiberion—"

"Are you questioning my orders, soldier?" Niall interjected. "Or are you suggesting that I would let him escape? The *traitor* who helped my father's assassin?"

The guards glanced to each other and then swam for the door, with one of them pausing only long enough to hand Niall the fob to shock me if I tried to get away.

Leaves rustled and then stilled when they sealed the door again.

"Cute," I muttered.

Niall ignored the comment. "Where's Chloe?"

"Go to hell."

The muscles in Niall's jaw jumped. He looked to Kirzan.

A patient expression on his face – though that damn, secretive smile never seemed far away – the old man sighed. "It doesn't have to be like this," he said, speaking in Yvarian. "Just give us the girl. We can make this go away."

I looked toward the windows. The guards out there would probably be on edge, just in case I attempted to make a break for it.

But that didn't mean they could catch me. Or that they or Niall would have a chance to shock me before I got out of range.

I shifted slightly on the windowsill, getting ready to reach for the lighter patch of stone on the wall.

"That said," Kirzan continued. "We are not above using leverage."

My gaze twitched back to him.

From the satchel on his shoulder, Kirzan drew out a smaller, slimmer bag.

I froze, recognizing it.

"Ina is safe," Niall assured me. "But think about this: what would happen if we told Ren she wasn't? If we told him Chloe's allies had our sister – and that she just might die?"

I struggled to find my voice. I couldn't believe Niall was this stupid. This naïve.

This *homicidal*.

"He'd tear the ocean apart," Niall continued as if putting words to my thoughts. "He'd storm through every nation from here to the Atlantic and make what Dad did to Driecara look like a child's game. Come on, Zeke. Are you willing to risk all that?"

"You can't—"

"Give us Chloe and we won't have to."

I couldn't stop staring at him. Over and over again, it kept throwing me. This *thing* he'd somehow become.

"Niall," I tried. "You *know* what Dad did. You'd let that happen a second time? You'd let *Ina* be the cause of that?"

His jaw muscles jumped again.

"It won't come to that," Kirzan interjected smoothly, looking more to Niall than me. "Zeke will help us. Even *he* is not callous enough to risk such a horror."

I ignored him, fighting to regroup. "How do I even know you have her, Niall? You're going to tell Ren that; what if you're lying to me too? Ina could've dropped the bag and—"

"Your sister was found at a relay station not far from Santa Lucina," Kirzan interrupted. "She was attempting to call us. She wished to relay a message from that creature regarding some magical concoction that the girl claims will make her like us or a landwalker." Disgust showed on Kirzan's face briefly. "The creature thought to use it as a bargaining chip, I believe. She has threatened to take it unless we release you."

I struggled for words again. They couldn't know about that: the wizard Joseph and what Chloe had planned to get from him. Not unless their claim about having Ina was true. But Chloe also hadn't used it yet. She was trying to make a deal with the Sylphaen instead.

For me.

It was… hell, it was *insane*. What'd she think the endgame would be? She'd let them take her?

My wrists pulled at the shackles. She couldn't. I wouldn't…

I looked to the window. I had to rescue Ina. There was no telling what these psychos might do to her. But I had to stop Chloe too.

Kirzan cleared his throat, pulling my attention back to him. "Would you go make certain the others are ready?" he asked Niall. "We will leave in a few minutes."

Niall hesitated, still watching me. "Sure."

He handed Kirzan the fob and then swam from the room.

"They are so easy to control, your brothers," Kirzan mused when the leaves stilled again. His smile spread. "And you."

He set Ina's bag on a nearby table.

"As Niall said," he continued. "Your sister is safe. We are not monsters, after all, and there is every chance Ina will see the truth and convert to our cause as Niall has done. But the king… well, when he sees the blood we will put on her bag and hears the terrible tale Niall will tell, what he will do in response…"

Kirzan made a concerned noise.

I rose from the windowsill.

He held up the fob, his expression becoming cautioning. "Careful now." When I didn't move closer, he lowered the device again. "You only need to give us the creature, Zeke. That girl with whom you have so… disappointingly connected yourself. She is the only one who must die in this."

"Killing Chloe won't help you destroy that thing. You kill her, it only makes the Beast stronger."

Kirzan paused. "Who said anything about destroying it?"

I stared at him.

"Our ancestors were weak," Kirzan explained. "They surrendered to fear of the Beast too easily and thus bound our people to the sea. And those visionaries who did not agree, those with the *wisdom* to understand what we could become if only we were willing to make the necessary sacrifices… they were called fools. *Madmen.* But those visionaries were right. This girl is not simply some amalgamation of corruption that has released our ancestors' powers; she is something new. Prophecies speak of the potential to master the Beast. Of how children with our ancestors' abilities, but who were born into a world where the Beast exists and influences magic, could have a stronger connection to the creature. Even control it, perhaps. Our ancestors never had the courage to surrender their children to test this. They chose to create those foul creatures, the landwalkers, and damn us to this hell instead. And now, this abomination with her corrupted heritage and landwalker blood is all we have. But everything is not lost. Of herself and with only her own strength to draw upon, she is too weak. Yet with our purifying influence and her abilities spread among us all…

"We will be free, Zeke, as will all who believe and join us. We will be released of our ties to the water, of illness and pain. We will have power over the greatest force this world has seen: a creature without form, that can decimate cities and armies and bring the humans to their knees. And that will make us safe. Our children will be safe. They will never again know captivity and pain from the water like we have suffered these past centuries.

"And you will help us."

I shook my head. "You're crazy."

"Vision and the will to do what is necessary have often been mistaken for madness. But I assure you, you *will* help us. You already have."

Without looking away from me, he reached into his bag and drew out a small vial. My gaze flicked to it and my brow drew down. Dark liquid moved inside, glinting deep red in the light.

"Because of you," Kirzan said, "the second phase can begin at any time. Soon, we will rise as the most powerful force in the water, with the Beast at our command and the greatest nation in the ocean as our willing servant. The only difference will be whether your sister remains safe during this, and if your brother the king is spared the burden of genocide on his soul." His smile made my skin crawl. "Destiny is too powerful a force to resist, Zeke. Even as you struggle against us, you only clear the way for our cause."

I ignored the last, my eyes still on the weird, dark liquid. "What is that?"

Leaves rustled. Niall swam into the room, several guards following him. "They're ready."

Smoothly, Kirzan slid the vial back into his bag. "Excellent. After you, Zeke."

I didn't move. "What was that stuff?"

Niall glanced to Kirzan. I saw his jaw muscles jump.

My heart began to pound harder at the *strong* sense my brother knew and didn't like it. "Niall, what is it? What are they planning?"

"Enough." Kirzan looked to the guards. "Bring him. We have a sacrifice to collect."

The soldiers came at me fast. They grabbed my arms and the world disappeared back into darkness as they pulled a blindfold over my head again.

5

NOAH

I was getting used to this 'being up all night' thing, and that probably wasn't good.

Sighing, I scrubbed a hand over my eyes while I watched the morning sunlight creep over the yard, dragging long shadows from the house and trees with it. Beyond the bluffs, the ocean rippled with hints of pinkish gold from the coming light.

Ellie was already outside, sitting on the far end of the concrete patio and watching the sunrise. She'd come downstairs about a half hour ago, while the sky was still dark. With a mumbled explanation of being unable to sleep, she'd headed outside and hadn't moved since.

Aaron had followed only a few minutes later. I wondered if he'd been listening for her from the other guest room, or if he'd just had trouble sleeping as well, but now he sat a few feet from Ellie's side, casting worried glances to her when he probably thought she wasn't looking. Every few minutes, one or the other of them would speak, their voices soft enough that much of what they said barely reached my ears. The comments were short; murmurs of how the ocean was beautiful, or of how her grandfather wouldn't have understood that, or of how everything had been meant to help even if it had gone so horribly wrong.

I'd taken a seat farther from the sunroom after a while. There was little I could do to keep from overhearing them entirely, but I was still trying not to eavesdrop. I felt bad for the girl. She'd obviously loved her grandfather. It had to be hard, losing him when nearly everyone around you couldn't help but be the tiniest bit glad he was gone.

Aaron glanced to Ellie, clearly about to say something. I grimaced and headed for the counter to get some coffee started, if only to let the machine help cover their words. The cabinet yielded up a bag of the fair-trade dark roast that Dad favored so much, and in only a few moments, the noise of the coffee maker filled the room.

I sighed, leaning against the counter and returning my gaze to the yard. Ina had yet to come back, something that I knew would worry Chloe when she woke. It'd been hours since the girl left, far longer than she'd originally said. It worried me too. I hoped Ina was alright – and that this didn't mean those dehaian bastards might be on their way. I *deeply* didn't want them trying to break into my house or hurt Chloe again. I couldn't get my head around the rest of it, though – the part where Zeke was dehaian royalty – and I wasn't sure I wanted to. I'd had enough trouble being forced to put up with the guy who wanted the girl I cared about *before* I'd learned that, oh by the way, he was also a *prince*.

Though on some level it almost didn't surprise me, considering how much of a pain in the ass he could be.

But it was still ridiculous. And infuriating. Especially when here we were *yet* again, with Chloe worried about him because he was in trouble.

And I had to help her. What other choice was there? Leave her to handle everything alone? That'd be great – if I wanted to make sure she'd have every reason to end up with *him* once all was said and done.

But this… I didn't even have words for this.

I scowled, turning back to the counter as the coffee finished brewing. Regardless, I wanted to give Chloe a few more minutes of sleep before I suggested we leave to keep her safe. She'd been pushing her people's ability to go without rest for all it was worth, and hadn't slept since the night she almost died – something that, by definition, didn't exactly count in my book. If she tried to keep going like she had, she'd probably hurt herself.

So I was letting her rest, and hoping those Sylphaen guys and that storm from hell stayed away at the same time.

I retrieved a mug from the cabinet, and then glanced to the ceiling as the floor creaked in the vicinity of the guest room as if in answer to my thoughts. Leaving the mug on the counter, I crossed to the windows. Whether or not Chloe was the one who'd just gotten up, I didn't want to risk any dehaians who might be watching the house catching a glimpse of her. Tugging the curtains into place, I made sure there were no gaps and then returned to finish with the coffee.

A few moments passed. Chloe appeared at the corner of the hallway. She wore the same clothes as yesterday, since her only other outfit had disintegrated when she'd changed shape in the car. On her cheek there was a faint mark from the pillow that, honestly, was sort of cute.

I just wished the rest of her didn't look so upset at me.

"You told me you'd wake me up," she said.

I paused, the warm mug in one hand. "She's not back yet."

The worry I'd known I would see flickered across Chloe's face. Her gaze went to the window and the drawn curtains.

I started to scowl and quickly covered the expression with a sip of the coffee. It wasn't like I wanted the guy dead or something. Gone, yes, but not dead. But if she suggested going out there after him…

"Noah," she started.

I glanced to her and she cut off at whatever she saw in my eyes. A breath escaped her and, grimacing, she moved past me to the table.

I studied the coffee, not sure what to say.

"Are Diane and Peter alright?" she asked after a moment.

My mouth tightened. I'd wondered if she'd noticed that; the way Dad and Diane looked on edge last night. I knew what had happened; Dad had come back downstairs after the girls had gone to bed to warn me. Or chew me out. I still wasn't sure which. But the point remained that things here hadn't gone well after Chloe left the ocean and headed to Kansas.

Diane felt like people were following her in town. Maddox thought others might be lurking outside the bookstore where he worked. Our neighbors had reported seeing strangers lingering around and studying the neighborhood, almost as if they were casing the area.

It wasn't hard to guess that the Sylphaen were still here. Still waiting in case Chloe returned. They'd stayed away from the house thus far – most likely out of a desire to avoid Dad and Maddox since they knew what we were – although that hadn't stopped them from watching from a distance.

But I couldn't tell her that. It wasn't her fault they were insane.

Though I wasn't sure she'd take it that way.

"Yeah, they're fine," I answered, making it sound like I didn't know why she asked.

At her silence, I glanced over. She sat motionless, her gaze on the closed curtains and her arms folded on the table top in front of her.

Bringing the mug with me, I walked over and sat down. "Are you?"

She nodded dismissively.

I wasn't buying it. "Chloe?"

She hesitated and then gave a small shrug. "You know, just still a bit shaky from yesterday…"

Her brow furrowed, the worry strengthening on her face. She dropped her gaze to her folded arms.

I paused. She wasn't the only one. Something inside me still felt electrified, like a low-level current was running through my veins. I was trying to ignore it – after all, it could just be the near-miss with lightning that was to blame – but it was still disconcerting.

Especially when it hadn't actually started till after we'd gotten hit with a wave of magic so powerful, it'd driven me the closest I'd ever been to losing control since I found out I was greliaran.

Drawing a steadying breath, I lifted the mug again and took another drink of the coffee. I hadn't, though. I hadn't hurt her. And she'd been able to change back after a couple minutes. Residual shakiness didn't mean anything was still wrong.

"It'll be alright," I said, not looking at her. "It's probably just taking a while for us to get over the shock of changing that fast."

She didn't respond. From the corner of my eye, I saw her look away.

A moment passed.

"It's not only that, though," she said quietly.

I glanced back. Her gaze still on her hands, she seemed to be struggling to find words.

"I'm scared, Noah. I'm just—" A rough breath left her. "These guys… they kill people. They *have* killed people, just trying to get to me. Those girls? The ones people thought were kidnapped earlier this summer? The Sylphaen murdered them, just because they looked like me. Because they thought those girls might *be* me. And Zeke's dad? They poisoned him. I mean, yeah, they wanted control of Yvaria, but they also…" She swallowed hard. "They also used it to get to me. And now they have Zeke, and Jirral, and maybe Ina too, and I just—"

I reached over, putting a hand to her clenched fingers. Shifting her grip, she wrapped her hand around mine, holding onto me tightly.

"We'll help them," I told her. "We'll figure this out."

She swallowed again, looking like she was on the edge of tears. Her green eyes rose, searching my face, and gratitude and sorrow mixed in them so strangely.

"I'm so sorry, Noah," she said. "I'm so sorry about all of this. How messed up everything is. I didn't…"

I rose to my feet and pulled her up with me. Wrapping my arms around her, I held her while her fingers clutched my back.

A tiny sob escaped her.

"Why are you so kind to me?" she asked softly. "When everything's just so…"

My brow furrowed. I pushed her back a bit and bent to catch her gaze. Tears slid down her face and I lifted a hand, cupping her cheek.

Her eyes met mine, the question in them remaining.

And I couldn't think how else to respond.

I drew her closer and kissed her.

She tensed, her whole body freezing as though she didn't

know what to do, and then slowly, ever so slowly, she relaxed into my arms.

My hands tightened on her. I hadn't forgotten how good this felt.

But no memory could truly capture it.

My fingers slid up through the waves of her hair, pulling her closer, and then holding her as I drew back to meet her gaze again.

"That's why," I whispered.

She trembled, her chest rising and falling as though she was trying to catch her breath.

Footsteps sounded on the stairs.

Chloe blinked, her gaze twitching toward the hall, and I let her go. Stepping away from me, she hesitated and then lowered herself back into her chair. I let out a slow breath, my heart still pounding. Returning to the coffee mug, I picked it up again just to give me something to do with my hands.

"Hey there," Baylie called when she reached the end of the hallway.

"Hey," I replied.

She paused. "Everything alright?"

Chloe nodded tightly, her face still turned to the curtains. "Yeah."

I could tell Baylie wasn't convinced. "Okay," she allowed, eyeing us both while she walked farther into the kitchen. "Well, um… is Ina back?"

I shook my head. "Not yet."

Her brow furrowed with concern. "So what now?"

I looked away, not sure how to respond. We needed to leave, and now that Chloe was up, the sooner the better.

But I knew she'd never agree to that.

A greliaran moved into my awareness.

My gaze snapped to the curtains. What? Who could…

Confusion set in. It wasn't a greliaran. Not… not quite. The presence in my head was similar, but bigger. Darker. Angrier, if such a thing were possible.

And out over the ocean.

My heart started pounding again for a whole new reason. I looked to Chloe. She hadn't moved. She showed no sign of feeling anything.

I headed for the door. I couldn't open the curtains, not without risking someone spotting her. But I had to see this. I needed to make sure I wasn't going insane.

"Noah?" Baylie called.

"Hang on."

I pulled open the back door. On the patio, Aaron glanced toward me when I strode past.

"Everything alright?" he asked.

I ignored him, scanning the horizon.

Nothing. Sunlight on the water and a gentle breeze promising more warmth to come. Barely a cloud hovered in the brightening blue skies.

But I could feel it, out there and moving along the horizon. A presence, like a greliaran but the size of… of I didn't even know what. It wasn't coming closer, though, and while I stood there, it drifted away, heading farther west.

A breath entered my chest when it vanished. I didn't know if it'd noticed me. I didn't know if I was losing my mind. It'd been so clear, though. Massive and terrifying, but *absolutely* clear.

"Noah?"

I looked back. Worry in every tense line of her face, Baylie stood by the door, watching me. Still seated on the patio, Aaron and Ellie didn't appear much different, though their expressions had plenty of confusion thrown in.

"What is it?" Baylie pressed.

I didn't know what to say. If that'd been the Beast, surely we would have seen something. Last time that thing had shown up, it'd looked like the thunderstorm from hell.

Unless it was like a greliaran. Unless that was just *one* of its forms.

"Inside," I said, moving past Ellie and Aaron again. I heard them climbing to their feet behind me, while Baylie stepped quickly out of the way at the door.

"Is something wrong?" Chloe asked when I came in. Still sitting at the table, she had a hand clasped to the back of the chair and her knuckles were nearly white.

"Did you feel anything just now?"

She shook her head warily.

I took a breath, feeling vaguely crazy for the words I had to say. "I… I think I just picked up on you-know-what out there."

Chloe stared at me. "Did it notice you?"

"I don't know. I don't think so. It headed west and… and then I lost it."

I glanced back when Aaron shut the door.

"Ellie?" I asked. "You know anything about this?"

She shook her head. "Nothing I've read ever mentioned the greliarans being able to detect, you know…"

"So," Chloe said, her voice choked. "Not just changing that fast, then."

She returned her gaze to the closed curtains. I watched her for a moment, unable to read what I'd seen on her face.

"Anyone else felt funny since yesterday?" I asked the others.

Baylie shifted her shoulders awkwardly. "Maybe a bit shaky," she admitted. "But it was crazy out there."

"Yeah," Aaron agreed. "Yesterday was intense – and that's *before* you all nearly had your car blasted off the road by that thing. We didn't get hit like you did, and *we're* still on edge." He shrugged. "Even if the elders' historical records don't mention greliarans picking up on that thing, they could be mistaken. Maybe this is just something you didn't notice till now."

I looked away. I would have noticed this. Yesterday, with the Beast overhead and all hell breaking loose, I would have noticed this.

So something happened. Something in that blast wave changed us.

Or else I was a freak who coincidentally discovered a new ability a single day after getting slammed by magic from that thing.

Right.

I drew a breath, attempting to stay focused. Freak or not, something happening to us or not, I wasn't sure it mattered. That monster was near Santa Lucina and even though it'd moved west, that didn't mean it wouldn't come back.

Or that I'd have enough warning to get us all out of here before it found Chloe.

"We should go," I said.

A breath left Chloe.

"We can leave a note for Ina," I continued. "Tell her to call us if she comes back. But with that thing nearby—"

"It left, though," Chloe tried.

"And it could come back. Or that cult could be on its way."

"Or Ina could. Maybe she's just been delayed because she's avoiding the Sylphaen or something."

I grimaced. Somehow, I doubted that. But regardless, that didn't make this place safe, or mean I wanted to risk the Sylphaen or that Beast thing attacking my home. If I had my way, we'd be heading inland – *far* inland – where neither of those problems could hurt her.

Even if it wouldn't make them go away.

I glanced at Chloe. She was back to not looking at me.

This was stupid. She needed to be safe. And while I knew she wouldn't take that black gunk Joseph gave her – not now, when she thought she could use it as leverage over those dehaians – there still had to be a way to fix this and protect her at the same time.

"Can we give it a few hours?" she implored without turning around. "Please? Just in case she's on her way."

My grimace deepened.

"She might need us," Chloe pressed. "If it's an emergency and if she comes back and we're not here…"

"A few hours," I grudged. "And then we leave."

She nodded.

Hoping I wasn't making a terrible mistake, I headed to the patio to keep an eye out for crazy cultists and invisible monsters.

6

ZEKE

The blindfold vanished again and this time the entire ocean filled the void.

I grimaced while my eyes adjusted to the twilit water. My gaze swept the dehaians around me, finding Kirzan but not Niall.

"—all along the street and throughout the neighborhood surrounding those animals, understand?" Kirzan finished to the soldiers.

The Sylphaen nodded.

"Ah, Zeke," he continued, catching sight of me glancing around. "Your brother elected to remain in Nyciena. Ren was concerned at having him transport you to the northern border. Or," Kirzan smiled, "close enough. Deliver us the creature, and all will be well. You have only to convince her to follow you into the water, and these loyal soldiers will handle everything from there. Your kingdom will be safe and your family too. Surely that isn't too much to ask?"

His condescending smile made my blood boil.

He turned to the guard holding the chain of the shackles still encasing my forearms. "Bring him near the shore and then release him. I will await your success here."

The soldiers nodded.

"Oh, and Zeke?" Kirzan added. "Don't try anything. Our connections…" He gave a small chuckle. "We have hidden in plain sight among the humans for a long time. Remember that."

He motioned to the soldiers. One of them pulled me along while they swam.

I scanned the ocean around me, my forearms twisting in the restraints, though my skin felt raw from the hours of doing so. I wasn't going to give them Chloe, but I needed a plan to get out of this. Kirzan had mentioned animals. Hopefully, that meant Noah. I'd throw that guy at the Sylphaen any day. And meanwhile, these guys surrounding the house had to look suspicious as hell, so calling the cops was definitely an option.

But that was assuming the Sylphaen didn't try to break in and grab her the moment they heard the sirens…

I swallowed hard. Whatever. I'd figure it out. But there was no way I was letting them have Chloe.

Or Ina.

Or Ren, Nyciena, Yvaria and whatever the hell *else* they were after.

A shiver ran through me. Getting Chloe to safety was one thing, and I'd do it. Somehow, I'd do it, and rescue my sister as well. But equal to those issues was the problem of the

Sylphaen themselves. The fact they would *always* be a threat to us until someone stopped them for good. I couldn't take them on by myself, though. I needed an army. Soldiers. Something. But Ren was out and Nyciena was too. My friends weren't an option, just as they'd never been, and beyond the capital, there wasn't anyone with enough power to—

My thoughts came to a halt. Almost no one.

Except Mom.

I drew a slow breath. I hadn't spoken to her in months, maybe since my last birthday or before, but things with her had never been as tense as with Dad. Or at least not in the same way. But that was part of the point. If she heard Ren stood a chance of taking up where Dad left off... She'd abandoned Yvaria over what happened with Driecara and Miri. She'd move the ocean to keep it from happening again.

But meanwhile, I'd have soldiers to help me find Ina, get her to safety, and then head back to solve this Sylphaen situation once and for all. As a group, the Sylphaen were massive. Powerful and frightening. But they had a leader and if I got my hands on their '*Wisdom*' Kirzan, maybe that would slow them down long enough for me to figure out how to keep them from destroying my home.

And to hell with the idiot king of Yvaria who, rather than believe me for one *second*, had just let them in the damn front door.

Rage burned through me at the thought of how stupid Ren had been, and I struggled to push it aside. It was a long shot, going to see Mom. *Such* a long shot. Lycera was a tiny nation. The Queen, my aunt Lisalia, was sick and my cousin Kobi was too young to take her place. The whole kingdom was in flux. And they barely even had a military to speak of, since nearly all their protection came through an agreement with Yvaria.

I had no guarantee the Sylphaen hadn't infiltrated there as well.

Grimacing, I shoved the thought away. Maybe they hadn't. And in any case, Lycera did have *some* soldiers – even if half of them were old enough to be my grandfather.

My frustration grew. Whatever. They were still soldiers and they still might help me. I *was* the son of their regent, after all.

And while I was gone, as one political leader to another, perhaps Mom would be able to get Ren to stop this insanity and see sense where everyone else in the ocean had failed.

The seafloor drew closer. Most of the soldiers broke off from the group, circling wide to head for different parts of the shore, leaving five guys still guarding me. One held the thick chains linking the shackles, while the others kept watch on me from a few yards away on all sides. Knives and guns hung from the belts at their waists, and on their arms, spikes already edged out of their skin.

A dehaian raced through the water from the south, coming back from near where the others had gone. The ones surrounding me slowed, and I could see the confusion on their faces.

The dehaian pulled up beside us. "They know we're here,"

he said hurriedly. "The boy, the blond one, he… he knows we're coming somehow."

I watched them. Noah was there. Okay. Probably good. He'd never said a word about being able to pick up on dehaians, though.

Greliarans, on the other hand…

"He saw you?" the soldier demanded.

The other man shrugged. "I don't know how. We were on the beach, blending with the tourists. He didn't look toward us, but he rushed from the house a minute ago. He just studied the ocean for a few seconds and then brought the others keeping watch with him when he went inside."

My brow furrowed. That didn't make sense.

Another dehaian raced toward us from the same direction as the guard. The soldier holding me glanced toward the feeling, disgust on his face while he muttered something about discipline.

"Orders, sir?" the guard pressed.

The man spat an Yvarian curse and turned back. "The plan hasn't changed. We send this one in to get her and—"

Net pods slammed into them. The dehaians spun in the water, thrown by the impact and their own attempts to rip the tentacles away. I twisted out of the guard's grasp as more nets followed, narrowly missing me and sending the soldiers tumbling toward the seafloor.

Jirral rushed up to me. "Sorry for the delay, boy. Bastards took forever to avoid."

I stared at him while he grabbed the shackles. A Vetorian-style belt hung from his waist, complete with knives. From a small satchel on its side, he fished out a pick and set to work on the lock holding me.

"What are you doing here?" I asked.

"Told you I'd get us out of this."

A gasping scoff left me. "But—"

"Ren put me down in a holding cell with the mercenaries. Turns out a few of them owed me favors." He glanced up, catching my expression. "I get around, kid."

The shackles fell away from my wrists. Jirral took them, fastening them to a loop on his belt.

"So I'm guessing Chloe or Ina are nearby?" he said. "That why those guys brought you with them?"

"Chloe. They think she's up at a house on the coast. They're surrounding her."

"And they're want to use you to trap her." Jirral scoffed. "Well, let's go ruin that plan, shall we?"

He turned for the shore.

"Wait."

He glanced back, his brow furrowing.

I hesitated. I didn't want to do this. I'd rather do anything else. Over a decade of distrust was yelling at me and presenting every *single* reason I should never put anyone's safety in Jirral's care. He'd gotten people killed. He'd run when he should have fought. He'd argued when he should have acted.

And he'd come back across Yvaria to save our lives yesterday, when the greliarans and the Sylphaen had us surrounded.

It didn't mean he wouldn't screw this up, though. That my sister – the only sister I had left – wouldn't die.

Nausea twisted my stomach. I didn't have any other options.

"They've got Ina too," I forced myself to continue. "They caught her and they're holding her as leverage. I don't know where."

Jirral didn't move.

"I can get Chloe," I said. "But I can't leave Ina. You say you get around? You have connections? Find out where they have her."

He glanced toward the shore. "There are bound to be a lot of them up there."

"I can handle it." I let out a breath. "I'm going to get Chloe away from them, have her go back inland, and then I'm heading for Lycera."

"Your mom?"

"The Sylphaen have to be stopped and Ren won't listen. You saw him. You saw the court too." I shook my head. "Mom's the best shot I have. Just find out where they have Ina and then come meet me. We'll bring the soldiers to get her back."

His jaw worked around. I could see the resistance on his face. "I can still help you here. Look for Ina once these bastards are dealt with."

"And if they get a head start warning Kirzan that I've gotten Chloe away? Jirral, they've had Ina for *hours*. We're running out of time."

He grimaced. "You watch yourself up there."

"I will."

His mouth tightened as though he wanted to continue protesting, but after a moment, he gave me a short nod and took off for the open water.

I closed my eyes briefly, trying to slow my racing heart, and then swam for the coast.

7

CHLOE

I hadn't moved from the chair by the dining room table and I didn't know how long it'd been. Diane and the others milled around the kitchen, talking in low, edgy voices. Maddox had joined them briefly, though he'd disappeared again once he'd claimed a mug of coffee. I thought he might be keeping watch out front. Meanwhile, Chief Reynolds had wandered downstairs at some point and now sat at the far end of the living room, not saying a word. Peter had taken the sofa, his attention supposedly on a newspaper, though I could tell from the look on his face and the way his gaze twitched to the chief every few moments that he knew what had happened the day before.

And Noah was still outside. I wanted to tug aside a curtain to check on him, even if I knew Peter would hear if anything went wrong. But I hated being trapped here. I hated that I couldn't go out there and do something about this situation.

All of the situations.

My eyes closed. It'd come out of nowhere, Noah kissing me.

I hadn't been expecting it. And now, I didn't know how to feel. What to think. I couldn't stop this weird trembling inside, like the ground wasn't quite stable under me.

I wished he hadn't done that.

I wished he hadn't stopped.

My brow furrowed. My head hurt and sleep last night hadn't helped. I felt like it should have, but instead, it'd just left everything more real and overwhelming somehow.

A noise from the couch made me open my eyes. Peter stood, one hand to the curtain as he checked the yard outside. My heart started to pound harder at the look on his face. Everyone fell silent while he headed for the door.

Noah beat him to it. Yanking open the patio door, he strode into the house.

And Zeke followed him.

I rose to my feet, a breath leaving me. His forearms were bruised. He looked as tense as I'd ever seen him. His gaze went to me briefly when he came in, though it twitched immediately back to the door when Noah closed it behind him.

"Alright, you wanted to talk," Noah demanded. "What is it?"

"We have a problem," Zeke replied, his voice tight. "The Sylphaen—"

He caught sight of Aaron. His shock lasted only a heartbeat before shifting into outrage. "What the hell is he—"

"It's okay." Ellie hurriedly interposed herself between them. "He's helping. He's not—"

"I'm sorry," Aaron cut in. "What we did to you at Doctor Brooks' lab, I—"

"Shut up," Zeke interrupted. "Just—" He let out a breath and shook his head. His gaze returned to me, and I could see him struggling. "The Sylphaen are here," he continued. "They've surrounded the house."

My brow rose. "What?"

"They have Ina. If I don't bring you outside to them, they're going to tell Ren that your 'allies' are holding her. Make him think it's Miri and Driecara all over again."

My mouth moved, words failing me. Noah glanced between us questioningly, but from my expression, he must have understood just how bad that was, since he didn't say a word.

"But," I tried, "killing me won't stop that thing. Did you—"

"They know."

Words abandoned me a second time.

A humorless, incredulous noise left Zeke. "They think they can control it. That if they take what you can do and somehow give that power to themselves, they'll be able to use the Beast as a weapon again, and turn it against anything they want, human or dehaian."

My hand found the chair, steadying me while my gaze dropped to the floor. This was madness. The ancient dehaians had changed their whole world, and – if what Joseph said was true – they'd screwed over all the magic in it too, simply because they couldn't hope to control the nightmare they'd created.

And the Sylphaen wanted to try it again. Supply even *more* power to that homicidal thunderstorm and attempt what God-knew-how-many dehaians who'd actually *made* the thing hadn't been able to accomplish.

"Who are these people?" Peter asked.

"Those asshole dehaians who broke in here a few weeks back," Noah supplied. He turned to Zeke. "Listen, we can try to help your sister, but there's no *way* you're taking Chloe—"

"Do you honestly think for one *second* that I would do that?" Zeke snarled. He looked around at the others. "Call the cops. Come up with a plan. Do *something*. They'll figure out I'm not going along with this soon."

Noah glanced to his father.

"Cops," Peter stated. "To start."

He crossed to the cordless phone on the kitchen wall and then brought it with him while he headed for the front room.

Noah's gaze twitched to Chief Reynolds, but the man didn't move.

"How many of them are there?" Noah asked Zeke.

"I saw at least thirty."

Noah looked like he was trying to keep from swearing.

Maddox strode down the hall. "I count ten out front," he said when he came into the kitchen, and it took me a second to realize he'd probably heard our every word from wherever he'd been. "They're keeping a distance for the moment, and Dad's watching them, but this guy's right," he nodded to Zeke, "they won't stay there forever."

"Do you think they'll try to get in the house if they hear the cops coming?" Ellie asked nervously.

"I don't know," Zeke replied. "Maybe."

Noah turned away, running a hand through his hair.

"Are the cars blocking the garage?" Baylie asked.

Maddox's brow furrowed. "What?"

"The cars. Peter and Diane's are in there, right? And the chief's and mine… I think we parked far enough away from the door. What if we bundled Chloe up in the back of one, and did the same to somebody else in the other? Then if they try to get in, we could leave and, you know, drive like crazy in two different directions. Even if they have cars or motorcycles or whatever with them, they still won't know who to follow."

Everyone stared at her.

"What?" she protested.

"That's… not a bad idea," Maddox allowed.

"Yeah," Zeke agreed.

Baylie shrugged, looking embarrassed. "Like the movies, right?"

She gave Noah a tiny smile. A dry chuckle escaped him.

Peter came back. "Cops are on their way."

"I'll grab some blankets," Diane offered.

At Maddox's nod, she hurried from the room.

"So what do we do if the cops try to stop us leaving?" Zeke asked.

"If those guys try to get in here," Peter said. "I'll call the police again. Tell them what we're doing."

I bit my lip briefly. If the cops did attempt to stop us, and if the Sylphaen grew desperate and hurt someone to get to me…

"Will the cops listen?" I asked, the words coming out before I could stop myself.

Peter glanced to me. "One problem at a time."

His gaze twitched from me to Chief Reynolds and I could just read it in his expression. His body language. Over and over, his family had been in danger.

All because of me.

Noah cleared his throat. "Okay, let's get ready then." He glanced to the chief. "You too," he added coldly.

I followed Noah through the hall. The door to the garage stood to one side of the foyer, not far from the base of the stairs and the front entrance. Noah pulled open the door and then continued inside, pausing only long enough to hit the switch on the wall. The lights flickered on, revealing two sedans that took up only a portion of the space, with the rest left over for storage.

"Here," Diane said, coming up behind us. She held a stack of folded blankets in her arms.

Baylie took a few of them and then glanced to me. "Guess I'll ride in the other car, then."

I managed a nod, trying to ignore the worry bubbling up at the thought of the Sylphaen getting their hands on her.

Maddox looked to the garage doors. "Cops."

I couldn't hear a single siren, but it didn't matter. I headed for the closest car.

"Um, one thing?" Ellie said behind me.

I looked back to see her watching Zeke and Noah anxiously.

"If they see you both in the same car… I mean, Noah, they might know you and Chloe are, um, friends and they sent Zeke here because, you know, um…"

She trailed off.

I studied her for a moment. It never failed: Ellie and her ability to spot flaws in the plan. And, as usual, she was right. The Sylphaen wouldn't have any trouble knowing who to follow.

I glanced to Zeke and Noah, and found them eyeing each other askance.

Peter cut in before either of them could speak. "Noah, Maddox, that car with Baylie. Take your friends here too. Head left. Zeke and Chloe come with me and Diane. We'll go right. And you," he continued, his voice hardening as he turned to the chief. "You're staying with me."

A window shattered at the back of the house.

"Move!" Peter ordered.

We scrambled for the cars. Zeke climbed in behind me and grabbed the blankets from Diane when she handed them back from the front. Unfurling one, he wasted no time in covering me while the chief got in on the other side of the car.

I tensed beneath the layer of fabric, unable to see anything.

Beyond the car, someone shouted.

"Hang on!" Peter called.

A thud sounded on the door. Zeke yelled and grabbed me,

pulling me tight against him. Glass shattered nearby.

The car surged into reverse.

Wood crunched and metal screeched overhead. The sedan shuddered and then lurched to a fast stop before lunging forward. More shouting surrounded us, fading quickly as the car raced up the driveway. My breath coming hot and fast under the suffocating blanket, I gripped Zeke's side through the fabric, hanging on while sirens faded behind us.

A minute crept by. I could hear Diane on the phone, telling the police dispatcher what had happened. I wanted to look around and make sure we were okay, but I didn't know if it was safe to move.

Zeke's hold on me shifted and he pulled the blanket away. Cool wind hit my face, blowing through the missing window beside him.

"You alright?" he asked, brushing my disheveled hair from my face.

I nodded while I straightened. Scooting nearer to him and away from the chief, I glanced around. Broken glass littered the seat and the floor, while on the bottom of the empty window frame, traces of blood glistened.

I looked to Zeke. He didn't say anything, but just pulled me closer.

Up front, Diane thanked the dispatcher and then lowered the phone. Peter kept an eye to her with quick glances from the road while she tapped the screen a few times and then lifted the cell to her ear again.

"You kids okay?" she asked the moment someone picked up.

I watched her, wishing I had greliaran hearing to tell me what was being said on the other end of the line. Peter seemed to relax a bit though, and his hands eased from their death grip on the wheel.

"Noah, where are you?" Peter asked.

Diane paused while Noah replied.

"Okay," Peter responded. "Library's close to there. Meet us in the parking lot."

Diane waited again. "See you soon," she said after a moment. She hung up.

"They're alright?" I asked.

Diane nodded.

Silence fell while Peter kept driving. His hand rubbing my arm, Zeke didn't let me go.

My gaze slid to the chief, eyeing him askance as the seconds crept on. He'd been quiet for over a day, barely even seeming to watch us. It was weird. Creepy too. He still had that look in his eyes like something was broken inside, and I didn't know what it could be.

I wasn't sure I *wanted* to know.

I shifted even closer to Zeke, hoping that we'd get to where we were going soon.

The car wove through traffic and the town, till finally we pulled into a parking lot near a large building of glass and steel. Massive windows glinted in the midmorning sunlight, while dozens of cars filled the lot. People trickled past the sliding doors, and a handful of teenagers lounged at the bus stop nearby.

I caught sight of Baylie and Noah leaning against the trunk of their car. Maddox stood near the driver's door, while Ellie was waiting for Aaron to climb from the back. From what I could see on the blue sedan's passenger side, the vehicle appeared intact, though Noah had his arm around Baylie as if comforting her.

Peter steered into an empty spot and then brought the car to a stop. Barely pausing to turn off the engine, he climbed out and headed for the others while Diane followed only a heartbeat behind.

Zeke pushed open the door and moved to get out.

"You're lucky, you know."

I froze at the sound of the chief's voice.

"She lived to be twelve. You've made it longer."

I glanced back.

"My cousin," he explained without looking away from his hands. "Lucy. She was like you. First one born alive in thirty years. Harman Brooks kept her going long as he could." He paused. "I was there when she died."

I shivered.

"It's strange, what we do to protect people. My family tried everything to save Lucy. It didn't matter. And now, with everything that's been done to save you," he shook his head, "that doesn't matter either."

He sighed. "You're going to die out there. What you are…

It's going to mean the death of you. Or these boys will. The dehaian and the greliaran." He chuckled humorlessly. "Killers, both of them. It's just a question of which one gets you first."

Zeke took my hand to pull me from the car. "Come on."

The chief snagged my arm, stopping me. "They'll tear you apart. Or he'll make a thrall of you. Lucy's mother. Women who are with them. They go mad before they die and the doctors barely save their chil—"

"Enough!" Zeke snapped.

"Oh, you know something about that, do you, boy?" the chief retorted, heat entering his voice for the first time as he turned to us.

At the look in his eyes, my shivering grew stronger. I tugged my gaze away, glancing to Zeke.

My brow flickered down at his expression. It wasn't what I expected. There wasn't anger like there'd been at my parents' house. No intensity, either.

It was just flat. Guarded.

Like he was hiding something.

"I know we're done here," Zeke answered tightly.

"You're a fool, girl," Chief Reynolds said to me. "A damned fool and what happens to you now is—"

The door on the other side of the chief ripped open.

"Let her go," Noah growled.

Chief Reynolds' gaze slid over. Noah's jaw muscles jumped at whatever he saw in the man's eyes.

I yanked my arm from the chief's grip. He glanced back to

me, and disgust twitched across his face. He held up his hands, his expression becoming contemptuous.

Quickly, I climbed out after Zeke. My heart was pounding and it wasn't till I reached Baylie that I could even look back at the car.

The chief stood by the sedan, but he made no move to come any closer.

"You okay?" Baylie asked me.

I didn't respond. The chief wasn't focused on me, not exactly anyway. He was back to studying the air ahead of him with that same creepy, blank stare he'd had since yesterday. Zeke and Noah were nearby, though. They never quite looked at each other, but they seemed to have come to an identical decision, with both of them stopped between me and the chief. Ellie and Aaron still waited near the passenger side doors behind me while, a few yards farther into the parking lot, Peter and Diane were speaking to Maddox in low voices. From what little I could overhear, they seemed to be making plans for what to do now that the Sylphaen had broken into their home yet again.

"Um, yeah," I managed, turning back to Baylie. "You?"

She shrugged. "I guess. The blanket meant I missed most of it."

At her gesture, I glanced over at the driver's side of the car.

My brow rose. Something had torn through the metal near the wheel well. Blood speckled the blue paint.

"Maddox said they tried to use those spike things," Baylie explained. "Take out the tire."

I swallowed hard.

"What now?" she asked. "You, um, want to head farther east or—"

She cut off as a cop car pulled into the parking lot, its lights flashing. It wended through the lanes toward us and then came to a stop nearby. The officer got out, leaving the lights spinning, and he gave us all a glance before heading over to speak with Peter and Diane.

I turned away fast, hoping he didn't recognize me as the girl who'd been theoretically kidnapped several weeks back. In the lot around us, people stopped and stared, while inside the building, others looked through the windows to find out what was happening. Down the street behind us, a young couple paused in surprise when they came around the corner, and then craned their necks to gain a better view of what was going on.

I wanted to get back in the car. I felt so conspicuous, standing here with all of us appearing vaguely terrorized. The sedans were inexplicable too, with their blood splatters, dented roofs, and shattered glass. Now that I looked, I could even see that the trunk lid of the car bore rips from spikes, like a Sylphaen had tried to hang on while Peter drove away.

What were we supposed to tell the cop? The madmen came after us with saw blades?

"Come on," Baylie murmured, nodding toward the strip of grass beyond the front of the car. I followed her, grateful for the chance to put any extra distance between myself and the police. Ellie trailed us, with Aaron coming a step behind, while

Zeke and Noah remained where they were, watching the chief, the cop, and everyone in the parking lot as though daring any of them to come near.

"So?" Baylie prompted, her eyebrow rising at me. "What now?"

I hesitated, unsure what to say. Zeke had to go; I knew that. Ina was in danger, every nation under the *ocean* was in danger… He had to leave.

And I needed to let him. Head back inland. Do the smart thing and stay away from the Beast, the Sylphaen, and everything else.

Again.

I looked away. What then, though? After I left, after I hid *yet* again… what then? I'd take the black gunk that Joseph had given me?

That'd been the plan. I'd almost done it yesterday and nothing had changed.

Except…

My gaze slid to Zeke.

The Beast was out there. I only had one way to stop it.

But that wouldn't help Ina. Or keep the Sylphaen from destroying anything and everything in their path.

Trembling spread through me. I could say that wasn't my problem. I could say I didn't care.

I'd be lying.

The Sylphaen had come after me again and again, and other people kept getting hurt. They *always* did. Those innocent girls in Santa Lucina. Zeke's dad. It was just luck we'd made it out of the house safely today. But what about the next time? I could take the potion, maybe turn into a landwalker, and then disappear. I could go back to Kansas or Colorado, or anywhere else at all, and pretend I'd never heard of the Beast or dehaians.

But that wouldn't stop the Sylphaen. That wouldn't make them believe I'd actually changed, and that they no longer had a chance of claiming their sacrifice.

They'd keep searching for me.

And Noah's family could be their next victims.

"I, um… I think we need to—"

"Excuse me, miss?"

The cop interrupted me. I didn't turn around. He could be talking to anyone.

He could be Sylphaen trying to make sure it was me.

"Miss?"

I wanted to run.

"Officer," Diane tried. "The girls have been through a lot and—"

"Chloe Kowalski?" he pressed.

I gritted my teeth, fighting not to swear, and then looked back at him.

His mouth tightened. "If you'd come over here?"

I gave a glance to Baylie, seeing much the same expression on her face as was probably on mine. Drawing a breath, I walked back around the car.

"Would you folks like to explain what this young lady is

doing here?" he asked the Delaneys. "You're the ones who reported her missing, correct? We received a report she was home in the Midwest."

Diane looked to Peter. "Well, you see, Officer. This—"

"Hey."

I turned at the sound of Noah's voice.

The young couple had crossed the street and were coming toward where Baylie and the others stood on the opposite end of the cars. Blond-haired and tan, they looked like a pair of beachgoers who'd decided to take a stroll through town.

My brow furrowed and my heart started to race. There was something weird about… something, though. The way they moved, maybe. I couldn't put my finger on it.

And it didn't really matter. Noah seemed to see it too.

"You hear me?" he called, striding toward them. "What're you—"

The young woman charged forward faster than should have been possible. Her hands snagged Baylie and whipped her around, pinning her arm behind her back.

Aaron rushed at her. The man intercepted him and shoved him back, propelling him to the grass a dozen feet away.

A knife blade flashed in the sunlight, coming to rest on Baylie's throat.

I froze and for a heartbeat, the world froze with me.

"Try anything and she dies," snarled the blond man.

The woman muscled Baylie forward, the knife remaining where it was. Ellie retreated while the woman circled the car, and Noah snagged the girl's arm when she came close, yanking Ellie behind him. In the parking lot, I heard someone shout. Footsteps pounded while people raced away.

I couldn't take my eyes from Baylie.

"We just want the girl," the man continued while they came closer.

"Hey now," the cop tried. "Take it easy. Whatever it is, we can talk—"

"Shut up," the woman snapped.

Baylie winced as the woman pressed the knife tighter to her skin. I tensed.

"We won't ask again," the man growled.

I trembled. We were too far away to reach her. Even the cop didn't stand a chance of grabbing his gun before the woman cut Baylie's throat.

And she would. Something in her eyes… there just wasn't any doubt.

Baylie's gaze locked on mine.

I couldn't do this. I couldn't lose Baylie to them, cut up and bloodied like all the nightmares my imagination was tossing at me right now. But if I did anything here, if *any* of us did, over a dozen people would see me and Zeke with spikes on our arms or Noah's family with fire in their skin.

"Now!" the woman ordered.

I didn't care.

"Okay," I called.

Noah's gaze went to me, incredulous and denying, and

Zeke's didn't look much different. I walked toward the woman, and pulled from Diane's grasp when she tried to grab my arm to stop me.

"Young lady," the cop warned, "just stay—"

"Shut up!" the man barked. He looked back to me. "Get over here."

"Chloe…" Noah growled.

"Let her go." I continued toward them slowly. My heart was pounding. I had no idea what I was going to do.

I couldn't watch my best friend die.

"Stay!" the man yelled at Zeke when he started forward to intercept me.

Keeping an eye to his companion, the man inched forward, one hand extended to snag me the moment I came near.

I looked to the cop. His hand hovered by his weapon and he flicked his gaze from me to the others and back, just waiting for an opening.

A ragged breath left me. I could feel my forearms stinging, ready to let the spikes out.

And if I got close enough… if I surprised them…

So many questions would need to be answered.

It didn't matter.

"Please," I tried, the note of begging in my voice anything but feigned. "Please don't hurt her. I'll go with you."

Contempt twitched over the man's face. He jerked his chin at the woman while he came toward me.

She shoved Baylie away, sending her stumbling toward the

others. The man closed in, moving to grab my arm.

The spikes rushed out. I lunged forward.

He twisted sideways, avoiding the blades. I spun, trying to catch him with one arm while keeping the woman away at the same time.

I wasn't fast enough. Using my momentum against me, he yanked me around and then wrenched my arm behind my back. I cried out as numbness shot down to my fingertips and the spikes retreated by reflex. Gasping with pain, I fought to pull away from him.

His hold tightened and a knife appeared at my throat. I froze.

"Now—" The man nodded to his companion. "—give her the keys."

When no one moved, he jerked my arm. I couldn't stop a choked noise from escaping. My shoulder felt like it was on fire.

"Keys!"

"No," Zeke said. "You won't kill her. You need her alive."

A scoff left the man holding me. "You sure about that, your highness? So sure you'll risk watching her die?"

The knife bit my skin. Blood trickled hot down my neck as if to prove his point. I closed my eyes, tears stinging and my head pounding from the pain of his grasp. I'd been so stupid. So stupid and desperate. I'd thought I could stop them. I'd thought I could get them away from me and Baylie and—

A shiver coursed through my body, strong and electrifying.

The man's hold on me vanished and the knife clattered to the concrete. I stumbled forward, my eyes opening, and I turned.

He'd fallen to the ground. Curled into a fetal position, he gasped, his eyes wide and his hands clutching his middle. Garbled, choked noises escaped him while his body convulsed like he was being electrocuted.

My gaze rose to the woman. For a heartbeat, she stared at the man and then her eyes lifted to me, horror on her face.

"Just stay there!" the cop yelled.

I looked over. He had the gun aimed at her, though from the way his gaze twitched to me, he didn't seem sure which one of us to target anymore.

A panicked sound escaped the woman. She spun and took off, racing between the cars and down the street so fast, I heard the cop swear in surprise.

I retreated from the man on the ground. Foam came from his mouth but the spasms were fading. His eyes rolled up into his head and he barely seemed to breathe.

"Chloe!" Baylie cried.

She ran up and threw her arms around me, ignoring the way the blood on my neck smeared on her. Feeling like I was moving on autopilot, I hugged her in return.

Zeke and Noah came after her. Circling the car quickly, Noah pulled open the passenger door and then reached inside, retrieving a handful of napkins from the glove compartment.

"Here," he said when he came back. Baylie released me and stepped back while Noah put the napkins to my neck. "It's only a nick. Just keep pressure on it."

I nodded tightly, holding the napkins where he'd placed them.

Noah's hand moved down my arm, not letting go of me. Nearby, Zeke grimaced at the sight and looked back toward the cop.

The man was heading for us. Gripping his radio, he called for assistance, relaying our location and a request for an ambulance.

"Excuse me," he said, pushing past the onlookers in the parking lot. He kneeled down, checking over the man on the ground.

The guy had stopped shaking. I trembled while the cop felt for a pulse and then rocked back on his heels. He glanced to me before turning his gaze to the parking lot.

People were coming closer. Sirens wailed in the distance.

The desire to leave was overwhelming.

"Miss," the cop began. "What did you—"

"Pardon me, officer." The chief strode up to us. He fished his wallet from his pocket and then showed his badge. "Chief Barry Reynolds, Reidsburg Police. If I could talk to you?"

The cop regarded him skeptically before he straightened. He walked over to join Chief Reynolds several yards away, and kept an eye to us while the chief began speaking to him in a low voice.

My gaze twitched to Noah, whose brow rose a bit as the seconds crept on.

"He's claiming they were addicts," Noah relayed quietly. "Part of a gang from back east. He's claiming your… uncle? Your uncle owed them money and they've been trying to kidnap you to force him to pay."

Noah glanced back to me, his expression clearly questioning whether we should trust this help.

I didn't know what to tell him. I supposed even the chief wouldn't want other cops digging too far into anything involving dehaians and, by proximity, landwalkers as well.

"Did the cop see me, you know, with the spikes?" I whispered.

"If he did, he's not saying anything."

I let out a breath.

"What happened?" Baylie asked softly.

I gave a helpless shrug and looked to Zeke, my brow rising in tacit repeat of the question.

His jaw worked around, his gaze flicking from me to the body.

"Zeke?" I pressed.

"I have *no* idea."

An ambulance pulled into the lot, bringing its blaring sirens and flashing lights and cutting me off before I could speak. Two cop cars followed a heartbeat later, and at the sight of them all, the officer turned from Chief Reynolds to wave them over.

I shuddered. I just wanted to get out of here, and with good reason. The Sylphaen… they were here too, in the middle of town. I mean, yeah, they'd found me quickly before. The one who'd put me in the hospital weeks ago had worked at a bookstore I'd visited, for pity's sake, and the ones who'd tried to kidnap me at the Delaneys' cabin, they'd managed to hide as EMTs. But this was still ridiculous.

Speaking of which, though…

My gaze went to the ambulance. To the crowd that was forming and the cops who were on their way as well.

The shuddering grew stronger. "I… I, um—"

"Run," Noah murmured.

I looked to him in alarm.

"I'll keep up. Just run."

Baylie made a protesting noise. "But where are you—"

"This could be a contingency plan," Noah interrupted. "The cabin was a setup too."

A breath left Baylie.

At my glance to him, Zeke nodded.

I scanned the parking lot again. Peter was striding toward us. I could tell from his expression that he'd heard us and didn't like Noah's suggestion. Reluctant agreement showed on Maddox's face, though, while he watched us from the corner of his eye. Diane seemed wary at the sudden manner in which her husband and stepson were acting, and looked around as though trying to figure out what could have changed.

And the cops were walking over here.

We were out of time.

"Miss?" the officer called.

I ran.

Streets and buildings and startled people flashed past while we raced down the sidewalk and it wasn't until we were a dozen blocks away that we slowed. I cast a quick look back when we came to a stop, noting with relief that Noah wasn't too far behind us.

"Over here," Noah said, breathing hard as he caught up. He nodded toward an opening between two shops.

I followed Zeke into the tiny alleyway. Brick walls formed either side, with a few half-hearted attempts at graffiti scribbled upon them. A trio of tall, plastic garbage totes were clustered to our left, and as narrow as they were, the bins still barely fit between the buildings.

"So what now?" I asked, keeping a nervous eye to the street.

Neither of them answered me. I glanced over.

Zeke's mouth tightened. "You still have whatever Joseph gave you?"

I gave a small nod.

He didn't quite look at Noah. "You should take it," he continued to me.

"What about the Sylphaen?"

Zeke made a noise of frustration. "What kind of plan was that, Chloe? What, you'd just let them take you if—"

"No. Of course not. We were going to run. I-I know it wasn't great, but—"

I cut off when he scowled and turned away.

"You should just do it," Zeke pressed, not looking at me. "Stop the Beast while you can."

"It's not going to stop it all at once. It took years for the Beast to go away after what the dehaians did."

He didn't respond.

I looked between them. Noah was watching the street and I couldn't read anything from what I could see of his face. Zeke didn't turn toward me, his eyes on the other end of the alley.

And I didn't even know what I was arguing. Yes, I needed to take the potion thing that Joseph had given me. I knew that. But the potion wouldn't stop the Sylphaen. It wouldn't keep them from hurting other innocent people for however long it took them to figure out I wasn't coming back. And that was *assuming* I became a landwalker. I could become a dehaian like Zeke – unable to leave the ocean for long, unable to go much more than a hundred miles inland without excruciating pain.

Ren was still out there. He wanted to put me on trial, and possibly execute me after it was done. And, again, the Sylphaen wouldn't stop.

They'd almost killed Baylie.

My stomach churned, the adrenaline fading and letting the panic in. Forcing myself to breathe, I struggled to shove it away.

"What are you going to do?" I asked Zeke, working to keep my voice steady.

He didn't respond.

"Zeke?"

"I'm going to Lycera."

"What's in Lycera?"

"My mother. She's in charge there, more or less."

My brow drew down at the phrasing. "And she… what? Has soldiers? People who can stop the Sylphaen?"

He paused. "Yeah."

My expression didn't change. There was something weird in his tone. In the way he still wouldn't look at me.

"Zeke."

He turned, his face tense. "I'm going to fix this, okay? I'll take care of it. Just…" His gaze went from me to Noah and back. "I need you to be safe too, and using whatever Joseph gave you is the best way to do that right now."

I swallowed at the look in his eyes. I wanted him to be safe as well. Him, Noah, everyone. I didn't want to risk this hurting any of them. And if I left, if I let Noah take me back inland somewhere and drank that gunk Joseph had given me…

It wouldn't help. Not really. Not this. The Sylphaen could kill Zeke, or Jirral, or Ina, or anyone else they wanted. They could go after Diane, or Peter, or anybody here before they figured out I was gone.

They'd almost killed *Baylie*.

Somewhere inside, I felt like I was screaming.

I fought a breath down. They hadn't, though. Baylie was okay. I hadn't watched anything happen, because nothing had, and everything was fine, and…

And the people I loved were still in danger.

Another breath entered my lungs. Love was a big word. A

complicated word that I wasn't sure I wanted to think about right now. But I cared for Zeke. Noah too. Both of them in a way that was still a mess in my head and I hadn't had a single moment to sort it out. But I could have lost Zeke today. The Sylphaen brought him back to catch me, but that didn't mean next time they wouldn't kill him instead.

And I couldn't risk that. Couldn't risk that he'd go out there, and I'd never hear from him again.

Not when I could have done something to help.

My gaze dropped to my hands, as though I could see the shivery, strange feeling still tingling through my skin.

I didn't know what I'd done, but regardless, I couldn't run. It wouldn't matter. I'd learned that lesson in Iowa. You ran and ran, and the bad guys… that didn't stop them. It never stopped anything.

They'd just be waiting for their next opportunity to come after you and everyone you cared about again.

"No."

Zeke's brow drew down. "What?"

"No, I'm going with you."

Noah looked back at me. "Chloe, you can't—"

"I am *going!*" I snapped at them both. "I know it's crazy. I know it's dangerous. I don't care. I'm done with running from these guys. I am done with hiding. I am capable of more than they think and I am going to use that to stop them."

They both stared at me.

"I killed that man back there." My stomach somersaulted

with nausea at the words. "I didn't mean to, but I did. And they're scared of me for a reason." My gaze went between Zeke and Noah. "I want them gone. I want people to stop dying because of them, getting hurt because of them. Because all they want is to get their hands on me and they keep killing people to do that. You say there are soldiers in Lycera? Fine. Let's go get them."

Zeke hesitated. "There aren't that many," he admitted. "And they're fairly old."

I watched him for a second. "They're a start."

He didn't take his eyes from me, seeming speechless.

"Chloe," Noah tried. "That Beast thing will pick up on you out there. Anything you do—"

"Joseph said I could hide. That as long as the Beast wasn't close, I could go in the water, try suppressing that signal thing, and probably be okay."

"*Probably* being the operative word here!" Noah protested. "And if that crazy turtle was wrong, you could die!"

"I have to stop them, Noah. They broke into your house again. Diane seems terrified and maybe that's just a coincidence, but I'm guessing it's not. And just now, they might have—" I couldn't bring myself to say the rest. With effort, I regrouped. "I can't keep doing this. If there's even a *chance* to stop this out in Lycera or wherever, I'm going to take it."

Noah was silent.

I turned to Zeke. "How long will we need to get there?"

Zeke's expression had barely changed. "Chloe…"

"How long?"

His jaw muscles jumped. "Maybe a day. It's on the southwest edge of Yvaria, though. We'll have to go through it to reach Lycera."

The words made me shiver. I worked to give no sign. "Alright, then let's get—"

"Take me with you."

I looked back to Noah. "What?"

"Take me with you," he repeated. "You brought him to Kansas. Bring me to this place."

I stared at him.

"That was different," Zeke argued. "We're already able to handle breathing underwater or on land. You aren't. You'll drown."

Noah didn't look away from me. "Maybe not. Ellie said dehaians like you used to bring people underwater with them. So try it."

I shook my head. "Noah, I don't—"

"If Chloe does anything out of the ordinary," Zeke snapped, "the Beast will find her. You'll get her killed."

"I can pick up on it. I can tell where it is before it notices her."

"*What?*" Zeke demanded incredulously.

Noah ignored him. "I can help, Chloe."

"But if something happens to me… Noah, you'll die."

He paused. "Then I better make sure nothing happens to you."

I couldn't respond. He just watched me, waiting, and I couldn't think what to say. It was one thing to risk my own life. Even if I was terrified, I was still willing to do that if it meant that I'd keep the people I cared about safe.

But risking him…

"You'll slow us down," Zeke said.

Noah glanced to him. "You've never seen this done. How do you know?"

I swallowed hard. "Noah, please. I don't want you to get hurt."

"And I don't want to lose you."

My gaze fell away. There was so much in those words, it made me ache inside.

But I didn't know about this, about what could happen or what magic like this would do to a greliaran. It could kill him. Make him lose control. Make him unable to ever come back to land again.

It could do anything.

"Chloe, I know it's dangerous. And I don't care."

I looked up at the repetition of what I'd said only moments before.

He met my gaze. "Let me help you."

I wanted to say no. His brow rose.

"Okay," I whispered.

Gratitude showed on Noah's face. His lip twitched up in a small smile.

I couldn't hold his gaze. I turned away, a breath pressing

from my chest.

"Where's the safest place to get back in the water?" I asked, my voice choked.

It took Zeke a moment to reply. "Probably outside town. But, Chloe, this is crazy. And it doesn't solve anything with the Sylphaen. If you go down there – if *either* of you go down there – then what?"

"You were going to get the soldiers. What was your plan after that?"

He made a frustrated noise. "Head north. Find someplace to hide and then bait their leader Kirzan into thinking you were nearby, so he'd come to where I could get my hands on him. But the point was to make him *think* you were there, not to put you in a place where he could actually *find* you!"

I hesitated. That'd been a crazy plan. With just a few soldiers, and old ones at that, it'd been a crazy plan. The Sylphaen were *massive*. Their leader probably wouldn't go anywhere without loyal acolytes all around him, and if they believed I was someplace they could finally capture me…

They'd brought dozens today alone.

A handful of old soldiers wouldn't be a match for them. They'd die, and Zeke would too.

Zeke was desperate, though. I could see it on his face. Ren must not believe the Sylphaen existed, not if he still had Niall around. Not if he'd let his soldiers arrest Zeke.

And Zeke was like Ina, in his way. He was trying to save what was left of his family.

I just couldn't let him die to do it.

Running my hand through my tangled hair, I looked away. I didn't have a plan either, though. My way added three people to the mix, leaving God knew how many Sylphaen against a few old soldiers and us. And *us* wasn't much. A dehaian, a freak, and a greliaran in a place he'd never been meant to go. For pity's sake, even on *land* that was a suicidal…

My racing thoughts slowed. On land…

A shiver ran through me. It was madness. It'd never work.

It would stop them once and for all.

"How many greliarans do you know?"

Silence greeted the words. I looked up.

Noah was staring at me. "*Huh*?"

"Greliarans. You said once that you don't keep in touch with the others. Is that true for all of them? There aren't *any* you can reach?"

"Chloe," Zeke protested. "What are you doing?"

"Dad might know a few from when he was younger," Noah allowed. "He doesn't talk about those days much."

I nodded. "Call him. See if he can get them to meet us."

"Chloe!" Zeke snapped.

"A trap," I replied. "That's what I'm doing. We go to Lycera like you said. We get those soldiers, and then we come back to land. Let this Kirzan guy and all his Sylphaen know where we are. Get them to meet us on the coast. The soldiers hide in the water, let them pass. When the Sylphaen come out to grab me, we end this. The soldiers block their retreat and the greliarans…

handle the rest."

Zeke stared at me. Blinking, Noah looked away, seeming taken back.

"Niall's out there," Zeke said, his voice tight. "He'll come with them."

"We'll find him. Stop the greliarans from killing him."

He hesitated, and then gave a small nod.

Silence fell between us.

"Guess we just need to get back to the ocean, then," Zeke managed.

I nodded as well, though I dropped my gaze away rather than continue looking at him. It was just too hard, given what might happen to his brother if something went wrong. Niall *would* come with the Sylphaen. He'd do his best to bring me back for their ritual.

And Zeke wanted to save his family.

Drawing a breath, I forced myself to concentrate. I meant it, though. We'd help Niall. We'd figure out how to protect him and not get ourselves killed at the same time. But first, we had to get out of here. So far no one had commented on the three of us in this alley, and no cops had spotted us either, but we still had limited options. Baylie and the others were presumably back at the library, and I could guess that the police wouldn't be too eager to let them leave. I felt bad, getting them stuck like this, even if there hadn't been a choice.

I just hoped no one got in too much trouble for us taking off like this.

"So… taxi?" Noah suggested.

I looked back at him. He shrugged.

"Yeah," I said.

I returned my attention to the street, watching the passersby while Noah took out his cell phone to call a cab and get us out of here.

"You sure you want me to leave you here?" the driver asked as he pulled the taxi to a stop on a curve of frontage road.

In the back seat between Noah and Zeke, I attempted a smile when the man looked over his shoulder at us skeptically.

"Yeah," Noah replied. "This is where our friends are meeting us."

"For a picnic," the driver stated, repeating the lie we'd told him when he picked us up in town.

"Well, yeah." Noah shrugged. "They said it was nice out here."

The man stared at us.

"They don't like the city beaches," I tried.

His gaze moved between me and the others. "Uh-huh."

Noah pulled his wallet from his pocket and took out some money quickly. "Thanks for your time."

He pushed the cash at the driver and then drew me with him when he opened the door and left the car. Zeke climbed from the other side.

I let out a breath when the man drove off, heading toward a junction with the main highway.

"Call your dad?" I suggested, glancing to Noah.

He nodded. Taking out his cell, he started away from the road.

My gaze drifted to the water. Waves tumbled against the beach and then swept out again, dragging bits of sand and gravel from the shore with them. Parched scrub brush and weathered bushes in tones of faded green and yellow separated the road and the coastline, and rough boulders dotted the narrow expanse.

I swallowed hard. I hadn't really seen the ocean back at the Delaneys' house in Santa Lucina. All the curtains had been closed and I'd been trying to stay away from the windows besides.

But the urge to just walk into the waves now was overwhelming.

"Come on," Zeke said quietly.

I blinked, tugging my gaze from the water. Focusing on trying to reduce whatever signal I might be giving off, I followed him toward a cluster of boulders and bushes. We crouched behind them, the branches and rough rocks concealing us from view of the road and the water alike. Only a narrow line of sight remained to where Noah sat beside another boulder, talking to his father on the phone.

Salt from the waves carried through the breeze. I shivered.

"You alright?"

I glanced over at Zeke. His brow rose.

"Been a while," I managed.

He nodded.

The sounds of the water and the distant highway mingled in the air. Behind the other boulder, I could see Noah arguing with his father, his words lost to the white-noise rush of the waves.

"So Joseph really said you could hide?" Zeke asked. "That you could keep that thing from finding you in the ocean?"

"He said I could make it harder for the Beast to locate me. Suppress... whatever it is I'm sending off."

Zeke didn't respond for a moment. "I really wish you'd reconsider coming with me. I can get the soldiers and bring them back here myself. You don't need to come."

"I can still help. Stop anything from—" Fear threatened to choke me. I battled past it. "I'm going to end this, Zeke, and keep everyone safe too. I don't care what it takes."

He paused. "And if I do?"

The words were soft and when I glanced over, I trembled at the look in his eyes. Deep. Worried. It stole my breath.

And I didn't know how to answer him.

Footsteps crunched on the gravel.

"He'll do it," Noah said. "He's not happy, but he will."

I nodded, struggling to bury my discomfort. "Where are we going to meet them?"

"At my uncle's place. Dad's going to call up there. See if he can arrange something of a truce with Richard."

He grimaced at my expression. "We know the area and it

has those traps. Seemed like the best option."

I managed another nod. "Suppose we should get going then."

Avoiding both of their gazes, I pushed to my feet, pausing only to check that nothing had changed and no one had stopped their car nearby. The frontage road remained empty, however, and the vehicles on the highway flew past at such speeds, it was obvious nobody was attempting to stop at the sight of us.

"What about that potion thing?" Noah asked.

My brow furrowed. "What about it?"

"You can't bring it with you. I mean, it's not like you can take it. If you do and you become a landwalker while you're down there..."

My stomach rolled.

"Here." Noah nodded to the gravel behind me. "We can leave it. My dad's already coming to pick up our stuff. He can get that too."

He pulled his wallet and phone from his pocket. I stepped aside while he moved past me. Removing a few grapefruit-sized rocks from around the base of the boulder, he tucked the wallet and phone where the stones had been. His shoes followed, and then he reached for the vial.

I hesitated, reluctant to let go of the slight advantage it provided us against the Sylphaen, even if only on land. His brow twitched up.

Trying not to grimace, I tugged it out and then handed it to him. He placed it by his wallet while I slipped from my flip-flops and Zeke removed his shoes as well.

And then they both went to take off their shirts.

My gaze fled, locking onto the rocks, the sand, onto anything else at all. From the corner of my eye, I could see them stuffing the shirts into the tiny crevice. I didn't move, resisting the urge to wrap my arms around me as if to hold my clothes on. Awkward wasn't the half of it. Right now, a scale swimsuit just didn't feel like enough covering, and I'd rather let the ocean take my clothes than deal with their attention during the time it'd take me to get into the water and change form.

I heard Noah pick up the rocks again and arrange them around our things to conceal everything from view.

"Ready?" he asked.

I nodded, still avoiding looking at either of them.

We headed for the ocean. The soles of my feet changed in response to the gravel as I followed Noah and Zeke toward the water, and when the tide swept in around my ankles, it was all I could do not to let the rest of my skin do the same. Drawing slow breaths to fight the shivers running through my body, I forged farther out among the waves and felt them push at me as they rolled into shore.

Zeke tossed a quick glance toward the highway and then dove fast. Surfacing a moment later several yards away, he threw me an impatient look.

I turned to Noah.

He gave me a tight smile.

I dropped below the water and kicked away from the seafloor. The change raced through me, disintegrating my clothes and transforming my legs into a tail. I couldn't restrain a gasp of relief at the feeling, as though my body had been under pressure without my realizing.

And now that pressure was gone.

Spinning in the water, I returned to Noah's side and broke through the waves again.

His hands caught me. My tail moved to steady us both while the tide sucked us toward the deeper water. His shorts were soaked and his hair was as well. The water rolled around us, sweeping as high as his shoulders and nearly pulling him from his feet.

"So," he called over the noise of the waves. "What now?"

I bit my lip. It'd just taken a thought to help Zeke come inland or get the landwalkers to the coast.

This felt a lot more complicated.

Holding onto his arms, I tried willing him to be able to come with me. To be able to breathe and see and survive where I could.

"Come on," I suggested.

He let me pull him beneath the water. For a moment he hovered there, and then he choked and kicked backward, surfacing again quickly.

I rose fast to find him coughing and swiping saltwater from his eyes.

He shook his head. I swam closer, taking his arm again.

"Chloe," Zeke called.

I glanced back.

"It didn't work," he continued. "Come on. We need to go."

"Try again," Noah said.

I turned to him.

He met my eyes. "Ellie said you could do it."

"She said I *might* be—"

"Chloe, try again."

A grimace crossed my face. Ellie really hadn't said that. She'd told us that, in stories, the ancient dehaians had been able to bring sailors underwater with them. But I wasn't really like them. Not entirely. After all, no one talked about ancient dehaians *killing* people like I'd just done. Those stories only told about the dehaians kissing sailors and then taking them down into their world.

I paused.

There was that.

I glanced to Zeke, seeing the worry and impatience in his expression. Discomfort twisted through me, and I felt my face turning red. "Um… there's one more thing to try."

My gaze went back to Noah. He took a quick breath while I kicked backward, pulling him down with me.

The water closed over our heads. We floated for a moment, inches from each other and rocking with the tide. His brow furrowed, questioning.

I drew him to me. My lips pressed to his.

He seemed to freeze, as if he was as shocked as I'd been when he'd kissed me this morning. And then the tension faded. His hands released my arms to take my back, bringing me closer.

My heart raced while my body moved against his, steadying us and keeping us below the waves. Electricity ran through my skin like I was changing all over again.

I recognized the feeling.

My eyes opened. I pulled away from him.

He stared at me, breathless.

And reality caught up to him.

He drew another breath, his eyes widening. His lips curled into a smile.

"It worked," he said and then he blinked at the sound of his voice, no different than in the open air. His smile grew.

I felt Zeke coming toward us. I turned.

His expression made me look away again.

"Ellie said in those stories—" I started.

"Yeah," Zeke interrupted flatly. "I remember."

I wasn't sure what to say. Blinking fast, I glanced back to Noah. Though he was breathing like me and his voice carried in the same way mine did, his body hadn't changed. His legs still kicked under the water, fighting the current to hold him nearby.

And I knew he wouldn't be able to keep up with us.

"Well, um…" I put my arm around him.

Noah's skin was warm against my side. I could feel his muscles beneath my hand.

My face flushed. Shoving the observations out of my head quickly, I didn't meet either of their gazes. "Guess we should go."

A heartbeat of silence followed.

It felt like a year.

"Yeah," Zeke agreed.

I felt him turn in the water. His tail kicked hard, sending him racing away.

My eyes still avoiding Noah's, I followed Zeke deeper into the ocean.

8

WYATT

Noah's neighborhood was a haven for rich idiots who wanted to surround themselves in luxury and hide it from common sight behind fancy walls and trimmed hedges. Shining Mercedes and BMWs sat in the driveways, when they weren't tucked inside garages big enough to be middle-class houses. The spacious yards were trimmed down to grass carpets that didn't have enough cover to obscure a child.

It was no place for greliarans.

Which I supposed meant the Delaneys felt right at home.

With Clay a few steps ahead of me, I walked down the sidewalk, my gaze scanning the houses. We'd hitchhiked to get here, catching rides with truckers since our SUV had been destroyed by what that green-skinned freak had done. It'd taken us the better part of a day and a half to make the trip, but now we'd finally reached the Delaneys' neighborhood.

I wasn't sure if the fish girl would be here. She could have gone anywhere after leaving the forest. But I did know that she'd had that pretty-boy Noah with her yesterday, and this seemed the most likely place to which he'd retreat after scampering away from that storm.

It might not have been much to go on, but it was better than wandering all over the nation or returning home like Dad probably would've insisted we do.

My lip twitched. Moron. I'd gotten us closer to her in a day than he'd done in a week. And that wasn't the only thing that'd changed.

I glanced to the coastline. The black storm had dissipated hours ago, back by the coast near that weird turtle-guy's house, and it'd mostly taken the whispering with it. I still felt it in the air from time to time, however, similar to the presence of another greliaran but a thousand times the size. Unlike one of us, though, a sense of its proximity wasn't the only thing I picked up on. Vague emotions carried through as well — something that was disconcerting to say the least. I didn't know if Clay could feel it. I hadn't asked him and I wouldn't, since giving the slightest impression that I was slipping would be enough of an invitation for him to try taking control. But ever since I'd opened my eyes to see that churning mass of black clouds above me, the weird feelings had been in my head.

It was out there now, even if the sky looked clear. For a time, it'd vanished over the horizon and I'd lost it, which was nice. I couldn't care less about that thing except where it helped me kill the girl, and its irrelevant concerns were cluttering up my head. But now it was back and it felt... confused. It was hunting her too, that much I knew, and it hated her for reasons I couldn't even begin to understand. But it also appeared torn on where she was located. Over the past day, it'd gone back and forth, drifting closer to shore and then returning to the open ocean like it couldn't decide where to search for her trail.

The stupid thing was making it hard to concentrate.

"Wyatt?"

I tugged my gaze back to find Clay staring at me. "What?"

His brow furrowed. "I asked you how close you wanted to get to the house."

I bit back a curse. And there was my point entirely. That big emotional cloud of hate really wasn't doing me any favors.

"I heard you," I retorted. "I was thinking."

He didn't respond.

I covered my irritation with a glance around the neighborhood again. We couldn't just keep going like this. In a few more moments, we'd come into view of the Delaneys' house; it lay just beyond the curve of the road. They might look out the window and spot us. We'd hidden our presence as a matter of course the minute we'd neared town, and when it came to sneaking around in such silence that even our kind would have trouble hearing our footsteps, I'd bet there wasn't anyone better than us. But that didn't mean Noah and his family couldn't get lucky.

"Circle back around the next block," I ordered. "Come at the house from the other side and stay out of sight behind the neighbor's place. I'm going to head to the park. Follow along that hedge separating it from the house. See if I can spot anyone through the back windows."

Clay looked like he wanted to protest. My plan left him doing little more than watching a garage and a wall. But after a moment, he just glared and then turned back to do as I'd instructed.

I smirked and walked toward the park.

Spreading out for about a grassy mile of winding sidewalks and sandy volleyball courts, the park ran up to the edge of the water. The rightmost side climbed in a gentle slope toward the Delaneys' house, though a tall line of bushes and trees separated the neighborhood from the public space. Voices carried over the distance in the park, and laughter did as well, while under the bright sunlight, people tossed Frisbees to their dogs or rollerbladed along.

And none of them looked my way.

I scaled the slope and then slipped into the brush. Maybe eight feet wide, the border hedge was dense enough to block any view of the house from the park, but it wasn't so tight that I didn't have room to maneuver. Moving carefully, I slipped deeper into the bushes and then paused when flashing lights came into view.

Cop cars sat in the circle drive. A few officers stood around them, while others came from the house. The door looked broken, as though it'd been kicked wide, and the bottom of the garage door was a shattered mess, like someone had driven through it before it fully opened.

A sedan pulled into the driveway and my brow furrowed. It was Uncle Peter's car, though the roof was dented and scratched, and one of the windows was shattered. Aunt Diane's vehicle followed his, looking equally beaten up. The cars came to a stop and when Peter climbed out, I heard him call to the cops.

Diane and others got out after him. I restrained a growl. The fish girl wasn't with them. Neither was Noah. The cops were asking about her, though, saying something about a girl running away with two guys back at a library. Peter seemed to be deflecting the questions as though he didn't know how to explain.

I glanced around. She'd run. Okay. Maybe she was heading for the water, then. There were several beaches in town, but on foot – even with the scale-skin's speed – she'd probably head for the closest one from where she'd taken off.

Which was… I grimaced, unable to recall the location of the library in Santa Lucina. I wasn't even sure I'd known they *had* a library in this town.

Tires rumbled on the driveway again. I looked back. Another car pulled up, entering the wrong way in the drive and coming to a halt a short distance from my hiding space. My brow climbed.

The girl's parents. Whatever the fish had done to them back at our house still held because they didn't appear the slightest bit sick from the ocean only a few dozen yards away. Leaving Peter with the cops, Diane hurried toward the couple when they left their car, and Noah's stepsister came after her.

"What is this?" the girl's father asked anxiously. "Where's Chloe?"

"She's…" Diane cast a look back at the police and then lowered her voice even further while she motioned them closer to the bushes. "She's fine. But we had a break-in. The people like the ones at the cabin came after her again. She, Noah, and another boy left when the police arrived."

"Where'd she go?"

Diane hesitated. "We're not entirely certain," she answered carefully. "They ran into town and—"

She glanced back as Peter escorted the cops into the house.

"Listen," she continued to the girl's parents in a rush. "The kids are in the water. I can't go into more detail right now, but they have a plan to stop this. After we're done with the police, we're heading out to meet them."

The couple paused.

My brow furrowed. Noah was *where*? For that matter, what the hell were the fish and my cousin planning to stop? That storm thing? *Me*? Fat chance on either account. The bitch was dead the moment I got my hands on her, to hell with whatever that cloud monster wanted. After all this work, nothing – and that included any scale-skin plan – was going to keep me from what I deserved.

But that did raise the question of what Noah thought he was doing.

Glancing around, I inched closer.

"Your son is in the ocean with her?" the woman asked.

Diane's face was tight with barely hidden worry. "Yes. I don't know how."

The woman looked to her husband.

"Are you guys okay?" the stepsister asked, her tone and expression both guarded.

For a moment, they didn't respond.

"Yes," the man said finally. "We…"

"Nothing hurts," the woman explained when he trailed off. "And we just…" She hesitated. A helpless expression crossed her face. "We thought perhaps she'd come back here. We didn't know where else to go."

Awkward silence fell briefly.

"Do you think, maybe…" the woman continued to Diane, almost sounding desperate. "Maybe we could help? Whatever's going on, we just want to help her."

The stepsister's face darkened. "I saw your *help*, Mrs. Kowalski. I watched Chloe almost die from it."

"Baylie…" Diane cautioned.

"No," the girl retorted. "No, these people let a psycho run *experiments* on Chloe. They didn't listen, they *never* listen, and she nearly—"

"We know," the man cut in. "Baylie… we know."

The girl eyed him warily.

"We made a mistake," he continued while his wife looked away, her face crumpling like she was trying not to cry. "A lot of mistakes. And Chloe… Baylie, our daughter saved our lives." He glanced to his wife again, including her in the statement.

"She risked herself for our sakes, even after…" He shook his head. "You're right. We should have listened. But we want the chance to see her again. To tell her we're sorry and that, no matter *what* she is, we love her. So please," he looked to Diane, "allow us to come with you. Allow us to help our child."

The awkward silence returned. I scowled. These emotional morons just kept going on, but they hadn't said a word of where the fish was headed.

It was infuriating.

"They're going north," Diane said.

My lip twitched. It was like the woman could hear my thoughts. And the girl's exact location would be…?

"But—" Diane glanced around, almost as if checking whether anyone was nearby – not that she'd even *know*, the human. "Let's get inside, shall we? Continue this conversation else-where?"

The girl's parents nodded. With Diane and Baylie, they walked into the house and shut the door.

It was all I could do to restrain a growl of frustration. With all the cops blathering on out here, I couldn't hear a damned thing. But I needed that information. I wasn't going to let that girl get away from me this time.

But then, she wouldn't do anything till her family was there – or, at least, not take off for someplace else in the meantime. And these people weren't smart. Hell, most of them were human or landwalker, which put them about on the level of half-dead rabbits in terms of survival skills. They didn't know

I was here, and I was good enough at hunting and stalking that chances were, they never would.

So I'd be careful. I'd stay out of sight and listen hard, and make sure that idiot Clay did the same. The cops had to leave sooner or later.

And the Delaneys would slip up eventually.

NOAH

In all my life of knowing about dehaians, I'd never imagined I'd be swimming through the ocean with them.

Keeping my arm around Chloe's shoulders, I cast a glance to her while we raced along. Her green eyes glowed in the darkness, and her skin glistened like it was dusted with gold. At my side, her long, cream-scaled tail undulated in the water, propelling us along at speeds that felt like they should've been impossible.

But then, all of this should have been.

I didn't know how deep we were, though it didn't seem to matter regardless. Something about the same magic that enabled her to bring me here kept the pressure at bay. There was barely a drag from the water as well; it just seemed to bend around her, allowing us to rocket along and keeping anything in it from hurting our eyes or skin at the same time.

Though she didn't seem to notice. Or perhaps it was so

familiar to her at this point, she just ignored it.

She seemed to be able to navigate, however, while I could hardly see a thing. The water around us was nearly black, as though we were flying through a nighttime world of dense fog, with only an occasional flash of flotsam and detritus shooting past us to break the monotony. I didn't know if letting my greliaran side out a bit would change that, but having her so close in her dehaian form worried me. I wasn't willing to risk relaxing my control just to sharpen my vision. Thankfully, my hearing helped. I'd realized as the minutes crept on that I could at least pick up changes in the sound of the water when Zeke altered direction ahead of us.

Chloe, though… Her glowing eyes twitched across the murk like she was watching something. It made me wonder what else was nearby that I couldn't see.

Her hold tightened on me and we shifted direction, bringing her side into contact with mine. There wasn't anything on her now but scales and skin, the latter of which was soft and strangely warm despite the cold water around us.

Which, now that I thought about it, was another thing that probably should have been affecting me. It had to be freezing down here.

Meanwhile, though, it felt great to be this close to her again. Distracting as hell, yes; I was supposed to be keeping watch for the Beast. But great. And when she'd kissed me…

Damn, I wanted more of that.

We shifted direction again, heading deeper. The darkness

intensified, stealing even my glimpses of her next to me. Drawing another breath, I attempted to focus on any sense of that thing being nearby, rather than my blindness or the incredible feeling of her body moving beside mine.

Minutes crept by, turning into endless, black hours without much to distinguish them. Chloe's glowing gaze darted to me from time to time, and her arm adjusted on me every so often, almost as though she was afraid I'd slip away.

And then suddenly she tensed. I floundered when she pulled up fast, coming to a halt with her gaze on something ahead of us.

Clutching onto me tightly, she jackknifed in the water. I gasped, hanging on while she rocketed back the way we'd come and then dove sharply down. A heartbeat passed and then, just as quickly, she veered up again, bringing us to a stop.

Her side pressed against mine and I could feel her breathing hard. Her fingers pressed to my lips, silently telling me to stay quiet. My eyes scanned the murk, seeing absolutely nothing.

I scowled. My greliaran side could do anything down here, including get her killed. I didn't know what would happen if I let it out.

But in the meantime, I was blind. We were obviously in trouble, and I was blind.

Hell with it.

I let my vision grow sharper and held on for dear life to the rest of the greliaran traits fighting to get free inside. My eyes stung, as though the heat from them was affected by the water.

I winced, biting back a grunt of pain, but after a moment the burning faded.

The murk took on more definition. The darkness pushed back the slightest bit, revealing the grayish sand of the seafloor.

Chloe glanced to me and I felt her tense. Worry flashed over her face, painful to see.

"Okay?" she mouthed.

I nodded.

Hesitantly, she echoed the motion and her grip tightened on me again.

Zeke appeared out of the blackness, and I could tell from his face that something was wrong. His eyes went wide at the sight of mine, and quickly, I held up a hand, trying to keep him from doing anything that'd make me lose control.

He paused. Nodding to the left, he took off again.

Chloe pulled me after him. Gray sand rushed beneath us, dotted with small rocks and strange creatures and yielding up nowhere to hide. Beneath my arm, Chloe's sides moved rapidly with her panicked breaths. I could feel her shaking.

I didn't know what we were escaping from, but the desire to protect her from it made it *incredibly* hard to keep my skin from changing.

Piles of jumbled chaos raced into view. My brow furrowed and it took me a moment to figure out what I was seeing.

A ship. The broken remains of one, anyway. Toppled on its side, the thing was a mess of holes through what had once been the hull and decks, including a massive tear that probably had been what killed the vessel in the first place. Draping protrusions like knobby icicles made out of rust hung from the railings, while mollusks and God knew what else encrusted every available surface, further obscuring its original shape.

Chloe shot upward, pulling us above the wreck and past the debris littering the ocean floor. Turning quickly after Zeke, she brought us both through a gap in the hull.

The darkness grew thicker around us. Metal poles stuck out from the shadows like bony fingers that swayed and creaked faintly when our presence disturbed the currents. Chloe's hold on me tightened, her body still shaking. I put my free hand to her side, trying to calm her despite the fact I didn't know what we were escaping from.

Or how I'd stop it if it came to hurt her.

I pushed the thought away. I'd figure something out, even if I couldn't move as fast as a dehaian in this murk.

Seconds slid by. I didn't hear anything but the whispers of the ship and the water moving past the opening overhead.

The current stirred when Zeke reached over, touching Chloe's arm. Her breath caught. His glowing blue eyes met hers for a moment and then, with the tiniest flick of his tail, he crept upward to the gap in the ship's hull. Chloe watched him, trembling.

Another moment passed. He turned, looking back at us. Chloe drew a breath and together, we followed him.

"How much farther?" she whispered when we reached Zeke.

He grimaced. "A few hours."

I glanced between them. "What happened?"

"Soldiers up ahead," Chloe answered. Her brow rose at Zeke. "Is there a way around them?"

His grimace didn't fade, but he nodded. "There are some ravines and caves to the south. Soldiers might be watching them, but at least the terrain will give us places to hide till we can get close enough to pass the border."

"You don't look too sure about that plan," Chloe said.

He paused. "South's closer to other borders too. Vetorians might've slipped through near there."

Chloe swallowed.

"Who?" I asked.

"Mercenaries," she explained. "They sort of work for the Sylphaen."

I shook my head. "No way then. We have to go another—"

"You know how to navigate down here?" Zeke snapped.

"No, but it doesn't seem like you're doing so great a job either."

Zeke started forward. Chloe dropped her arm from me to put herself in his path.

"Stop it!" She looked between us. "Both of you. Please." Her gaze went back to Zeke. "Caves. Okay. And the Lyceran border… it won't be a problem?"

It took him a moment to pull his glare from me. "No," he answered her. "Lycera's border isn't heavily guarded, since they're one of the few nations that haven't had problems with Yvaria in the past hundred years. We should be able to get through without trouble."

Chloe nodded, though when she moved to take my arm again, I could see the worry on her face.

Zeke's gaze twitched back to me. His jaw muscles jumping, he turned and started swimming for the south.

I watched him. He didn't like Chloe being this close to me.

A microscope wouldn't have been able to find how little I cared.

Minutes stretched again as the gray sand continued, the surface speckled with rocks and tiny creatures that bolted when we sped past. Other than the wreck behind us, nothing much of interest had revealed itself and I couldn't help but wonder, given how little there was to see, what the dehaians' cities were like. Chloe hadn't mentioned anything she'd seen from the last time she was down here.

But then, maybe there just hadn't been much to tell.

Up ahead, I heard Zeke adjust his course in the water, and a heartbeat later, Chloe followed suit. Even with my sharpened vision, I couldn't see him through the murk, though thankfully my hearing still made up a bit of the difference.

Though the three of us weren't the only sound out here.

My brow furrowed. It wasn't quite like the whispering noise the dehaians made when they cut through the water. More like a whine, so *incredibly* faint and infrequent that I could barely catch it before it seemed to be behind us and gone again. And I knew it wasn't the Beast; I felt nothing different about the ocean nearby. It was just a weird, quiet sound.

I looked around, even if the darkness was so thick, I could hardly see beyond the two of us. "Chloe?"

She glanced to me, worry on her face.

"Do you know of anything that'd make a whining—"

Dehaians appeared out of the empty ocean floor on all sides.

Chloe gasped, attempting to turn. Zeke shouted her name. With ruthless speed, the dehaians leveled weapons at us that looked like guns.

And fired.

10

CHLOE

Pods of nets and vines struck us, pinning me against Noah and sending us both plummeting to the ocean floor. I heard Zeke shout for me, and then the vines crawled over my face, blinding me and nearly cutting off my ability to breathe.

My heart racing, I shoved against the net, fighting desperately to break its hold. Nothing changed. The tentacle-like ropes clung to my skin everywhere they touched, and stretched with my movements like rubber from hell. I couldn't get my hand to my face to remove the vines. Every motion just made them stick worse.

At my side, Noah snarled. I gasped.

"Noah," I whispered. "Breathe. Please. We'll be okay."

I prayed he believed the lie. I didn't think that for a moment myself, and the sound of laughter beyond us just made the doubt worse.

He shuddered. "Who…"

I hesitated. He wouldn't like the truth. "It's going to be

okay," I tried a second time.

He paused, and then his hand moved, finding my side. I'd landed mostly with my back to his chest, though my hips and tail were twisted at an awkward angle. But he felt comforting holding me against him nonetheless.

The net rocked when someone grabbed it. Water rushed through the tiny openings in the vines as we began to move.

I trembled. The Vetorians had just come out of nowhere. One minute, the seafloor had been empty for miles, and the next, they were all around us as though they'd appeared from the water itself.

But Noah had noticed something. I wished I'd had more time to react to what he'd been trying to say.

They must have been hiding behind veils, though. Those weird, bubble things that blocked any view of Nyciena and travelers alike. It was the only way to explain how the ocean had sprouted dozens of Vetorians from nothing.

And now they had us.

I pushed the thought away fast. They had to let us out of the nets eventually. And then we could do something about this. I wasn't sure what, but it'd be something and then we'd be fine.

After all, we weren't in Sylphaen hands yet.

Noah's grip on me tightened. He'd felt my shaking grow worse. Drawing a partially stifled breath past the muffle of the vines, I attempted to focus on staying calm while feeling for anything in the water around us.

The nets made it nearly impossible. Shapes moved past the tiny openings in the vines, and I couldn't tell if they were dehaians or rocks. We rose and fell while the Vetorians carried us, and I lost all sense of how deep we were in moments. I couldn't see anything – a vine lay over my closed eyes – and the Vetorians barely said a word. Zeke was likewise silent. I had no idea where he was at all.

I tried not to think what that could mean.

The Vetorians dove lower in the water again. A hard surface thudded into us. Sand puffed through the gaps in the net, making me choke. For an eternal moment, nothing happened, and then the vines moved near my face.

Someone yanked the sticky tangle from my eyes. I winced.

A Vetorian woman hovered above us. Her brown eyes flicked from me to Noah and an expression twisted her face like we were some kind of refuse she'd dredged up from the seafloor. Scars marred the bronze-flecked skin of her midsection and sides, the marks almost ritualistic in their regularity, and stones glinting with green ore hung from braids in her brown hair. Shoving us back to the sandy ground, she scoffed.

I turned as much as I could, searching for Zeke.

He was trapped in a net several yards away, at the edge of what felt like an opening in the seafloor. Dozens of Vetorians floated around us, but as I watched, a dark-haired man with splotched scales like a koi fish cut the vines from Zeke's head and then tugged them aside.

Scowling and still encased in the net from the neck down,

Zeke struggled back from the man. Twisting in the vines, he scanned the water, and relief flashed over his face when he spotted me.

At the sight of him, though, the Vetorian man sputtered something, the language indecipherable but the shock behind the words more than clear. The woman looked over and surprise took the place of her disgust.

She turned back fast, her knife coming up to aim at me. "Name."

I stared at her.

"What is your *name*?" she demanded.

The knife rested on my neck, the point pricking my skin. Behind my back, I felt Noah tense.

"Venika," the man near Zeke snapped. "We don't get paid if you kill them."

Disgust returned to the woman's face, but the knife moved away. She jerked her chin at the others, and several came closer, taking up the net and hoisting us from the ground again. We swung between them while they swam over the edge of the ravine, revealing a deep canyon that descended into blackness with caves pockmarking its walls.

I shivered and felt Noah's grip on my side tighten again – out of tension or to comfort me, I wasn't sure. Up ahead, the mercenaries holding Zeke headed toward an opening halfway down the cliff wall, and a moment later, the ones around us followed.

The cave mouth passed us and I blinked when a veil did as

well. Blue-white light glared in my eyes, emanating from a pair of torches on either side of the entrance. Four dehaians were there, carrying stone spears and clearly serving as guards. Ignoring them, the Vetorians dropped the nets to the floor and then Venika appeared, a knife in her hand again.

With quick motions, she sliced at the vines around us while the dark-haired man did the same to the net holding Zeke.

Venika tugged the ropes away, sending me falling to the side.

"What the—" she began when she spotted Noah.

"He's sick," Zeke interjected quickly. Shoving away from the nets, he started to swim toward me. The dark-haired man's knife brought him up short. Grimacing, Zeke glanced from me to the others. "He can't fully change right now."

Venika eyed Zeke for a moment, and then returned her gaze to Noah, the ever-present disgust strengthening. "Stay away from him, then," she told the others.

Looking like she'd almost rather kill Noah than leave him there, Venika retreated toward the entrance while the dark-haired man did the same. The four dehaians near the torches moved to take up places in front of the cave mouth, blocking us from escaping.

"Go find Kreyus," Venika ordered the dark-haired man.

I stopped breathing. Wait, I… I'd heard that wrong.

"What did you say?" I managed while the man left the cave.

Venika ignored me.

I struggled up from the ground and swam toward her. Zeke

sped over to stop me. I shoved his hands aside.

"What did you say?" I repeated, my gaze still on Venika.

"Shut it," she retorted tiredly.

I stared at her. I had to be missing something. Maybe the name was like Joe or Bob to dehaians. Or, again, maybe I'd just misheard.

There was no way my biological father was here. This. A Vetorian working for the Sylphaen.

"What is it?" Zeke asked.

I shook my head. I couldn't even speak the words. I had to be wrong.

A group of dehaians swam past the veil at the cave opening, and the Vetorians guarding us instantly drew themselves up to attention at the sight. Men and women alike, the newcomers were even more covered in scars than the rest, and not all of the old wounds looked as ritualistic as the ones on Venika. Their scales were shades of brown or rust, and their hair was much the same.

But the one at the center…

My insides quivered.

Dark red hair. Gold flecks to his skin. Scales like burnished bronze, but with an iridescent sheen. His green gaze swept across Zeke and Noah and then landed on me with nothing but ice in his eyes.

"There wasn't anyone with them?" he asked Venika.

She shook her head.

His eyebrow twitched up as though he found that surprising.

"Post extra guards on the canyon walls, in case anyone comes looking. And Ezio," he glanced to the dark-haired man, "contact the client for payment."

Ezio nodded.

The red-haired man turned and swam back the way he'd come.

"Are you Kreyus?" I called.

He continued on.

"Please!" I cried, starting forward.

The guards' spears brought me up short.

Pausing, the man glanced back. "What is it to you?"

I trembled. "Did you go on land a little over seventeen years ago and… and meet a woman named Susan?"

His brow furrowed. "What?"

"Susan. Her name was Susan. Did you—"

He swam toward me again and I recoiled at the look on his face. Dark. Threatening.

And so very, *very* angry.

"Who the hell are you?" he demanded.

I struggled to find my voice. "Her daughter."

He stared at me. "Susan's daughter couldn't become dehaian."

My trembling grew stronger. The phrasing. *Couldn't become dehaian.* Humans weren't able to have children with dehaians. Jirral had mentioned that ages ago. But this guy hadn't said that. And he wouldn't have known to say anything different. Not unless…

He turned to leave.

"I am," I called. "I-I am her daughter. I'm half-landwalker. I survived."

The man stopped. The other Vetorians glanced to him, confusion and curiosity clear on their faces.

He looked back at me again.

"I changed for the first time this summer," I continued, fighting to keep my voice steady. "I lived in Kansas before that."

"This is a trick," Venika muttered.

Kreyus didn't respond. His brow flickered down, his gaze still on my face, and then he looked away sharply. "We're done here."

He swam off.

"Please!" I called. "Please don't let the—"

Venika rushed at me, knife in hand. Zeke pushed me back, putting himself between us.

"Shut up," Venika spat, a look in her eyes like she'd stab us both if I breathed in a way she disliked.

I didn't make a sound.

Venika's gaze went from me to Zeke and she scoffed. Watching us contemptuously, she swam to the entrance and then jerked her chin at the guards.

The men moved aside. She left the cave.

Zeke let out a breath and glanced back at me.

I couldn't meet his gaze. Turning, I swam toward Noah and then sank to the ground.

Zeke followed. His tail curled beneath him as he sat by my

side.

Silence fell.

"Thank you," I said to him quietly, "for… you know, protecting…" I nodded to Noah.

Zeke's brow inched up.

My gaze fell away again. Right. Noah wasn't the one he'd been protecting.

I closed my eyes.

"Chloe," Noah tried. "You… you really think that guy's your dad?"

I shifted uncomfortably. "They said my… my whatever… that his name was Kreyus. And to look at him, he really…"

My words ran out. I didn't know what they would've been anyway.

"You need to stay away from him," Zeke said, his voice tight.

I glanced up.

"He's a Vetorian." A humorless noise left Zeke. "Hell, he's in *charge* of Vetorians. And…"

Trepidation quivered through me at the sickened, angry scowl that flashed across his face. "And what?" I prompted warily.

His mouth tightened. "Nothing."

My heart started pounding. I knew that look. 'Nothing' had nothing to do with it. "Zeke…"

"It's just something your dad… Bill said. Or didn't say. I…" He shook his head.

"What was it?" I pressed.

Zeke hesitated again, like he was trying to find words for something he really didn't want to repeat. "Bill made it sound like your mom might've died from aveluria magic."

I stared at him. I couldn't quite breathe. My lungs just kept catching while my brow rose.

Noah muttered a curse, turning away.

"That's part of why the aveluria thing scared them," Zeke continued. "Why they wanted me gone."

My mouth moved, working to find a response, and finally a breath managed to emerge from my chest. The chief had brought up something about that too. About the women who were with them and the way they died.

Zeke hadn't wanted him to say it.

"What did Dad tell you?"

His grimace returned. "Chloe, I—"

"What?"

He hesitated. "That he could bet some of the stories about dehaians were true, like the one that got your mom pregnant and then killed her."

I trembled, my gaze falling to the rocky floor beneath us. That wasn't quite saying aveluria was responsible. It *wasn't*.

But it was *so* close.

"You just… don't push this, okay?" Zeke urged. "Stay away from him. We'll get out of—"

"Why didn't you tell me?"

At his silence, I looked up again.

He gave a small shrug. "Would you have wanted to hear that? On top of *everything* else, that your dad might've…"

I shook my head, my stomach churning. No, and I didn't want to hear it now either.

He would've basically *raped* her.

The churning in my stomach grew worse. I straightened fast, struggling to fight the nausea.

"Chloe," Noah tried, putting a hand to my shoulder.

I shoved him away and rose. I didn't want anyone touching me. I didn't want anything.

Except out of here.

My gaze flashed to the Vetorians, but the sight of them just made it worse. I retreated to the rear of the cave, stopping only when I reached the back wall. I leaned on it, one of my hands bracing me against the rough surface as if to keep the world from falling away from me.

I closed my eyes. It might not be true. It might be a misunderstanding. Maybe she'd really loved him. Maybe she'd just missed him terribly.

There could be another reason she died.

I wasn't sure what I wanted it to be, though. Me? Giving birth to me?

Or aveluria from him.

A sob swelled in my chest. Grimacing furiously, I tried to fight it down. A Vetorian and a murderer. That was my father. A Vetorian, a murderer, and someone who was going to hand me over to be killed by the Sylphaen. And for money. That was it. Just to get his hands on goddamn *money*, he was going to call up those psychotic cultists, tell them I was here, and let them slaughter his own damn—

The water vibrated. I lurched forward, a crunching noise making me open my eyes.

Around my hand, the rock was broken. Shattered into a vaguely oval depression, like someone had plowed into it with a battering ram.

A choked noise left me. Carefully, I retreated from the wall.

My hand tingled. I looked down.

A current whipped around it, spinning like a tiny tornado around my forearm and fist, and sparkling like electricity was trapped within.

I gasped, flinching back.

The current vanished.

For a heartbeat, I couldn't take my eyes from my hand. My skin looked the same. Everything looked the same. The quivering sensation was still in me, just as it'd been since we escaped the Beast yesterday.

But then, what'd just happened hadn't felt like it'd come from that. At least, not *entirely*. It'd felt like when I helped Noah get down here or when I'd brought Ellie and the landwalker elders to the coast. It'd felt like *me*, not something foreign coming out of me. Like my own abilities, only amped up about a hundred fold.

And yet... and yet I'd...

Oh my God, I'd just bashed in a *wall*.

With effort, I tugged my gaze to the rest of the cave, my body still shaking.

Zeke and Noah stared at me, their faces equal pictures of wary alarm.

And the guards weren't much different, except for the addition of the fear in their eyes. With white-knuckled fists, they clenched their weapons.

My shaking grew stronger. The four Vetorians at the cave entrance inched backward.

"Noah?" I asked.

"Uh-huh?"

"Do you feel that thing anywhere around here?"

He paused. "Um…"

"*Do* you?"

"No."

The current spun up around my hand again. I didn't take my eyes from the guards.

"Get out," I ordered.

The men glanced to each other.

I started toward them.

They bolted from the cave.

"Chloe," Zeke tried. "You don't know what this—"

A gasp escaped me. I didn't want to hear it.

"The Beast, Chloe," Noah added. "It could still—"

I shook my head, but the current vanished.

My teeth were chattering. Shivers ran through me so violently, I felt like I might shake apart. But this quivering wasn't coming from the magic. For some reason, it just didn't feel like the magic at all.

I wanted to find him. I wanted… I just wanted to *know*.

Breaths hitched when they tried to enter my lungs. I looked back at Noah and Zeke. "Come on."

Zeke hesitated. "Come on where?" he asked carefully.

"I want to talk to him."

"Chloe," Noah started.

My gaze snapped to him. He cut off.

"I want to talk to him."

Noah glanced to Zeke, who seemed equally unwilling to argue further. Without a word, Zeke reached over, hoisting Noah's arm across his shoulders and keeping his eyes on me the entire time.

I swam out of the cave, leaving them to follow.

The Vetorians were waiting.

My gaze ran over them and the weapons they held. Hovering between the canyon walls, over a hundred men and women watched me, their hands adjusting nervously on their guns and knives. But I couldn't find Kreyus among them. Venika or Ezio either. These just seemed like the Vetorian version of soldiers, regrouping to stop our escape.

"Where is he?" I asked.

The weapons rose.

"I want to see Kreyus."

They didn't respond. At a thought, my hands tingled and water moved around them, spiraling up my arms. Electricity sparked and crackled inside the whirling current, dancing like lightning despite the fact we were underwater.

"Guys," Zeke urged. "I *really* think you ought to back off…"

"Stand down," Kreyus called.

The Vetorians above us moved aside. Kreyus sank past them and I could see the caution in his eyes. His gaze went from my face to the swirling water, and then he held up his hands. At his back, Venika and Ezio took up positions on either side of him, their knives drawn.

"What do you want?" he asked.

"To talk. Just us and you."

He gave a careful nod and then motioned to another cave nearby.

My eyes narrowed. I couldn't see within it. Couldn't feel much there either, which meant it was probably disguised by a veil. Anyone could be inside.

"Out here," I countered. "Send them away."

He hesitated and then jerked his chin toward the canyon rim. "Up top."

Turning, he started for the ledge.

The electrified water twisting around my hands, I trailed him. Still helping Noah, Zeke followed, and the Vetorians pulled away, letting us pass.

Kreyus glanced back when we reached the top of the ravine. "Over here."

He nodded to a collection of boulders.

I gave the rocks wide berth, watching while he swam toward them, but nothing waited behind the stones. Warily, I continued toward him, still keeping an eye to the canyon. Ignoring me, Kreyus sank onto one of the boulders.

"Hey," Noah hissed to me when he and Zeke came closer. "Like the damn *sun*, remember?"

I hesitated, recalling the metaphor Joseph had used. Reluctantly, I willed the current to disappear and focused on suppressing whatever the hell was happening inside me.

It was difficult.

"So," Kreyus prompted, looking for all the world like he was hosting a pleasant after-dinner conversation in some lounge, rather than sitting on a rock in the middle of nowhere. "You wished to talk?"

"How many of your people are trying to circle us right now?" Zeke cut in before I could speak.

Kreyus glanced to him, saying nothing.

I shivered. "Susan."

Kreyus returned his attention to me, the same congenial expression coming back to his face. "What about her?"

The shivering grew worse. Desperately, I fought to keep the magic from escaping.

He seemed to see my struggle. "Listen," he offered. "I don't know who you are – or *what* – but this isn't going to work. My people will stop whoever's coming after you and whatever you hoped to gain from this ruse—"

"What?" I demanded.

"This. You're not my daughter, or Susan's. You can't be. It's imposs—"

Rock chips shattered from the boulder beside him.

Kreyus didn't even flinch.

I drew a ragged breath, fighting to get myself back under control. "How would I know about her, then? How would I—"

"Because this is some kind of trick. I'll grant that you look the part. You're quite a talented actress, and the information you've gathered is impressive as well. But his brother has been hunting us for months, both before and after he assumed the throne." Kreyus nodded toward Zeke without taking his eyes from me. "And King Renekialen especially wants to capture me. Why you brought the prince with you, I don't know, but regardless—"

"Ren's not behind this," Zeke interjected.

Kreyus gave him a look like he didn't believe that for a moment.

"I *am* Susan's daughter," I insisted. "Her brother, Bill Kowalski, and his wife raised me. I grew up in Kansas and—"

"This won't—"

"I'm not lying, you son of a bitch!"

I choked on a sob. My palms hurt from how hard my nails were digging into them and my whole body shook with the effort of not losing control.

Kreyus stared at me, appearing slightly taken aback.

"Chloe," Noah tried gently. "Come on. This guy isn't worth—"

I shook my head and turned away, not wanting to hear it right now. I'd intended to ask him about the aveluria. To learn for certain whether he'd done that to her.

And I couldn't even get him to believe—

"Chloe," Kreyus said.

"What?"

He didn't respond. I looked back to find him studying me, his brow drawing down.

"What?" I demanded.

"Susan," he replied. "Her likes. Dislikes. What are they?"

A strangled laugh rose up, painful with its irony. "What? So I can *prove* that I'm her kid?"

He waited.

"She's *dead*." I bit off the words. "She died when I was born and my parents—" The laugh returned. "They think it was aveluria that killed her. You."

He didn't move. I couldn't read anything from his face.

I turned away again, disgusted. We needed to go. Do what we had to in order to get around those Vetorians… and just go.

"I would never have hurt Susan," Kreyus said quietly.

I stopped.

"Never," he repeated. "I cared for her, and doing something like that… I wouldn't. Not to her. I swear that on all I hold dear."

My gaze slid back to him.

"But if you are who you say you are," he continued. "I've

heard the old stories. You shouldn't be alive."

"Yeah," I replied. "I get that a lot."

He paused. "How did you survive?"

I watched him. There'd hardly been anything in his voice. Maybe curiosity. Maybe not even that.

"I don't know."

"And what you can do?"

I hesitated. "Means your people better not try anything."

Kreyus studied me for a moment and then, of all the reactions in the world, an amused smile twitched across his face. "Yes," he agreed. "I suspect you're right."

He pushed away from the rock. I retreated distrustfully.

"Susan's daughter," he said, his tone almost musing. "Susan's *dehaian* daughter."

Kreyus' brow rose and fell as if he still couldn't quite wrap his mind around it.

I didn't take my eyes from him.

"Come back to the canyon with me," he continued. "I think we have more to discuss."

I shook my head. "I'm not staying. Your 'client'—"

"I will stop the messengers."

"The hell you will," Zeke countered. "Vetorians don't pass up a chance to make a profit. Not when you have—"

"There is a bit about us you have to learn, your highness," Kreyus interrupted. "And since it appears *Chloe* may be who she claims… well, you might just have a chance."

Wary confusion tangled through me as much at the way he

said my name as the rest of his statement.

He motioned toward the ravine. "If you would?"

I glanced to Zeke and Noah. This could be a trick. Kreyus had to know I wanted him to believe me.

Sort of desperately.

I shivered at the realization. I did. I *really* did. Even if I'd just met him, even if he was a Vetorian… having him think I was lying was somehow *so* much worse.

My head moved in a tight nod. "Okay."

He swam for the canyon, leaving us to come after him.

"Chloe," Zeke began.

"I know."

I looked back. Zeke grimaced, while Noah had a pained expression on his face, like he wanted to argue but couldn't.

Swallowing hard, I followed Kreyus back to the ravine.

❧ 11 ❦

ZEKE

I was losing count of the reasons I was concerned for Chloe, and it was starting to drive me crazy.

With Noah's arm slung over my shoulders and the overwhelming urge to leave him on the seafloor gnawing at me, I followed her toward the canyon. It wasn't only that she was here, in the ocean where the Sylphaen, the Beast and, obviously, the Vetorians could easily find her. That'd been bad enough.

But now...

I didn't know what was happening to her. And not just because of her sudden and impossible ability to do things to the water. *With* the water. To the rocks and everything around her. That was, well... honestly, it was a bit terrifying, but the problems went deeper than that.

There was the look in her eyes, like something had snapped.

Like after Harman's experiments and the kidnapping of her parents and all that she'd endured these past several weeks, she'd finally, *finally* been pushed too far. It'd started after the

Sylphaen grabbed Baylie. That man had collapsed and died, and something had just… changed in Chloe's eyes.

I didn't know if she realized it. But it worried me for her. About her. I didn't want her to lose herself to the chaos her life had become. I didn't want to lose who she was.

And that wasn't the only thing.

My gaze tracked toward Kreyus. Vetorians were chaos with scars; that'd been one of the first things I'd ever learned about them. Other descriptions were even less flattering, ranging from barbarians to berserkers to Yvarian insults that even grown adults hoped their mothers would never hear them speak. But the hatred was understandable. They raided villages. Kidnapped or assassinated people. They were known far and wide as opportunistic, bloodthirsty scum.

Though they, of course, just called it business.

And that was the problem. In the wilds of the Prijoran Zone – that mess of barren hills and valleys and wasteland far to the west – it *was* business. The tribes out there had been attacking each other for centuries. There was no industry, no agriculture or successful hunting trade. To survive, the tribes simply preyed on each other and anyone else who happened along, meaning that as sick as it was, murder and theft were the primary skillsets of people out there.

The Vetorians, though, they'd taken advantage of that. They'd refined those skills into a salable product, available to the highest bidder. From what I'd learned growing up, they operated out of cells based mostly on tribal affiliation – although outsiders could join successful groups who had greater potentials for profit – and of them all, their leaders were the most brutal. Through force and bloodshed, the Praelex of a Vetorian cell maintained absolute control, like a wild animal keeping the smaller members of its pack in line.

And Chloe was related to one of them.

I grimaced while we swam down into the canyon. The resemblance between her and Kreyus was uncanny. Even if I hadn't known them at all, I'd have bet money they were father and daughter – a fact which might have forgiven Ren his assumptions, if not for everything else he'd done, and how he'd never listened to any story but the one he'd already decided was true.

The stubborn ass.

I pushed the thought away. It was shocking, though, how likely it seemed that this man was Chloe's father. She had his hair, his eyes. Even the gold dusting to their skin was the same. And the way he'd hinted at Susan being a landwalker from the start – and based his objections to Chloe's claim on that detail – gave even more credence to the possibility.

Of all the people in the world, though…

She may as well have been the kid of a *Sylphaen*.

Ahead of me, Kreyus veered off toward a cave, paying the other Vetorians no attention despite the way some still fingered their weapons as if awaiting the order to attack. Like the previous cave, a veil guarded the entrance, and when we passed it, the darkness gave way to sudden brilliance of several torches spaced along the wall. A mat of seaweed rested at the far end of the space, the bed wide enough for two people.

Venika looked up when we came in. On the ground in front of her lay a collection of weapons. In her hands, she held a wickedly curved blade and a sharpening stone.

"Go tell Ezio to stop the messengers," Kreyus ordered before she could speak. "No one is to inform the client of anything until I give approval, understand?"

Her brow furrowed as if she did anything but.

Kreyus' brow rose in response.

She nodded. Her gaze flicked over us, the disgust in her expression tempered by a new sort of caution, and then she swam outside.

Ignoring her departure, Kreyus headed for the weapons.

Quickly, I shrugged Noah's arm from my shoulders, wanting to be able to move fast in case the man tried anything. Kreyus didn't spare us a glance, though. Gathering up the weapons, he returned them to a bag and then carried them to the far end of the cave.

Hovering near me, Chloe watched him. "So is she your, um…"

Kreyus turned back. "Venika and I have an understanding."

Chloe seemed to absorb the statement. She gave an uncertain nod.

He swam over to take a seat on the floor. Motioning to the space around him, he waited for us to do the same.

I reached out, touching Chloe's arm carefully to draw her

attention. She tensed and glanced over. I nodded for her to sit on the other side of me, away from him.

She didn't say anything, but just slipped around to sink down between me and Noah.

Kreyus studied us while we joined him. "And you?" he asked her.

Chloe's brow furrowed.

"Your… friends." His gaze flicked between me and Noah. "A prince and a young man who is… sick."

I could hear the question in the final word. The doubt.

And he confirmed it a heartbeat later.

"Or does this also have something to do with you?"

Chloe shifted uncomfortably on the stone floor. "I don't really—"

"Of course," Kreyus cut in. "My apologies. How about we start with your questions? I'm sure you have plenty."

"You believe me?" Chloe asked, her voice tight.

He paused. "What else did Susan's family tell you about me? Besides the mistaken belief I hurt her with aveluria, that is."

Chloe glanced to me and Noah. "Nothing, really," she admitted. "They only knew your name."

"And yours as well."

Chloe's brow drew down again.

"Kloyamina," Kreyus said. "Or Chloe for short. It is a dehaian name, as much as a human one. Rather like Zeke." His gaze flicked to me again and then returned to her. "And it was your grandmother's."

Chloe seemed to freeze.

"It could be a coincidence," Kreyus continued. "Or another part of a ruse. But how could the Yvarian king know I had told Susan that name? It would be something of a gamble for him to include such an apparently inconsequential detail, would it not?"

She appeared to struggle to find her voice. "That was my…"

"Your grandmother, yes. You rather look like her, to be honest. Your scales, your eyes."

A hitched breath left Chloe like she was struggling not to cry. I reached over and her hand fumbled into mine. Her fingers crushed down, her grip trembling. On the other side of her, Noah put a hand to her back and in spite of myself, I tensed. I forced my attention back to Kreyus, and caught the way his eyes narrowed slightly at us all.

Chloe didn't seem to notice.

"D-did you know about me, then?" she asked. "I mean, even if you didn't think I'd survive, did you—"

Kreyus shook his head, the curious expression vanishing as though it'd never been. "Susan chose that herself, and must have told her family her wishes before she died. She and I… we were only together a short time. The pain of the ocean was too much for us to stay together longer. I had no idea she was pregnant when we parted ways."

"But," Chloe tried, "how did you even…"

"Meet her?"

Chloe nodded.

He smiled. "Where I come from, strength is one of the most respectable traits to have. Physical strength, yes, but mostly endurance. Bravery, daring, those are also prized. And when I was a young man, I was challenged by friends to sneak all the way through Yvaria. To cross to their beaches and then return. This was… well, risky to say the least. The former king, his great uncle," Kreyus nodded to me again, "was in the later years of his rule, and he held Yvaria with an iron fist that had only grown more merciless as time went on. Vetorians found in their waters did not fare well. But backing down from the challenge was to some degree a worse option, so I did it. I reached the beaches of California and once there… I kept going. I figured this could be the only time I ventured that far successfully, so I may as well take advantage of it. By walking and hitchhiking, I made it to a small town in central California, and that was where I first saw Susan.

"From the moment I laid eyes on her, I could tell there was something different about her. Something unique. We started talking and…" He chuckled. "Next thing I knew, an entire day had gone by and we were sharing stories like we'd known each other our whole lives."

His smile returned. "That should give you an idea of what we had, Chloe. Dehaians… we keep what we are a secret. Even the craziest, most reckless among us wouldn't risk letting a non-dehaian know what we are. It wouldn't even be suicide; it'd be signing up for torture at the hands of humans if the wrong ones learned the truth. But I told her. And she told me about the landwalkers. She was a fighter, your mother. Despite what she was, she'd come so far and she fully intended to go farther. It was incredible."

"And," Chloe started. "You both… you stayed…"

"Three days. That's what we had before the pain became too much for us. When we were together, it seemed to get better, but even that couldn't last. I told her I would come back. That I would find a way to see her again. And then she returned home, and so did I."

He sighed. "It took four years. But when I made it to land again, her phone number belonged to someone else and Directory Assistance had no record of Susan in her town. I wasn't certain what to do and, after a while, I had to return to the water. Accept that I'd lost touch with her, and hope that we could reconnect someday.

"I never anticipated this."

I didn't take my eyes from Kreyus when he finished. I wasn't sure what he was playing at, telling Chloe this story, but I couldn't believe it was actually kindness.

He'd been willing to hand her over to the Sylphaen less than an hour ago.

"And now you're a Vetorian Praelex," I said.

From the corner of my eye, I saw Chloe turn to me with an expression like she didn't want me to stop him from continuing.

But Kreyus just gave me the same, mildly amused look as when I'd asked about the Vetorians surrounding us before.

"For the past seven years, yes," he acknowledged. "And a

highly successful one, at that. But where I come from, your highness, your father is known as a genocidal tyrant, and your brother has displayed a clear willingness to follow in his footsteps. I'd be careful before passing judgment."

"My father wouldn't hand his own child over to a *client* to be murdered."

"But he would murder countless others, simply for being part of a nation with which he had a quarrel. Besides, that's the distinction, is it not? Believing Chloe was my child, well, that took evidence. And now matters have changed. You *were* correct in saying that Vetorians are interested in profit. We have families to feed, after all, and the so-called 'Prijoran Zone' offers few options for doing that. But we do prize one thing above money, and that is blood. Among my people, there is nothing more important than loyalty to one's tribe. To violate that means no other tribe can trust you. Even *Vetorians* cannot trust you, because you are capable of betraying them to a higher bidder. These markings are not simple vanity, highness," he gestured to the scars on his sides, "they are evidence of where our loyalties lie. They broadcast what we've sworn to protect — and what we've betrayed if we are found aiding others elsewhere. And those who *do* violate their oaths…" He smiled. "You think us cruel to our enemies. Trust me when I say we save the worst for the disloyal among our own."

His expression made my skin crawl. There was no regret. No compassion or qualm. He might as well have been discussing the fact that the Earth occasionally needed rain.

Chloe was related to a shark.

"You see us as barbarians," Kreyus continued, as if reading something of my thoughts in my face. "Yet we only do what we must to survive. And I would hazard a guess that my daughter knows this lesson. I can hear it in her voice. See it in her eyes." His gaze flicked to Chloe. "You've been forced to kill. Most likely to save your own life or that of someone close to you, I would imagine."

She fidgeted uncomfortably again, saying nothing.

Kreyus looked back to me. "There is more than a little of the Vetorian in her."

My brow twitched down, a suspicion creeping over me that made me want to grab Chloe and get the hell out of here right now.

"So… in that case, what's next?" Noah asked, a heavy note of caution in his tone, like the guy might've heard the same implication as me. "You're not turning her over to your client… you let us all go?"

"As tempting as it would be to hold the prince hostage in exchange for our own people in King Renekialen's custody, we are in his territory, and therefore surrounded. The benefits do not outweigh the risks, and we will free our people some other way. Thus, you two may do what you wish. But as for my daughter…" He glanced to her. "The bounty was for Chloe and, as you all may have guessed, it is a large one. Outside of the Ivalaen tribe and this cell of the Vetorians, she is in danger. So I would propose she come back with us. We can protect her.

We *will* protect her. She is one of our own. And besides," he finished with a touch of a smile, "she and I have years to make up for."

Chloe's fingers tightened on mine. I could feel her trembling.

"And this interest in helping her," I said, barely able to make the words into a question. "It doesn't have anything to do with what she's capable of?"

"Chloe is free to do as she chooses with that," Kreyus replied calmly. "I admit I am intrigued and would like to know more, but that is her information to share."

I said nothing, somehow doubting those words. What I'd seen her do…

This guy was essentially a warlord. Or, as he'd probably claim, a businessman. But whether or not he *actually* believed she was his daughter, Chloe's newfound abilities would make her one hell of a weapon for him to use.

And I wasn't buying that paternal compassion bit for a minute.

"I-I can't," Chloe answered, her voice choked.

Kreyus gave her a curious look.

"The Sylphaen," she continued. "That 'client'? It's not just them after me. There's a…" She glanced to me and Noah again. "A thing. It's magic. It's called the Beast. It's after me too."

He paused.

"You've heard about that," I said, not even bothering to turn the words into a question this time. His expression was more than enough of an answer.

"We are not as uneducated as rumor would have it, highness," Kreyus replied. His mouth tightened. "But I thought the Beast was only legend."

"I've seen it," Chloe said. "We both have." She nodded to Noah. "It tried to kill us yesterday."

I couldn't hide my alarm. Neither of them had mentioned that.

Discomfort flashed over her face as if she could feel my stare. "It, um… it's hunting me," she said. "It feeds off what I do, and while I *can* hide a bit, I can't keep it from finding me forever. I'm a danger to anyone I'm near. I'm just here to stop the Sylphaen because…" She swallowed. "Because you're right. They've come after my friends and me. I've killed a few, but it's just a matter of time till someone I care about dies."

Kreyus regarded us thoughtfully. "And may I ask what your plan is for handling these Sylphaen? Unless I've missed something, I would hope the three of you aren't intending to take them on alone."

I hesitated when Chloe looked to me. He was teasing at the edges of a question without asking it outright, and it just made me want to leave more. The fact he knew some of what Chloe could do was bad enough. But if he learned about the greliarans, and if the Vetorians ever attempted to make a deal with them like Niall had obviously tried with Noah's relatives…

"Um, we're going to Lycera," Chloe started.

"Your mother," Kreyus filled in, glancing to me.

"Yes." I left the answer at that and, after a heartbeat, his eyebrow rose.

"Lycera has precious few soldiers, your highness. You know that."

I didn't respond.

He nodded slightly. "Fair enough. Well..." He looked around the room as if gathering his thoughts. "Then allow me to present an alternate suggestion. The border between us and Lycera is heavily guarded. I realize this hasn't always been the case, but before you call me a liar, consider that King Renekialen has been on a crusade against infiltrators for quite some time. Even relations with his closest allies have become strained thanks to him."

I struggled not to scowl. For one thing, I suspected where Kreyus was going with this. And as for what he claimed... damn Ren, it was probably true. He'd been railing against Vetorians and goodness knew what else even *before* Dad died, and now, a few weeks later, he was a mock-trial away from sentencing Chloe to death over it.

It was only too easy to imagine that he'd screwed up our connections with everyone in the ocean as well.

"So," Kreyus continued, "if you *are* determined to go to Lycera, perhaps we can be of assistance to you. We've had repeated success in evading the king's border patrols. We can escort you to Lycera and make certain no one attempts to capture you, both during your trip, while in the capital city, and on your way to wherever else you intend to go."

"And in exchange?" Noah prompted before I could speak, a dry note in his voice that I was fairly certain wasn't my imagination.

Kreyus gave no sign of noticing it. "In exchange, I would ask Prince Zekerian to act on our behalf. The Prijoran Zone needs infrastructure. Centralized government. Options for residents to move from poverty to relative self-sufficiency. Among other things, this requires resources for education and food cultivation beyond what we currently possess. In the past several decades, Yvaria has been highly influential in convincing other nations to forego any trade or negotiation with our tribes. They claim their sanctions are a result of the Vetorians' actions, yet this has only turned joining the Vetorians into the premier method for supporting a family in our land. I would like the prince to assist us in changing this, and set the 'Prijoran Zone' on a path to no longer being the pariah state of the ocean."

I stared at him for a heartbeat and then glanced to Chloe. I didn't want to upset her. I had no idea what she was thinking about this. But I also couldn't agree to what he proposed, and not just because it was madness.

Ren would never listen to me. Not about anything and *certainly* not about aiding the very people he thought were responsible for Dad's death. And lying to Kreyus in order to secure our safe passage to Lycera and the capital… it wasn't smart. Kreyus was *absolutely* the type to retaliate when he realized we had no intention of keeping the bargain and of getting the hell away from him at the first opportunity.

Yvaria's people and villages would suffer in the fallout.

"I'm supposed to believe you'd undermine the Vetorians' supply of volunteers and destroy your entire economic and political system for… what?" I asked. "Charity to the other tribes in the Zone?"

Kreyus chuckled. "Of course not. The Vetorians will continue, and through me, the Ivalaen tribe will become the primary conduit of communication between other nations and the tribes. This isn't charity, highness. It's politics."

I watched him. He looked like an anglerfish, luring its prey with its light till it could swallow them whole.

"Now," he continued, "I realize you won't be able to speak with your brother about this issue. Not only is he miles from here in another direction entirely, but rumor has it he despises you."

It was hard not to bristle at the words.

"But your mother reportedly does not hold the same opinion," Kreyus said. "And, as regent of Lycera during her sister's convalescence, High Lady Coriana is more than capable of putting into place the infrastructure and recognition we seek. Once she has authorized agreements with us, it is likely that neighboring countries will follow suit. Thus, I want you to convince her to do so."

"You'll undermine Yvaria's position with the other nations," I stated.

He smiled as though he was enjoying this. "Not if they join the others in recognizing us."

I knew that was a bunch of crap. By following rather than leading in the decision to open a dialogue with tribes in the Zone, Yvaria would appear to be bowing to the pressure of other nations. It was a perception issue, but Dad had taught us a lot about those.

In so many ways.

"What choice do you have, highness?" Kreyus asked.

My gaze flicked briefly to Chloe. This wasn't just about Ren or Yvaria. It was about Ina and the Sylphaen too. If they made Ren think she was in danger, my brother's response would do more to damage our relations with other countries than this ever would. Ren could already be sending soldiers to goodness-knew-where right now, all on the belief that Chloe's allies had Ina there.

And meanwhile, my sister was a hostage whose safety rested on an empty promise by Niall and the leader of the Sylphaen.

My jaw tightened. We'd lost so much time getting to Lycera already.

"I'll present your plan to my mother," I said, "but on the basis that she has to convince Ren to go along with it before formal acknowledgment of anything or anyone in the Prijoran Zone can be made."

Kreyus' eyes narrowed.

"Lycera's recognition alone gets you nothing," I argued. "The Vetorians and the Ivalaen tribe will look pathetic, gaining only the notice of one of the smallest, weakest nations in the water. You said it yourself, Kreyus. Lycera barely has an army.

They depend on Yvaria and, to be honest, even with my input the odds of you getting the Lycerans to go against the King of Yvaria are… well, 'slim' is putting it mildly. You want the Prijoran Zone to cease being a pariah, you need Yvaria. I have leverage with my mother; she has leverage with Ren." I shrugged. "This is the best plan all the way around."

Kreyus watched me for a moment, his smile long since gone. Keeping my expression as calm as I could, I tried to give no sign of how my heart was pounding. We were still trapped here. This could go wrong incredibly fast.

And then his gaze flicked briefly to Chloe. My hand tightened on hers.

"Very well," Kreyus allowed. "But highness, for *your* sake I hope your mother has the influence you claim. You are asking us to take quite a risk, hinging this agreement on her ability to affect your brother's decisions."

I could hear the threat. Merciful waves, I could hear the threat and more than anything, I wanted to get us out of here right now. But even without the border guards and the Sylphaen and everything else, we weren't likely to get far.

I'd seen the sheer number of Vetorians this man had at his command, and he clearly didn't intend to let someone with Chloe's abilities out of his sight.

Kreyus rose. "Now, if you all would come with me? I have a daughter to present and travel arrangements to make."

Chloe hesitated and then reached over, taking Noah's arm across her shoulders. I saw Kreyus' gaze twitch between us and

I tensed again when curiosity tinged his expression a second time.

He swam from the cave without a word.

I let out a breath as we followed him. That could've gone better. We could have avoided the Vetorians entirely, for a start, or could have left after reaching the top of the canyon with Kreyus. Either would have been a better option, since now we were stuck traveling with a bunch of Vetorians – a fact that, if we were found by Ren's soldiers, as good as sealed Chloe's death sentence.

But Kreyus also hadn't tried to take Chloe or force her into helping him with the impossible abilities she suddenly possessed. And sure, odds were, Kreyus knew that wouldn't have gone well, but the point remained.

It could've gone better. But damn, could it have gone worse.

Now I just had to figure out how to deal with this ridiculous agreement we'd made.

12

CHLOE

With Noah holding one arm over my shoulders and Zeke close by my side, I trailed Kreyus toward the entrance of the cave.

"You alright?" Noah whispered.

My gaze twitched toward him, not making it over fully before snapping back to Kreyus.

I didn't know what I was. Kreyus was brutal. Cold. Pragmatic in a way I'd never seen from anyone. I had no doubt, just no doubt at *all*, that if I hadn't been his daughter and he hadn't decided to believe me, we'd all be on our way to the Sylphaen right now.

And he wouldn't care. He'd know they were going to kill us, and I really suspected he wouldn't care. His priorities… they frightened me. I wouldn't want to be on the wrong side of them.

He was my *father*. The guy that somehow, my mother had cared for enough to… and he was like *this*.

Noah's hand rubbed my shoulder. This time, I did manage

to look at him.

The corner of his mouth rose in a sympathetic smile. Closing my eyes briefly, I drew a breath and then nodded.

We passed the veil and returned to the canyon.

The Vetorians had dispersed across the cliff sides. From near cave openings and in the shadows of the rough walls, they watched us. Venika and Ezio waited nearby, and their guarded expressions were scarcely different from what they'd worn this entire time. I couldn't tell if either of them had heard us through the veil or not.

"The messengers are back as requested," Venika told Kreyus.

He nodded.

Venika twitched her gaze from Kreyus to me, clearly waiting for an explanation.

Kreyus scanned the Vetorians along the canyon walls. "We have a change of plans," he announced to them all. "It appears the client who hired us for a bounty left a detail from the contract. The reward was put out for one of our own. An Ivalaen and the child of a Vetorian. My daughter, Chloe."

The eyes of every Vetorian in the canyon turned to me. Water quivered by my hands. I fought the magic down, working to keep from destroying anything by accident.

"Kreyus…" Venika started, her voice low and edgy.

"She has given sufficient proof," he replied quietly.

Venika glanced to me and I tensed. Nothing seemed like it'd be sufficient proof for that woman. She sort of looked like she hated me.

"All the information she has supplied has been confirmed," Kreyus said, raising his voice to be heard by the others again, "and her knowledge of her mother surpasses what any petty king could hope to possess. Thus I claim her as my child."

I shivered. Something about the way he spoke those last words… it felt like there was more in them than a simple acknowledgment that I wasn't lying.

A *lot* more.

But I wasn't sure I wanted to know what it was. For that matter, now that he'd decided to believe me and had sworn he'd never used aveluria on my mother, I wasn't sure I hadn't made a mistake. Maybe I should have taken Zeke up on leaving when we'd been at the top of the canyon and we'd stood a chance.

"We have come to an agreement," Kreyus continued. "Her associate, Prince Zekerian Ociras of Yvaria, has agreed to assist us in exchange for safe passage to Lycera and beyond. We will provide this. Along with Venika and a small team, I will escort them to their destination. The rest of you will return home — assuming, of course, that a profitable detour does not appear along the way."

Chuckles rose from around the canyon. I felt Zeke shift in the water next to me.

"Braxus," Kreyus ordered, "take your brothers and go on ahead. Find us the best route to Lycera. Trevion, have someone prepare a place for my daughter and her companions to stay until the scouts return."

Kreyus turned toward me.

"What is she?" came a nervous call from somewhere on the cliff walls.

The other Vetorians fidgeted uncomfortably, as if they wanted to know the answer but were deeply glad they hadn't been the one to ask the question.

Kreyus paused. His gaze slid back to them. "Chloe vel Kreyus valya Kloyamina, the daughter of your Praelex."

Silence pressed down on the canyon.

"You heard him," Venika called into the tense quiet. "Now move!"

The Vetorians scattered.

She glanced to Kreyus, bowing her head in the same way I'd seen people in Nyciena do to Zeke or his family, though in this case, her expression practically telegraphed the fact she expected an answer to the question herself.

His lip twitched at the look. "Later."

Venika seemed to relax ever so slightly.

Kreyus turned as another redheaded dehaian swam up, a pair of muscled Vetorians with silver and gold mottled scales behind him.

"We have located a space for your daughter, sir," the redheaded man said.

Kreyus nodded and then glanced to me. "Go with him. And Trevion, bring them food soon as well."

"Yes, Praelex." Trevion looked to us. "This way, please?"

I bit my lip and followed. There was something in the way

the man was acting toward us. *Me*, and I recognized it.

Again, it bore similarities to the way people in Nyciena behaved around Zeke's family.

Trevion led us down along the cliff wall with the pair of muscled dehaians at his side, and he didn't stop till he reached a cave nearly at the bottom of the canyon. Even to my eyes, the water was almost black down here, and the cave was nothing but a darker shadow in it.

I looked upward. The open ocean felt awfully far away.

So did any chance of escape.

Leading the way, Trevion swam into the cave. Without any other option, I trailed him inside.

I blinked when another veil passed around us, revealing the sudden light of four torches on the wall. At fifty feet deep and only about twenty wide, the cave felt like a large room, albeit with rough, pitted surfaces all around. Chips and cracks in the dark rocks of the floor caught glints of the fire's blue-white glow, while the larger chunks of stone in the walls and ceiling cast strange shadows all around. Two mats of seaweed lay by the rear wall, and otherwise the cave was empty.

"You should be safe here," Trevion said. "We will bring food shortly, and another bed, if you require it."

I could hear the question in his tone and see it in the way he looked between us again. "Yeah," I managed. "Thanks."

He nodded and then turned, swimming from the cave. The muscled dehaians remained, taking up positions by the entrance.

I glanced to Noah when he slipped his arm from my

shoulder. He was watching the Vetorians almost as if sizing them up for what he'd do if we needed to fight. Meanwhile, the pair just studied us with a gradient of disgust and distrust in Zeke and Noah's case, and respectful caution in mine.

A shudder ran through me. This was madness. All of it. Just madness.

"How long will it take your scouts to find a way to Lycera?" Zeke asked them, a hint of challenge in his voice.

The Vetorians regarded him flatly. "Several hours," one of them stated.

Zeke grimaced.

Seconds ticked by. Trevion returned, a large and covered container of brown stone in his hands and another dehaian behind him with the rolled mat of a bed in his arms. As the other man swam past us to place the mat on the floor, Trevion paused in front of me.

"If you would?" he said over his shoulder to one of the guards.

I tensed while the man came closer.

Trevion removed the lid from the container. Cut pieces of raw fish were piled inside.

"Choose three pieces for him to sample," Trevion said to me.

My brow furrowed.

"To prove there's no poison," Zeke murmured.

I glanced from him to Trevion.

"A custom of the Prijoran Zone," the man elaborated.

I struggled to regroup and then pointed to three pieces at random. The guard picked them up and ate them in rapid succession.

A heartbeat passed. The Vetorian bowed his head and returned to the entrance.

Trevion placed the cover back on the container and then set it all down on the cave floor. "If you need anything else," he said to me, "simply ask one of them."

He motioned toward the guards.

I managed a nod.

Without another word, he swam from the cave. The man who'd brought the mat followed him.

I glanced to Zeke and Noah and then sank down next to the bowl. I hadn't eaten anything since we'd grabbed a meal on the way to Santa Lucina the day before, and I didn't know how long it'd be till we had food again.

But I wasn't exactly hungry, not with how my stomach had become a ball of lead.

I didn't look up while Zeke and Noah took a seat on either side of me. Reaching over, Zeke lifted the cover away from the stone container.

"Freshest sushi on the planet, huh?" Noah commented quietly.

Zeke hesitated. "Suppose."

Neither of them seemed inclined to continue. I could feel them watching me while the paltry attempt at conversation died. In silence, they started eating.

I made no move to join them. I couldn't believe this. Out of the entire ocean… to just *stumble* across my father like this.

It was insane. I'd figured maybe I'd look for him someday — though lately it'd been contingent upon whether I remained dehaian when all this was done. But if I had, if I'd taken Joseph's potion and become like Zeke, then… then, yeah. In the back of my mind, I'd figured it'd be a thing I would eventually do.

But this…

I didn't know what to make of it. Kreyus was like a mob boss, a pirate, and a cutthroat politician all rolled into one. He terrified me, really, and not just because of his cold priorities. I was related to him. I was… I'd *come* from him. I didn't even know what that meant. What that made me. A Vetorian? One of the Ivalaen tribe?

Chloe vel Kreyus valya Kloyamina.

Whoever the hell *that* was.

I shuddered. I didn't know what to think. How to feel anymore.

And I really just wanted to speed up the world, so that we could get to Lycera, get back to the coast, and finally bring all this insanity to an end.

Hours had passed since we arrived. The guards had changed shifts twice, bringing new, muscle-bound dehaians covered in scars to watch us and the canyon both. The three of us had stayed to the back of the cave, putting as much distance between us and them as possible.

It was probably late up above the water. Maybe midnight or sometime past. Noah had fallen asleep a while ago, two days of being awake finally dragging him down. I knew I should probably rest too, even if I'd gotten a bit of sleep the night before. Like the food, there was no telling how long it'd be till we'd get the chance to stop again. But I couldn't keep my thoughts from spinning. From circling back to the madness of the past few hours and worrying at it like a sore tooth. Since earlier today, I hadn't lost control of whatever the hell I could do, but I could still feel it inside me, like I was filled to the brim with magic and the barest pressure would just make me explode.

And Kreyus hadn't come back. It made me nervous. Everything he'd said aside, he could have lied to us. He could be bringing the Sylphaen.

He could be doing anything.

I wanted to go out there and find him. I wanted to make sure he wasn't betraying us.

And I wanted to get moving so I could return to the coast and end this. End being here. End being around this mercenary who was my father.

Zeke shifted on the mat at my side. I kept myself from glancing to him. I didn't know what he thought about all this. We'd barely spoken in the hours that'd passed. It was obvious he wasn't happy about the deal with the mercenaries, or about how things had ended up. He'd been pretty impressive, though, in how he'd handled Kreyus earlier. He'd seemed as if negotiating like that was second nature to him.

He just didn't seem thrilled in the slightest at its resolution.

And I wondered what he thought of me, now that he knew I was the kid of a Vetorian.

I closed my eyes, trying to ignore the tangle of fear the thought caused in my chest.

"Chloe?" Zeke whispered.

I hesitated. "Yeah?" I replied without looking at him.

He didn't respond. I dragged my gaze over to him. With his back to the wall, he was sitting on the seaweed mat, his attention on the guards at the other end of the cave.

"What is it?" I asked, keeping my voice down in the hope the Vetorians couldn't hear.

"Yesterday. You said the Beast almost killed you?"

I winced.

"What happened?" he pressed.

I gave an awkward shrug. "It found us."

Zeke raised an eyebrow, clearly waiting for more.

"Joseph said I screwed up his sensors. What I am did that, I mean. And I guess I screwed up his defenses too. The Beast picked up on us. It attacked Joseph's place. He had a lot of magic pent up there somehow, and when the storage for it exploded, the blast hit us. And I don't know what happened then. I started being able to break stuff like I did earlier, and Noah can feel where it is… I don't know."

"You're okay, though? You feel alright?"

I looked down.

"Chloe?"

"Yeah."

A moment passed. From the corner of my eye, I caught him studying me.

I looked away again, discomfited. I was okay from the magic or I wasn't, but either way, I couldn't know until something went wrong. True, I felt like I wanted to explode, and yet whenever I *did* break something, it didn't seem to come out of the magic pent up inside me. Not exactly. Instead, it just felt like *me*.

And as with everything else in the world right now, I didn't know what any of that meant.

"Does the water feel weird when I do that?" I asked him.

Zeke hesitated. "Yeah. Not painful, though. Basically like the first night I saw you. And then it fades. Like now. You're trying to suppress it?"

I nodded. He shrugged as if that had to be the explanation. I dropped my gaze to the seaweed below me.

A moment crept by.

"And otherwise," he prompted carefully. "This stuff. You doing alright about that?"

I didn't respond.

His hand reached over, taking mine. I tensed, looking up at him.

"What?" he asked at my worried expression.

"Are *we*?" I tried warily. "Alright, I mean. Now that I'm…"

My gaze went to the guards. I couldn't even get the words out.

He seemed to read my meaning anyway. "This doesn't change anything."

I hesitated.

"Chloe," he insisted, "it doesn't. Not to me. You're still you, I promise."

"But what Kreyus is calling me. What he *is*. Zeke, I'm his daughter. What does that make me? I mean, he says he sees Vetorian in me and I—"

"That's not you. That's just what he wants."

I wished I could believe the words. That being Kreyus' daughter was simply genetics, which had power over my hair or skin or whatever, but nothing to do with who I was inside.

It just didn't feel quite that easy. I'd *known* I wasn't like Mom or Dad… the Kowalskis or whatever the hell I should call them now. I'd known I wasn't crazy and that, whatever was wrong with them, it couldn't be genetic. But choosing to be crazy because you were a control freak, and being this… it felt different.

I shifted uncomfortably on the seaweed mat. It *was* different. I'd killed people since all this started. Actually *killed* people. And yes, I'd been defending myself and yes, I hadn't had much choice at the time, but that didn't change the facts of what I'd done.

I'd just been surviving. But now I wondered if there was more to it than that.

"You're *not* him, Chloe," Zeke said. "I swear. Just because your father has chosen to be a certain way, just because you're related to somebody, that doesn't mean anything about who *you* are."

I paused, hearing something in his tone.

His brow furrowed. "What?"

"Is that how you felt?" I asked carefully. "About your dad, I mean?"

Zeke looked down. I winced, regretting the words.

"Yeah," he answered after a moment. "Maybe, I guess. At least once I got older and really began to understand what he'd done, anyway. People used to look at us like they were scared of us. Like they thought that, if they said something wrong or did something wrong, Dad would—" He shook his head.

"But Ina, me... we're not our father. And you're not yours. Any of those traits that might be in us, we get to decide how we use them. What they become. We're not our parents' choices." He paused, his fingers tightening on mine. "And you're *not* a Vetorian. You're not Ivalaen. You're not anything but you. Chloe Kowalski. The girl who's taken on the Sylphaen, and the greliarans, and all sorts of psychopaths. The girl they can't stop, and the girl I—" He cut off.

"What?" I asked.

He glanced to the guards, to Noah, and there was something strange in his expression. Something that made my heart start to pound when I realized what he might have been about to say.

"The girl I crossed the ocean and half a continent for," he finished, his voice tight. "The girl for whom I'd do it all again."

I trembled.

He let out a breath. "Chloe, I—"

Venika and Kreyus swam into the cave.

"Braxus and his brothers have returned," Kreyus said. "We leave in five minutes."

I blinked, the moment falling around me. After all this time of waiting, everything suddenly felt like it was moving too fast.

Though maybe that was only because of what I suspected Zeke had been about to tell me.

I managed a nod. Trying to keep my face neutral, I reached over and nudged Noah.

"Time to go," I said, working to give no sign of how my heart was racing.

Noah glanced toward Kreyus and then moved to get up from the mat.

I drew a breath, grateful he hadn't noticed anything. Taking his arm over my shoulders again, I started for the cave entrance.

A moment passed before Zeke followed.

I couldn't be certain if that was how he'd meant to finish that sentence, or how he'd intended to follow it up. It could've just been my imagination.

But it really felt like he'd been about to say he loved me.

And I had no idea what to say in return.

Several dehaians were already waiting for us when we reached the flatlands above the canyon, and they nodded respectfully at the sight of Kreyus. While he swam over to speak with them, I hung back with Zeke and Noah, and tried not to fidget uncomfortably when Venika remained only a few yards away, watching us.

Hate really was a mild word for how that woman looked at me. Of all the Vetorians, she was the only one who seemed to have no issue with glaring at me like she'd cut my throat if she could.

It was strange.

And worrisome.

I felt Noah tense beside me.

"What?" I whispered, not looking away from Venika.

He didn't answer.

I glanced over quickly to find his gaze twitching across the water. "Noah?"

"I thought… maybe to the north when we just came up here. But…"

My heart started racing all over again. "But what?"

Noah exhaled, shaking his head. "Nothing." He glanced to me. "You suppressing that whatever-it-is?"

"Best I can."

His mouth tightened as if he wished there was more to be done, but he nodded.

I drew a breath, trying to calm down.

It wasn't easy.

A dozen more dehaians rose from the ravine behind us. At the sight of them, Kreyus motioned for us to come over to join him. With the other dehaians trailing us, we swam over to the group of Vetorians.

"Braxus, report," Kreyus prompted.

A beefy, fiery-haired dehaian who looked like everything you'd cross the street to avoid swam from the group behind us. He bore a patch over one eye and on his brown scales, old scars that looked blatantly like knife wounds cut strange patterns. Two more Vetorians followed him, both of them possessing enough similarity to him in their appearance that I guessed these were the brothers Kreyus had mentioned earlier.

"At the moment," Braxus said, his voice deep and quiet, "the soldiers appear not to have noticed our presence. They're spread out from here to Lycera, however, moving in shifts to patrol the border. I recommend sticking to this side of the canyon and then heading south when it ends. The terrain is fairly flat from here to Lycera, however. We needed to hide more than once while scouting, and I suspect we will on the way back again as well."

Kreyus nodded. "In that case, Chloe, the prince and their friend will stay by Venika and me, while the rest of you divide up so you're close to someone equipped with cover as well. I want two groups, one in front and one behind us, and until the canyon is past, the caves are the first point of retreat."

He glanced around quickly, as if checking for questions from his people, and then he nodded. "Go."

Half the Vetorians spread out and started along the line of the canyon's edge, heading south, while Braxus and the remainder hovered nearby, waiting for Kreyus to move.

Kreyus looked to me. I couldn't tell what he seemed to be confirming. Without a word, he nodded to Venika.

She swam after the others. We followed her, with the remaining Vetorians coming behind us.

Minutes passed in silence. I couldn't stop my gaze from slipping to Noah. He hadn't seemed to have noticed anything between Zeke and me earlier – a mercy in the midst of everything else going on – and he wasn't looking toward me now. Instead, his eyes just moved over the darkness, his brow faintly furrowed.

Realization hit me. Since we'd left the camp with its torches, he was probably back to struggling to see – if he could even see at all.

I bit my lip, guilt following on the heels of my understanding. Though greliarans had been partly created with magic from dehaians, they didn't have all of our abilities any more than we had all of theirs. And regardless, it wasn't like he could change his eyes even a little bit with Kreyus and the others around. He was enduring a lot just to be here and let us know if the Beast came close.

It scared me to think of what the Vetorians might do if they found out about him.

I made myself keep breathing. Thus far, Kreyus hadn't pressed the issue, though I couldn't expect that'd continue forever. But at the moment, we were okay. We were heading for Lycera, we were going to get those soldiers, and then…

Then things would be easier. Once the Sylphaen were dealt with, it'd just be a question of taking the potion Joseph had given me and seeing what happened. Maybe I'd end up landwalker and have to leave, regardless.

And maybe I'd end up dehaian – a reality that felt like it was growing more complicated by the minute. I felt like the poster child for overload right now, between trying to sort out the hell of my feelings for Zeke and Noah, and surviving run-ins with the Sylphaen or the Beast.

Or the Vetorians.

My gaze slid to Venika. With knives strapped over her chest, she watched the water as though waiting for the opportunity to kill it. She appeared to be in her late twenties, and probably a decade younger than Kreyus if not more, and her entire body was covered in ritualistic scars.

I wondered if Kreyus would expect me to come back with him, if I became fully dehaian after this was all over. To become some part of his tribe, scars and all.

I wondered what he'd do if I said no.

Shivering, I tugged my gaze back to the water ahead. I'd cross that bridge when I came to it. *If* I came to it. It might well be that I'd have to leave the ocean, and there wouldn't be a question of living with Vetorians or not.

Funny how becoming a landwalker, while still horrible, suddenly felt like it'd be *so* much simpler.

I scowled, pushing the thought away. I needed to concentrate. The Beast could still pick up on me if I wasn't careful.

And I *really* didn't want to think about this anymore.

The canyon came to an end and the Vetorians turned, cutting across the end of the rift and continuing toward the south. Flat terrain rushed beneath us, peppered with infrequent rocks, strange life forms, and not much else. With his arm over my shoulders, Noah held onto me while on my other side, Zeke stayed close, his gaze scanning the emptiness.

Up ahead, the Vetorians pulled to a fast stop and motioned some kind of signal back toward us. Venika muttered a curse and then she dove toward the seafloor.

"Soldiers," Kreyus relayed quietly.

My heart pounding, I followed him down, Zeke right behind me.

Half a dozen Vetorians crouched with us on the sand while another tugged a stone from a satchel on his belt and then sped around us all. A veil rose in a curtain of bubbles that sealed over our heads. Setting the stone down on the seafloor, the man watched it as a small, blue light began to flicker on its side.

Seconds crept by. Noah's arm remained on my shoulders, and I could feel how tense he was from the way his hand gripped me.

My breath caught as the light on the stone shifted to red. My gaze snapped up to the murky water above.

Dehaians ghosted out of the darkness. There were so many of them, I couldn't even count them all. Belts crisscrossed their chests, the marks on them familiar from my time in the palace in Nyciena, and more than a few bore weapons. I swallowed hard, watching while the soldiers slipped past us, heading back the way we'd come.

A minute passed, and then another. The last of them disappeared to the north.

I let out a breath I hadn't realized I was holding and looked to the others.

Venika met Kreyus' gaze, her expression even angrier than normal.

His mouth tightened briefly. "Everyone will have hidden before the soldiers arrive."

The woman didn't respond.

Taking up the stone again, the Vetorian man made short work of the veil. I rose from the sand with Noah, and then paused when I saw Zeke watching the man.

"Yvarian," he said shortly with a jerk of his head toward the tool.

Venika gave him a poisonous smile, and in her expression I could just read what'd happened to the veil stone's previous owner.

Zeke could too. His jaw muscles jumped while he started swimming again. I hurried to catch up.

He didn't say a word when I joined him.

We continued through the water. Time wore on, filled with frequent waves of more soldiers appearing and forcing us to hide again and again. Zeke never spoke. He just watched the

Yvarians pass from behind the shelter of the veil without a single expression touching his face.

And meanwhile, the Vetorians studied us from the corners of their eyes. The scrutiny made me edgy, and it only grew worse while the miles passed. Me, they treated like royalty. But Zeke?

Son of their enemy. Brother of the man who'd been hunting them for months.

I veered a bit closer to his side, and avoided his eyes when he glanced to me questioningly.

They wouldn't touch him. Or Noah. Not if there was a thing I could do about it.

A Vetorian from farther ahead sped back toward us.

"Slow up," Venika ordered in a low voice.

Noah tensed, glancing to me through what had to be near-blackness to his eyes.

"Vetorian," I whispered.

Venika glared at me for speaking, while Kreyus' eyes became tinged with curiosity.

The Vetorian rushed up to us. "Border guards are watching Lycera," he said. "Up from the ground to a quarter mile below the surface."

Zeke looked away like he was trying not to swear.

"This changes nothing," Kreyus replied. "You know what to do."

The man nodded and then raced back the way he'd come.

"How many of them are you going to kill?" Zeke growled.

Kreyus met the question with a mild look. "None, if this goes well."

Zeke's furious expression remained.

Shouting broke out in the distance. On the edge of my senses, I felt dehaians suddenly race through the water toward us. I glanced nervously to Kreyus and Venika, but they just watched the murky water when suddenly, the dehaians up ahead seemed to scatter in every direction at once.

"Go," Kreyus said.

Venika took off and the other Vetorians followed suit. Holding onto Noah, I sped after her with Zeke staying close to my side. Overhead, more people shouted, and I could feel them moving in the water, twisting like eels while they fought. Others tried to dive to catch us, but they were quickly intercepted by additional dehaians charging at them from farther above.

And then we were past them. The shouting faded behind us.

Breathing hard, I glanced back. No one felt like they were following.

"You alright?" Zeke asked me, keeping his voice low.

I nodded. "You?"

Zeke echoed the motion.

"Noah?" I whispered.

He shrugged. I could read the motion, and the tight expression on his face. He hadn't seen anything, or felt it either. We'd probably just been racing pell-mell through blackness as far as he was concerned. I gave him a smile, hoping he could at least spot that in the dark.

"Lycera coming up," Zeke said quietly.

For a moment, nothing seemed to change. My brow furrowed while I studied the water ahead of me, and then suddenly, I picked up on a second line of dehaians in the distance. Far fewer than the ones we'd left behind, these seemed to be barely moving in the water, as though they hadn't noticed or didn't care about the fight going on behind us.

But they were armed. To the teeth, they were armed. The shapes of weapons I could sense around them hinted at swords, guns, shields, and things I couldn't even identify.

Zeke made an angry noise. "*Idiot…*" he muttered.

He caught sight of me when I glanced to him. Grimacing at my expression, he shook his head. "Nothing."

I watched him for another moment, but he just kept going, a look on his face like he wanted to pummel somebody.

The dehaians ahead of us drew their weapons and my focus snapped back. Two of them swam toward us.

My brow furrowed when they emerged from the murk. They weren't like the soldiers of Yvaria, all bodybuilder-sized and deadly-looking. They seemed instead like the Lyceran leader's desperate attempt to arm anyone who could carry a knife. One didn't seem to even be my age, with baby-blue scales and even bluer eyes, while the other was grayed and wizened enough to be his great-grandfather. Their assortment of weapons appeared as mismatched as they were. The swords and knives all bore remnants of mollusks on them, like someone had dredged the blades up from the seafloor.

If not for their expressions, which were *furious*, the two would have almost seemed pitiable.

"Stop there," the old man barked. "This border is closed. Get back where you came from."

"We wish to claim sanctuary," Kreyus replied.

"Say what?"

"Sanctuary," the boy repeated to the old man loudly. "Why?"

He snapped the last at us, glaring.

Kreyus smiled like he was glad the young man asked. "Because Prince Zekerian Ociras of Yvaria requests it."

He motioned back to Zeke. The boy's gaze followed the gesture and his blue eyes went wide.

"Surely you wouldn't want to explain to High Lady Coriana that you'd turned her son away?" Kreyus finished.

"Why do you have Vetorians with you?" the old man demanded of Zeke.

"He hired us," Kreyus answered before Zeke could respond. "You've heard, yes, of the Vetorians infiltrating—"

"You lot didn't come through here!" the old man snapped.

"Of course not," Kreyus countered smoothly. "But in Yvaria, they have so many problems with Vetorians. Yet who better to protect a prince fleeing from his home country than the infiltrators accused of attacking it?"

The old man's brow furrowed. I could see him struggling with the logic of the statement – mostly because there wasn't any.

His younger companion didn't seem far behind. "We're not to let any Yvarians through…" he tried, regrouping.

"*Including* the son of your own High Lady?" Kreyus pressed.

The boy looked to his companion worriedly.

"Damn Yvarians," the old man growled, almost as if to himself. "If it's not accusing us of harboring Vetorians, it's asking us *to* harbor Vetorians." He scoffed. "Well, fine. Maybe *this'll* prove we're your allies, since over a century of peace clearly wasn't good enough for you."

I saw Zeke's jaw muscles clench.

"You lot stay under guard, though," the old man continued to the mercenaries. "Not having you make things worse."

"Of course," Kreyus replied as if he wouldn't dream of having the Vetorians with him do anything else.

The old man made a contemptuous noise. With a jerk of his head, he motioned back the way he'd come.

We swam toward him.

"Well, then," the old man spat at Zeke when we reached him. "Welcome to sanctuary in Lycera, your highness."

❧ 13 ❧

NOAH

The dehaians had been swimming for hours since crossing the border, though at least they'd left the bouts of hiding and fleeing for their lives behind. Stretched across my back, Chloe's arm held onto me, and I'd started to be able to tell how much trouble we were in solely based upon how much she was trembling.

Right now rated about a five out of ten – based hopefully on the Vetorians and the Lycerans around us and not on some other threat I couldn't see – but that didn't make things any easier. My greliaran abilities didn't count for much down here – a fact that had become more apparent with every near-miss at discovery by those soldiers. The reality ate at me, though there wasn't anything for it. I could hear the dehaians, it was true. I could also keep watch for the Beast, and warn her if it came toward us.

And I could rip to shreds any stupid dehaian that thought to grab Chloe while I was close enough to protect her.

I closed my eyes, fighting to keep my greliaran side under control. That part of me *hated* this. Being trapped in the darkness. Being stuck as essentially an invalid, unable to move fast enough to stop anyone who tried to hurt Chloe in all this water. The frustration had just gotten worse with every passing hour, till now it was all I could do to keep my eyes from changing, just so I could at least *see* past all this damned darkness, even if I couldn't do much else to keep her safe.

The relief would be short-lived, though. That fact was about the only thing holding my frustration in check. The Vetorians appeared edgy enough about Chloe, given those new abilities that seemed to be scaring even *her*. I didn't need to add a glowing, red-eyed monster to their list of 'things we probably want to find a way to kill'.

And I *really* didn't want all these dehaians to make me lose control. Not with Chloe so close by. My greliaran side was having enough trouble already. Chloe and Zeke had been one thing. It hadn't been too much of a problem to handle that.

But hundreds of dehaians… hundreds of dehaians who looked like a *threat*…

Oh God, that was hard.

Drawing a slow breath, I opened my eyes again, though the darkness didn't change much. I could hear the two dehaian guards ahead of us, and the Vetorians all around. Beyond them, the water seemed mostly silent, and except for that brief moment beside the canyon, I hadn't picked up on the Beast at all.

That last part worried me. I hadn't really thought about it

before, but it'd started to strike me as odd that I kept noticing the Beast while it never seemed to notice me. True, the damn thing *was* a thousand times larger than us, and maybe that was the explanation.

I just wished I knew for certain.

A buzzing noise in the water brought my thoughts up short. It was like the tiny whine I'd heard around the magical protection the Vetorians used to hide, but louder. Stronger.

I looked to Chloe in the darkness. "There's a—"

"We're coming up on the veil around the Lyceran capital," she whispered.

My brow furrowed. Veil. Okay, that gave me the word for it. But the thing sounded *huge*.

The whine drew closer and then passed us. Like in the Vetorians' caves, the darkness vanished, replaced instantly by the glare of blue-white light.

But this time, I couldn't keep from staring.

It was a field of massive rock spires and boulders, all of which had been turned into a city filled with dehaians. Long-leafed plants blocked what appeared to be windows and doors, all on the sides of stones large enough to be houses. Biolumi-nescent creatures swam inside crystalline balls by the doorways as though they were lanterns, while other globes hung from strands strung between the structures like Christmas lights. Torches burned with impossible blue flames from posts like streetlights and overhead, the bubbles of the veil glittered like a million tiny stars. Coral grew on the walls and rooftops, and in what appeared to be yards as well, until the entire place looked like an enormous undersea garden.

A breath left me. So this was what Chloe had seen when she'd come down here. Not a featureless world of sand and darkness.

This.

Her hand adjusted on my back, cutting my thoughts short. Regrouping as quickly as I could, I glanced to her.

She gave me a nervous smile. "You okay?"

"Yeah," I managed, working to sound casual.

She seemed to relax a little.

I tried not to grimace.

We sailed over the rooftops and streets as if we were flying. Some of the dehaians below looked up curiously, though most ignored our passage and none moved to question our presence. The Lyceran guards ahead of us – an old man and a teenager whose voices I'd only heard through the darkness before – headed toward a craggy sprawl of hills on the edge of town. Buildings, I realized, not just hills. The mounds were the same as everything else here; a large living space with stands of those green-leafed plants dotting their sides.

Only this place had guards hovering nearby.

"Prince Zekerian to see High Lady Coriana," the old man called when we approached the guards.

One of the soldiers turned and disappeared through the leaves behind him like he'd slipped past a curtain. None of the others moved a muscle.

Minutes ticked by. The Vetorians hovered around us,

scanning their surroundings like they were running a total of how much they'd get if they tried to sell it all. The Lycerans scowled at the sight.

The plants rustled when the guard returned. "This way, please," he said.

We followed him past the leaves and into a hall twice as high as the doorway. Bowls of opalescent glass hung from the ceiling, with blue-white flames flickering inside and gold-inlay starbursts surrounding their bases. The rock walls had been polished to a shine, and veins of minerals glinted with myriad colors inside their surfaces. Abstract designs of glittering jewels dotted the walls like art hung in a collector's house, while mirrors hung between them, reflecting the light and all the rest of it back at us.

I tried to keep my expression calm even though… damn. Just… damn. This was where she'd been staying. Or, somewhere like this, anyway. A palace. She'd been staying with dehaian royalty in a palace.

"Not as fancy as you're used to, your highness," the old man sniped. "But I heard rumor your brother wants to send you to the wastes, so I guess it'll have to be good enough, eh?"

I paused. And Nyciena was even more ornate than this. Huh.

Zeke didn't respond. At the end of the hall, another stand of leaves waited, this one flanked by two guards who looked more ceremonial than anything. They held stone staves in their hands with gold spear tips on the ends and they didn't look at us when we approached.

"Hey, Zeke!"

I glanced over sharply. Down a side hall to our left, a dehaian kid hurried toward us, excitement on his face. Blue-scaled with a mop of black hair on his head, the boy couldn't have been more than six at the most.

"What are you doing here?" the boy cried happily. "Did you come to see Aunt Coriana or— hey!"

He cut off when a harried-looking servant snagged him.

"Kobi," Zeke said to the kid, his voice tight. "Hey. I'll catch up with you in a bit, alright?"

The boy nodded, ignoring the servant as if he was used to their efforts to stop him. "Yeah, okay."

One of the ceremonial guards pushed the leaves of the door aside. I could feel the kid's eyes on us while we headed inside.

A throne room waited beyond, with a ceiling about forty-feet high supported by pillars of glistening stone. A dais held a throne at the far end of the space, but unlike in the hallway, there was nothing ceremonial about the guards hovering around it.

For a start, there were easily thirty of them.

On the throne, a woman sat. Her hair was black like coal, but her scales were pale silver and her eyes were icy blue. It wasn't hard to guess that she was Zeke's mother. Similarities in their appearance aside, I could see the worry breaking past her regal poise.

"Zekerian," she called, her gaze darting across us and the Vetorians. "What is the meaning of this?"

"My lady," Kreyus cut in, "I am Praelex Kreyus. Allow me to—"

"No," Zeke snapped. "Enough."

He pinned the man with a glare before returning his gaze to his mother.

"High Lady Coriana," he started, as if choosing every word carefully. "We need your help."

"And you brought Vetorians," she replied, her voice edging toward a question.

Zeke paused. "Not by choice."

Alarm flickered across her face.

"But we have come to an agreement," Zeke continued. "And we can discuss that in a minute. First, however, I need to speak with you about Niall and King Renekialen."

The tiniest of pauses preceded the title. I caught a flash of disgust on his face before he buried it again.

Coriana's own expression tightened with anger. "Your eldest brother is not someone I choose to discuss at—"

"Niall's joined the Sylphaen," Zeke interrupted, the formality falling from his tone as stress came through. "They exist, they're back, and they have Ina. I asked Jirral to find out where she's being held, and once he gets here, I'll need some of your soldiers so we can go after her. But meanwhile, the Sylphaen have threatened to tell Ren she's a hostage in whatever country they choose, and when he hears that…"

His mother stared at him. She turned to one of the guards.

"Find my daughter," she whispered.

"High Lady," Zeke pressed. "Please. I need to go after her. You know what Ren will do if he—"

Coriana held up a hand, cutting him off.

Zeke gave her a confused look.

The door behind us opened.

"Zeke!"

Ina darted through the water and barreled into her brother, hugging him hard. Moving more slowly, their grandfather swam into the room. Beneath the gaps in his vest, I could see a strange, red line visible on his chest. At the sight of me, confusion raced across his face.

"Jirral, are you okay?" Chloe called.

"Nothing a little sieranchine couldn't fix," he replied. He didn't look away from me. "But I must say it's a surprise seeing you here."

I didn't know how to respond.

"Yeah," Chloe filled in quickly. "He, um… he's sick. Or he'd, you know, change like normal."

In a heartbeat, every trace of confusion on Jirral's face vanished behind a mask that gave away nothing. "Oh yes. Of course. I'm sorry to hear that."

I managed a nod, but I could feel Kreyus' eyes on us. I wouldn't have bet a penny he believed Chloe's words.

"So, when—" Zeke tried, as if attempting to change the subject. "I mean, how did you—"

"Granddad found them," Ina told him, pulling back from the hug. "Those little reschiatas that—"

She blushed and glanced to her mother like she was embarrassed by what she'd just said.

"They had her in a cave in Yvaria not far from Nyciena," Jirral supplied into the pause. "And not all of them are as resistant to persuasion as Niall and his new best friend might wish."

"You bribed Sylphaen?" Zeke asked.

Jirral gave him a dry look. "I said persuasion."

My brow twitched up. However strongly I disliked Zeke, I couldn't help but sort of admire his grandfather.

Zeke just looked distrustful, however. He eyed Jirral like the old man had to be lying.

Jirral ignored the expression. "High Lady," he said with a bow to Coriana, "now that Prince Zekerian is back, might we have those soldiers to go after the Sylphaen's strongholds as we discussed?"

"Before that occurs," Kreyus cut in smoothly. "The prince and I have a few matters to cover with High Lady Coriana."

"That's not going to happen right away, Kreyus," Zeke countered. "We have to handle the Sylphaen before anything else."

"But, your highness. Your friend is sick. Surely we need to let him rest before rushing off again?"

Zeke didn't say anything. Kreyus smiled.

"Oh, I'm fine if we leave now," I offered into the silence. "Don't worry about me."

"Actually," Coriana began before anyone else could speak. "I would be curious to know what agreement you have made with this man, Zekerian."

"Excellent," Kreyus replied. "Thank you, High Lady. And then perhaps we can discuss the prince's plans for what to do next, and how we could be of assistance to him."

Coriana regarded him with a sardonic expression incredibly reminiscent of Zeke. "There is much to discuss, yes." She looked to the guards. "If you would escort the prince's friends to a guest chamber?"

"High Lady—" Zeke started.

"It is beginning to feel a bit crowded in here," Coriana stated.

Several of the guards moved forward. By my side, I felt Chloe go rigid.

"It's alright," Zeke assured Chloe, a look on his face like he could read something behind her tension.

A tight breath left her. Chloe nodded.

"This way, please?" one of the guards said with a gesture to the exit.

"Come on," I told Chloe.

We turned, following the Lycerans to the door.

"Venika?" Kreyus called.

I glanced back to see the woman jerk her head in a quick acknowledgment and then motion to a few of the Vetorians around us.

The mercenaries fell in behind the soldiers, keeping an eye to us as much as the guards nearby.

I tried not to scowl while we left the throne room.

14

WYATT

Every time I thought I'd gotten a handle on just how frustrating the Delaneys could be, they found a new way to irritate me.

They hadn't said a word about where the fish were headed. They hadn't even opened a window. Barring a few moments here and there, they'd scarcely come outside. Peter and Maddox were likewise hiding their presence, leaving me with only my hearing to depend upon for any warning that they were around.

And they weren't even all of my problems. Clay had been becoming an issue, fidgeting and grumbling and damn near getting us discovered on one occasion. I'd finally sent him farther into town, ordering him to keep an eye out for the fish on main roads, useless though that was. And meanwhile, that storm was almost enough to drive me nuts all on its own. It was still furious, and still confused on where to find the girl, and it kept appearing and reappearing on the horizon at unpredictable intervals like some kind of weather-based water torture.

It was enough to make me want to pull my hair out.

But really, the Delaneys and their friends were a bunch of cowards. I didn't know what had spooked them so badly, but they'd all stayed holed up in their house like rabbits. This morning was the first time I'd seen any of them outside for more than a few minutes, and patently useless didn't even *begin* to describe what was happening now.

I held back a growl. I barely remembered the black girl, except for some vague recollection of seeing her with the fish on the road near our house. But with her curly braids, petite figure, and big, tan-green eyes, she looked like a little doll – like something that would break easy and probably cry while you did it. She couldn't have been more than fifteen, maybe sixteen at the outside.

And she was doing nothing.

For the past ten minutes, ever since she'd left the house, she'd been standing at the far side of the backyard, right by the end of the hedge. With one hand holding back a branch, she'd locked her eyes on the park beyond the bushes, and short of a frustrated expression that passed over her face from time to time, she scarcely seemed to blink.

That cop-scientist guy was watching her from nearby. He'd always looked like an anxious bird, but there was something different about him now. With this weirdly protective expression on his face, he barely took his eyes from her, except for brief moments when his gaze would flick around like he was keeping watch.

It would have been amusing if it wasn't so annoying. I

couldn't move from my current hiding place in case they heard me. I couldn't do much of anything. I'd been tempted just to yank her into the bushes and take care of it, except that cop guy would yell and his cries would alert Peter or Maddox. My dear relatives might be lurking close to the windows, and would probably come rushing from the house if I did so much as sneeze.

Really, annoying didn't even cover it.

The back door of the mansion opened. I tensed, ready to get out of here if Maddox or Peter appeared.

Noah's stepsister came outside. I scowled. Twice now that bitch, Baylie, had gotten in the way of me capturing the fish. My cousin wasn't the only one I wanted to make pay for that, though I'd probably get more inventive with what I decided to do to her. Noah, I'd just kill.

The thought made my lip twitch, though otherwise I stayed motionless. She walked across the yard toward the black girl and the cop, casting a worried look to the ocean while she went.

"How's it coming?" she called.

The other girl didn't glance away from the park. She didn't even seem to hear the question.

Cop-guy gave an awkward shrug. "It's, um…"

A frustrated noise escaped the black girl. Letting the branch go, she turned from the bushes. "It's *not*. I just—" The angry sound came again. She shook her head.

"You said it took years, though," Baylie offered. "Right?"

The other girl grimaced. "Yeah, but we don't have that."

"Ellie," the scrawny cop tried.

"Joseph said I'd be good at this. That I'd… that I'd be *really* good, if I figured it out." She paused, looking away. "I couldn't help anybody yesterday. And Grandpa—"

"You couldn't have saved him," the cop said.

Ellie grimaced, not taking her gaze from the ground. "Maybe not. But I couldn't even *try*. Not with Grandpa. Not with those guys yesterday or anyone before them and I just… The elders will be there with us. Olivia's getting out of the hospital and Dave's bringing her. But I still want to help… if I can."

They were all quiet for a moment. My brow furrowed. The elders. *Landwalker* elders? How was the girl connected with them?

And how could I use that?

The elders had something. It wasn't magic like the fish – a power we could absorb into ourselves that felt better than any drug on the planet – but it was something that felt good too. I knew; I'd taken it in when I'd killed one of them on the road near our house. I hadn't told Clay about it, though. Secrets were a leader's prerogative, plus he'd gotten to kill two fish and I hadn't – the bastard. But if the elders were coming, maybe I could get my hands on more of that.

Though, how the little doll-girl fit in…

My confusion turned to suspicion. One of those landwalker elders, Doctor Harman Brooks, had died up by that weird turtle-guy's house. I'd found his body before Clay and I left. But he'd had a granddaughter. And now here was this girl, talking about

Grandpa and trying something. Staring at people and trying something.

She couldn't be an *elder*, though. She was barely a teenager. So she had to be Harman's granddaughter.

Maybe that meant she had that not-quite-magic thing too.

"So," Baylie began. "Um, about what Noah said."

My attention snapped back.

Ellie didn't respond.

"Do *you* feel anything?" Baylie asked.

Ellie shook her head. "Not really. We were pretty far ahead of the blast wave." She hesitated. "Do you?"

Baylie dropped her gaze away, her shoulder twitching in a shrug.

My brow furrowed again. Feel anything? What the hell was *that* supposed to mean?

"There was a lot of electricity," Ellie said, almost like she was apologizing for it. "Anybody'd feel shaky after that."

Baylie nodded, though she didn't look back at the girl. Another one of those awkward pauses crept past. I struggled not to groan. I finally had people out here, and not a one of them had mentioned anything useful.

"You want to practice on me?" Baylie offered.

Ellie turned to her in alarm.

"Anything to help, right?" Baylie shrugged. "Things could get pretty crazy, once Chloe and Noah get back."

Ellie bit her lip and cast a glance toward the park. "Those people *are* kind of far away…"

"So what do you need me to do?"

Still seeming uncertain, Ellie motioned to the grass. "Well, you should probably sit down, just in case, and then I guess—"

The door to the house opened again. Uncle Peter came outside.

I stopped breathing, waiting to see if he'd noticed me.

"We're leaving," he said.

"You, um…" Baylie glanced around. "It's okay?"

Peter hesitated. "I haven't heard from Richard, but we're going up there anyway." He scanned the bushes. I was still, as only my brothers and I knew how to be. "We're heading out within the hour."

The cop and the two girls followed him inside. I slipped back through the bushes to the park.

Richard. Up there. They were going north, then, and there was only one place they'd contact my father about traveling.

My lip twitched, exhilaration pounding through me. Finally, some useful information. The most useful of all, in fact.

They were heading to my home. I didn't know why, and I didn't care. The fish, my cousin, all of them were going to the one place I knew better than anywhere else in the world.

This was perfect. Hell, this was *Christmas*.

Now all I needed to do was get there first.

Striding across the park, I drew out my cell phone to call Clay and get his stupid ass back here.

We had some hitchhiking to do.

15

ZEKE

"—pending negotiation with the Yvarian king."

"My lady, you realize—"

"No, *you* realize. You realize I can't put Lycera in a position of openly supporting the very group Yvaria believes assassinated their king. We're *already* in a tense situation with them, and doing this would only serve to publicly confirm actions of which they've already accused us!"

Mom's shout carried through the throne room. I worked to keep my face calm. This was going worse than I'd thought – and I'd expected it to be bad. We'd been talking for half an hour, the two of us and Kreyus while Ina and Jirral hovered silently nearby, but there had yet to be a single sign of improvement. Mom had stared at me like I'd told her the ocean was draining when I explained what the Vetorians wanted, and on some level I couldn't blame her. Kreyus' plan was insane, and there wasn't a chance in hell Ren would take part in it. At least, not unless we could make the idiot believe the Sylphaen were real – something that felt about on par with the Beast transforming into a fluffy baby seal in terms of likelihood. Meanwhile, Kreyus expected me to support his side, which apparently meant pretending that political realities didn't exist.

Mom turned to me. "Honestly, Zekerian. What were you *thinking* agreeing to this?"

I couldn't stop a grimace. She acted like we'd had an alternative.

"I was thinking that we didn't have any choice," I replied, fighting to keep my tone level. "But there are points in what Kreyus suggests that are worth discussing once the current crisis is over."

"The current 'crisis', as you call it," Kreyus countered, "is nothing more than—"

"You're saying it wouldn't be easier to protect your daughter if the contract on her *life* was gone?" I cut in. "Or are you admitting it's not her *safety* you care about?"

Kreyus paused.

"Daughter?" Mom asked.

I hesitated, cursing internally. I'd said too much. But no one needed to go into the details of Chloe's identity yet, even if her appearance made it damn near obvious. At this point, Mom might have trouble coming to a conclusion different than Ren's.

"Which is it, Kreyus?" I pressed on. "You've got Vetorians crawling all over Yvarian waters, and more back home. And they all want a piece of that bounty. So what'll it be? Are you willing to let the Ivalaen tribe take on the *entire* Prijoran Zone over that contract, or can you just agree it'd be better to handle the Sylphaen and cancel the damn bounty first?"

He studied me for a moment. "You may have a point."

It was hard not to feel a measure of satisfaction at the words.

Even if it was short lived.

"But we *will* deal with our arrangement, highness. When the Sylphaen have gone and your brother has been convinced of our innocence in the former king's death, we will revisit this discussion."

"Once that happens is the only time there'll be a *chance* for discussion, Kreyus."

His eyes narrowed at my response.

"High Lady Coriana," he said, that pretentious formality returning to his tone. "My people need rest. If I may inquire as to where we might stay during our visit with you?"

I glanced to her, suspecting that she wanted to suggest the prison. Her face gave nothing away, however, and with an acquiescing nod to Kreyus, she said, "The chamberlain will escort you to the guest quarters."

She motioned to a dehaian by the throne room door.

Kreyus smiled. "Thank you."

He swam from the room.

A breath left me when the door closed.

"I thought Torvias taught you better than this, Zekerian," Mom said.

I didn't turn around.

"Making a deal with *Vetorians*," she continued. "How could you *possibly* have thought that would go well?"

"Over a hundred of them versus me, Chloe, and a guy who can barely swim." I looked back at her. "You tell me, what would you have done?"

Her mouth compressed. "Why didn't you have any guards?"

"Because Ren wants to stick me in the northern wastes and pretend that the Sylphaen aren't real." I shook my head. "They killed my *father*. He died right in front of me. They tried to kill Chloe, they convinced Niall to join them, they held Ina this whole time, and Ren refuses to believe they even exist. I didn't have a *choice*, Mom."

She paused, her gaze flicking to the guards. I struggled not to wince. I'd almost never called her that, not since I was a kid and propriety hadn't quite sunk in. And now… dammit, stress was catching up to me. I knew authority was like oxygen to her these days. Her sister, Queen Lisalia, was sick and Mom had been left to tend to the kingdom and my cousin Kobi alike. Meanwhile, the tension with Yvaria and her connection to that throne through us meant that people were undoubtedly questioning where her loyalties lay.

The last thing she needed was informality.

"High Lady," I corrected.

She gave an infinitesimal nod. "I can understand your position," she allowed.

I exhaled, a tiny bit relieved.

"But this agreement with Kreyus…"

"If the Sylphaen are gone, Ren will calm down," I said, still not sure I believed it myself. "The Vetorians are only in Yvaria because of the Sylphaen. Deal with them and this ends."

"Because of this contract on Kreyus' daughter?"

I hesitated. "Yes."

She regarded me. I held my breath, hoping she'd choose not to press the issue.

"And the young woman with you."

The hope died. "Chloe's a friend."

Mom paused. "Your friend seemed quite frightened of us."

"She's had a hard couple of weeks."

Mom studied me. I could tell she'd read between the lines, about Chloe's relationship to Kreyus at least. Anyone in their right mind could see how much they looked alike. But if I was lucky, she hadn't figured out the rest. My feelings for Chloe would only make the Vetorians' presence seem like an even bigger problem to her.

"I shouldn't allow you to stay here with them," she said to me.

I tensed.

"Traveling with Vetorians," she continued. "Zekerian, it makes the king's accusations of you seem—"

I let out a breath, relieved in spite of myself. "I know how it looks," I assured her. "And keep the Vetorians under as many guards as you wish. You won't have any argument from me. My concern is getting rid of the Sylphaen so that Yvaria, Lycera, and all the other nations of the ocean are safe."

For a long while, she was silent and it was everything I could do to appear calm. I'd told her that we had a plan to stop the leadership of the Sylphaen, that it would be put into action on the coast, and that soldiers were needed to guard us during it all. But I'd left out the part about the greliarans. Not only had Kreyus been in the room, but I didn't think it would've gone well to tell Mom that Niall's safety rested on us reaching her son before some psychopathic, glowing rock creatures did.

I could barely stomach that part of the plan myself.

"Very well," she relented. "But a decision to send soldiers through Yvarian territory…" Her mouth tightened. "It would be best for me to consult Queen Lisalia for her opinion. Give me time to speak with her, and then we'll see."

"Thank you."

She nodded, her expression making it clear that the audience had come to an end.

I turned and swam for the door, trying not to feel like I was bolting from the room.

Ina and Jirral followed me into the hall.

"We need to talk," Jirral said before I could ask the guards outside where the chamberlain had sent the others.

I hesitated. I didn't want to leave Chloe alone around here for a second longer than I had to, not with Vetorians who might want to take her away or Lycerans who might decide to treat her like a mercenary.

"Zeke?" Ina pressed, a note of pleading in her voice.

But I couldn't really argue either. Not with Ina. I had

questions for her too.

Fighting back a grimace, I nodded and then trailed them down a side hall. At a room I vaguely recognized as Ina's from the last time we'd stayed here, the two of them turned and slipped through the fejeria plants blocking the door.

"So what's going on, Zeke?" Jirral asked after I put a hand to the lighter patch of stone by the doorframe, sealing the plants behind me.

I wasn't sure where to begin. My gaze caught on the fading gash across his chest.

"What happened?" I asked, jerking my chin to the mostly healed wound. "You really attacked the Sylphaen?"

I couldn't keep the doubt from my voice. Annoyance crossed his face when he heard it.

Ina caught my tone too. "Zeke—"

"I did what I had to do," Jirral retorted. "Yes."

My mouth tightened. Anger took the place of his annoyance at the expression.

"Listen, kid," Jirral snapped. "I'm well aware you've believed I'm some kind of coward all these years – though by now, I would have *hoped* you'd have changed your mind. But there's something you need to get straight. I'm not the one you should be angry at. I'm not the one who screwed things up. Torvias did, and he *kept* screwing up by never teaching you kids to do better."

I bristled. "Excuse me?"

"There's a difference between being a ruler and being an

ordinary person, Zeke, and your father forgot that. Those Driecaran bastards made one hell of a mistake ambushing us on that trip and taking your sister, but Torvias made one fifty times worse. There were more lives than Miri's at risk back then. Innocent lives, and ones your father sacrificed when he went ahead and did things his way. He needed to *talk* to the Driecarans. Behave like a politician, not just a father. That's what I was trying to get him to do. That's why I kept pushing him to use diplomacy. Not because I'm a coward, but because he was a *king*. One that failed."

My heart pounded.

Jirral grimaced. "You think I wasn't out hunting Miri back then, even while I was trying to get Torvias to talk? I'm not above busting heads when my grandchildren are at stake, and that's exactly what I did. I have more people who owe me favors than most folks know in their entire lives, and I used every damn one of them. Hell, half of the reason I'm known outside Yvaria is because of what I did while trying to bring Miri home. But I'm just me. Your father was the leader of a nation. There's a difference between those things, and that's one lesson your father apparently never managed to teach you.

"I've spent every day of my life regretting that I took you, Ina and Miri on that trip, Zeke," Jirral finished. "Every damn day."

I watched him, uncertain how to respond.

"Zeke," Ina tried again. "Granddad went up against over a dozen of them just to reach me. He—"

"Don't," I said.

She fell silent.

I didn't take my eyes from Jirral. I wanted to hate him. That was the truth of it. I wanted to hate him with every fiber of my being, because it was easier. Really, actually easier.

It meant there was someone to blame. Someone who hadn't died in a genocide or caused one.

I turned away. She'd brought it up. Chloe, back in the cave. I hadn't been thinking of Dad when I talked to her about Kreyus. I'd only wanted to reassure her that she wasn't like him. But until she spoke, I hadn't remembered that way people had looked at us, or the fear in their eyes – like if they said or did *one* wrong thing to us, Dad would come after their families too. I hadn't remembered how we'd all started coping with it, without any of us ever really saying a word. Ren had become more Dad than Dad, as though by imitating our father he could prove that what happened to Driecara wasn't wrong. And the rest of us had blocked it out. Chased parties and sex and never thought too deeply about anything, just to prove to everyone that we weren't a threat. To prove to ourselves that life could be uncomplicated.

And then Chloe had come along, and suddenly I hadn't cared about uncomplicated anymore.

Jirral had saved her too, though. Shot the Sylphaen who'd taken her, and hid her in a cave so Ren's soldiers wouldn't find her. She'd be dead now if not for what he'd done.

I looked back at him. "Yeah."

Jirral froze, as if he hadn't expected the response. His brow twitched down, and then the nascent expression disappeared. He gave a tight nod.

I turned away again.

"So alright then," Jirral said, his voice brusque. "You're heading back to the coast?"

I nodded. "After we get the soldiers. We…" I grimaced, trying to decide what to say. I didn't want to lie to Ina, not with how she'd never forgive me if something went wrong and we couldn't help Niall. Mom wouldn't forgive me either, I knew.

But that was necessary. Without Mom's help, we'd have no soldiers. No one to guard against the Sylphaen escaping. And this… this was different.

My stomach twisted. Chloe wasn't the only one who'd changed because of everything that'd happened these past few weeks.

"Those things you shot nets at a few days ago," I continued. "The greliarans. They're going to be waiting for us. Idea is, they leave us alone and they get to kill the Sylphaen."

"Zeke…" Ina started, sounding incredulous.

"It's the only option we have."

She stared at me.

"These greliarans," Jirral said. "They can come underwater like us?"

I paused.

"That's one of them with her, right?" he pressed.

"Yeah, but… it's not his doing. It's Chloe. She brought him with us. He can just pick up on the Beast and tell if it's close."

"She's able to bring people underwater with her?" Jirral repeated.

"Among other things," I allowed.

He looked like he wanted more than that, but the old habit of not trusting him still made me pause. "She's discovering new abilities all the time," I continued with effort. "And some of them are fairly destructive." My mouth tightened briefly. "Kreyus has seen that, though. He knows that part of what she can do."

"And this deal with him," Jirral asked. "This business about a bounty on his daughter… am I right in thinking that's Chloe too?"

"Yeah. She just found out about him yesterday."

Ina scoffed.

I looked to her. "What?"

She shook her head.

"What?"

"Yesterday," she repeated. "Zeke, she's *actually* a Vetorian. Like, *really*. Ren said she—"

"This isn't about that."

"She's that guy's *kid*!" Ina cried. "You honestly think she 'just found out yesterday'?"

"I was there!"

"Oh, for the love of—"

"Ina, dammit, we've been through this! She's not—"

"Has Kreyus claimed her?" Jirral asked.

I tore my gaze from Ina to look at him. "What?"

"Said publicly that she's his child. Specifically that he 'claims' her."

My brow furrowed. I didn't like the sound of this and I hadn't even heard all of it yet.

And suddenly, I wanted to find Chloe even more than before.

"Yeah…" I allowed. "He told the Vetorians with them. All hundred or so of them. But I've never heard of 'claiming' in the tribes—"

"It's mostly a Vetorian practice, not a tribal one," Jirral said. "And it's only as significant as Kreyus makes it. But if he actually didn't know about her, that'd be the first step in making sure no other Vetorian thought to turn her in for that bounty. He's saying she's his property. Anyone who messes with her, messes with him."

I stared at him. Chloe damn well wasn't anyone's *property*, least of all his.

Jirral seemed to read something of my thoughts in my expression. "It doesn't mean he'll necessarily force her to do anything she doesn't want to do. But in Vetorian eyes, she's his."

My heart was racing. I wanted to get back to Chloe *now*.

"It seems unlikely that he'd put on a performance like that if he already knew about her," Jirral added.

"But not impossible," Ina countered, a touch desperately. "They both could have been doing it for Zeke's benefit."

I turned back to her, exasperated. "Ina—"

"What? That guy looks like a *psycho*, Zeke! Did you *see* all those scars? The people he has with him? He couldn't know you'd never been told about that stupid 'claiming' thing! He probably just—"

"I've heard of Kreyus," Jirral interrupted. "And while the topic never particularly came up, I can say no one ever mentioned him having a daughter."

My brow rose.

"I spent some time with the Ivalaen tribe a few years ago," Jirral explained. "I never met the man, but I heard stories. Praelex Kreyus is something of a favored son around there, considering how successful his cell of the Vetorians have been. As reputation has it, he's a hardcore pragmatist, a strong leader, and one hell of a businessman." He paused. "You did well in there, bargaining with him."

I hesitated, not sure what to say.

"They could have been putting on a show," Jirral continued to Ina. "But the chances are pretty remote. I'll go see what I can find out, though."

He turned to leave.

"This property thing," I said.

Jirral glanced back.

"Chloe's abilities," I continued. "If Kreyus thinks he can try to use her…"

"I'll see what I can find out," he repeated.

I grimaced, not remotely reassured. Jirral swam from the room. I started for the door as well.

"Zeke," Ina said.

My grimace deepened. I glanced back at her. "She's not one of them, Ina."

A wince crossed her face. "But Chloe just—"

"She's *not*!"

Ina blinked in shock.

I drew a breath. "Please, Ina. I'm not an idiot, alright? If I thought for one *second* Chloe was behind what happened to Dad—"

"You'd what?" she snapped, her hesitancy vanishing instantly into anger. "You'd *what*, Zeke? Turn her over to Ren? Let him *execute* her?" She scoffed. "No, you wouldn't, because you're a great guy who's loyal to a damned fault. But you *love* her, Zeke. You're *in* love with her and she's the daughter of a Vetorian warlord! Why can't you understand that's what's keeping you from—"

"Ina, stop!" I shuddered, my heart pounding. "Just stop, okay?" I repeated more quietly. "I…"

I looked away. I didn't want to get into this here, now, with her yelling at me. It just didn't feel like the time.

Because the truth was, I did love Chloe. I honestly *loved* her, and I'd come within a heartbeat of telling her that earlier because the words had gotten away from me. If those damned Vetorians hadn't come back when they did…

I wasn't sure what would have happened.

Or what she would have said in return.

"Zeke, you—"

"I do," I snapped. "Okay, Ina? I do. I love her like crazy and I *still* know she's innocent. *Please*, Ina. Trust me. I'm not blinded here, and if I suspected she was guilty, I'd… well, I wouldn't be defending her, I know that much. But she *is* innocent. I'm aware of what the evidence looks like, but I *swear* to you, it's not what it seems."

Ina stared at me, her blue eyes unreadable. "You know, I've never actually heard you say you love a girl before?" she replied softly. "Besides me or Miri, I mean."

I didn't know how to respond.

"Have you told her?" Ina asked.

"No."

Ina's mouth tightened. She dropped her gaze to the floor.

"Please," I said. "I need to go. If this guy tries to hurt her or force her to do anything—"

"You should tell her."

My brow furrowed in confusion.

Ina looked back up at me. "Zeke, tell her. If she's innocent – and I'm *trying* to trust you on that, okay? I'm trying. But if she really is innocent, if everything wasn't an act… then I saw it on her face when she told me her plan to get you out of Ren's custody. How scared she was for you." Insistence touched Ina's expression. "*Tell* her."

I tried not to grimace. We had Kreyus to deal with, and the Sylphaen as well. I couldn't get into my feelings for Chloe in the middle of all that. And besides, I didn't believe it'd go well, pressing her to talk about this.

Though maybe it was more that I didn't want to know her answer. I didn't want to know if she didn't feel the same way, or if she loved that other guy instead. Whatever Ina thought Chloe had seemed like a few days ago, I'd seen the way Chloe looked at him. And when I had to watch her kiss him…

The urge to grimace returned, along with a desire to repeatedly punch something – preferably him.

"It's complicated," I managed.

"Make it not be."

I let out a breath in exasperation. "Ina, I can't. There's other stuff going on, and that guy, Noah, he's always with her, in case he picks up on that Beast thing—"

"Oh, please. *Him?* Big deal. Go talk to the girl, Zeke. You let me take care of the glorified sonar."

A choked laugh left me in spite of myself. I doubted the guy would fall for Ina's brand of distraction, though. Not with how focused he was on Chloe.

"Come on," Ina insisted, starting for the door. "At least this way you'll know, right?"

I sighed. I didn't want to know. Not really. I didn't want to put myself out there, only to learn that she didn't feel the same way in return.

But I still had to find Chloe. And Ina probably wouldn't let up on this anyway.

Not quite able to believe this was a good idea, I swam with her from the room.

16

CHLOE

Zeke had said we'd be okay.

I was finding it really hard to believe that.

For the hundredth time in the past thirty minutes, my gaze twitched to the guards and Vetorians currently eyeing each other from opposite sides of the large guestroom. I was stuck between them, sitting at a table with Noah like the two of us were some weird island in a frigid and tense sea.

But then, this wasn't like last time, when I'd ended up being thrown inside a prison cell. I knew that. I'd been repeating it to myself nearly once a minute. But fifteen feet to my right, a dozen Vetorians I didn't recognize were studying me like they couldn't decide whether I was a threat or a possession, while an equal distance to the left, twelve Lycerans watched me as if convinced I was just another mercenary they might have to arrest.

Neither of them were doing much for my belief I was safe.

I drew a slow breath, working to keep my heart from racing. I hoped Zeke came back from the throne room soon. I was glad

204

Noah was here, but I was also worried what would happen if he had to do anything to protect us. What they'd do if the Lycerans and the Vetorians found out what he was.

And besides, people seemed less likely to try locking me up when Zeke was around.

"Hey."

I looked over to Noah.

"We'll be out of here soon," he assured me, his voice low enough that hopefully the others couldn't hear.

I nodded, willing myself to believe the words. My gaze returned to the window and the view of the capital beyond.

"You doing okay, though?" he continued. "You know, after what happened at the caves?"

I tensed, my gaze snapping back to him. I'd thought he hadn't heard Zeke and I talking. That he'd been asleep. But then, he was greliaran. That hearing of theirs… maybe it didn't matter.

"Chloe?"

I gave a tight shrug.

"You don't have to do anything you don't want to, you know," he offered. "Whatever Kreyus is to you… that's your decision to make, not his, okay?"

I hesitated. Oxygen made its way back into my lungs. So this wasn't about me and him, then. Or me and Zeke. Or anything like that at all.

Thank God.

I managed another nod.

He studied me briefly and then turned his attention to the Vetorians and Lycerans hovering on either side. "So I've been thinking," he began softly.

I tensed all over again.

"You ever consider it was ironic," he said, "how they called that thing the 'Beast'?"

My brow furrowed. That hadn't been what I'd expected him to say.

"Like it was their answer to—" His gaze twitched across the others again. He lowered his voice further. "You know, us. Like some grand 'anything you can do, we can do better'?"

I paused and then shrugged. "Maybe it was."

He was silent, his eyes slipping to the city beyond the palace window.

"I couldn't feel it, though," he said. "That day at Joseph's. It was just some huge storm. And now…"

I shifted uncomfortably on the seat.

"What?" he asked.

My gaze skirted around. I didn't want to think about this.

"Chloe?"

"I could."

From the corner of my eye, I saw his brow draw down.

"In the sky, I…" My head shook, more memories pouring in. Old ones, from a million years and only a month or so ago.

They made my heart race.

"I could feel it, Noah," I confessed. "Like it hated me. I could feel that. And even before then, too."

"Before?"

I glanced to the guards. I didn't want them to hear this. They probably wouldn't – we were barely even whispering – and if we moved it'd only draw their attention.

"In Santa Lucina," I murmured. "I had these... there were these dreams. Just about the ocean, like I *needed* to be here. And most of that was probably just the dehaian thing, it waking up or whatever, but there was this one..."

"What?" His voice was tense, urgent.

My gaze rose to his. "I saw it. In my dreams. I felt the Beast coming for me in the water, all dark and terrible just like at Joseph's. But I could hear it, like it was laughing."

He stared at me. I trembled.

"It's hunting you," he whispered. "Maybe those feelings are part of how it communicates or whatever. Back in Colorado, Dave said that the landwalker elders don't even know all of what that thing is capable of doing. And as for the dream when you were in Santa Lucina..." He shook his head.

"What?" I asked.

"Maybe it was just your instincts. I mean, the boat capsized and the water went crazy because the Beast was there. Weak, yeah, but there. Maybe all that danger just made your mind put a face to it – so to speak, anyway."

A tiny grimace tugged at my expression.

"Chloe?" he prompted.

"It feels like more than that."

He paused. "Like what, then?"

I shook my head. "I'm not sure."

Silence returned between us. His hand found mine across the table. I squeezed his fingers, a shuddering breath leaving me.

"It's like everything got supercharged that day at Joseph's," he murmured, his gaze on our hands. "You. What you can do. Me and the whole 'feeling its presence' thing. But then, what you did with that water… I can't help thinking about lightning. Storms. Ellie said the Beast is basically the ocean's magic made into a creature and maybe when that magic hit you—"

"But the dehaians," I tried, afraid of where he was going with this. "They said they could feel electricity in the water around me this whole time."

He was quiet for a moment. "True."

I looked down, my gaze skipping across the dark stone of the terrace. It wasn't the same, whatever they'd felt and this. It couldn't be. I hadn't killed people with a touch before. I hadn't punched in rock walls with a thought.

My entire body hadn't felt vaguely like a live wire.

But then, the Sylphaen *had* talked about me developing abilities, even if they hadn't specified *what*. Even Ellie had said that the landwalkers thought someone like me might have unusual skills. And everything that'd happened so far didn't feel like it came from outside me. Exactly the opposite, actually. And the Sylphaen had been scared of me. They'd wanted to use the neiphiandine injection to suppress whatever they thought I could do, and they'd never made it sound like the Beast was necessary to make those abilities happen.

Supercharged, Noah had said.

I shivered.

"You know what's odd, though?" he continued.

I waited, not really sure I wanted to hear the answer.

"It hasn't noticed you since that day on the beach."

I fidgeted. "Yeah, but Joseph said—"

"You could hide, I know. But twice now, I've felt it in the distance and… nothing. It moves on like it doesn't see you. Or me. Others… people like me… they'd pick up on my presence at the same time I felt theirs. But this—"

"Maybe we're too small. You know, compared to it."

He paused. "Yeah. Maybe."

I could tell that wasn't all of it. "What?"

His jaw worked around. "I can feel other greliarans, but over a distance, exactly *who* I'm picking up on fades. I can't always tell much beyond the fact it's *somebody* like me. And if the Beast did change us, if we've got some of its traits or whatever… if we're *connected* to it or something and it's not used to that…" He seemed like he was thinking out the words while he spoke. "Maybe we just feel like an echo. Like *it*. And maybe it's confused. Maybe that was even a bit of what happened that day with the boat to make you have those dreams, but comparatively, Joseph's was like…"

"Nuclear."

He looked back to me, agreement in his eyes.

I couldn't hold his gaze. Nausea churned at the implications of this. Implications I couldn't even *begin* to understand.

"You think the others are okay?" I asked softly.

He took a second to respond. "I don't know."

The shivering grew stronger. I was scared of what was happening to me. But equally as bad was the thought of what might be happening to Baylie. Magic wouldn't hurt me; probably not, anyway. But her…

I glanced to the city. We'd be back soon. We just needed Zeke's mother to agree to send the soldiers – something that hopefully wouldn't take much longer – and then we'd be on our way.

The thought did little to slow my racing heart.

"Could I ask you something else?" Noah said quietly.

My gaze slid toward him again.

He drew a breath. "Us."

My gaze darted away.

Noah paused. "Chloe, do you think we—"

Zeke swam around the corner, Ina at his side.

Already twisting, my stomach lodged itself into a complete knot.

"Hey," Zeke said to me. "Can I talk to you for a second?"

There was something in his face; I could just guess at the topic. For her part, Ina simply smiled and eyed Noah up and down as if she was trying to figure out how best to flirt with him.

And all around us, soldiers and Vetorians watched like they were the audience to some live-action theater production.

An incredulous noise left me, the sound strained. They wanted to talk. *Both* of them. About me. Us. The respective us-es that I hadn't figured out and didn't want to deal with right now.

Magic tingled in my hands and sent my heart climbing my throat. I shook my head at Zeke. I couldn't do this. I'd break something or attract the Beast or maybe just have a nervous breakdown, but regardless, I couldn't have these conversations *now*.

Pushing away from the seat, I fled the room.

Most of the Vetorians followed me.

Half the Lycerans did too.

Darting out the window, I raced over the terrace and down toward the garden below. Rock formations and enormous boulders filled the space, while rubble covered the ground with a million tiny bits of coral that'd crumbled over the years. Other coral grew from the debris, like stiff skeletons of bushes with branches that ranged from knobby to jaggedly zigzagged. Ducking down behind a twisting arch of stone, I sank onto a clear spot and tried not to feel like a freak for having taken off like I had.

The Vetorians and Lycerans circled my stone hiding place. In the water above, they hovered, watching me.

"Go *away*!" I shouted at them. "Can't you just give me a—"

"Clear out."

I turned sharply at the sound of a woman's voice.

Zeke's mother drifted around another rock formation, a pair of guards at her side. At the twitch of her chin, the Lycerans above me bowed and then swam away.

She regarded the Vetorians, her brow rising. Pausing briefly, the nearest one seemed to weigh his options, and then he jerked his head at the others. They retreated to the far edge of the garden, still watching us.

Coriana ignored them. With her guards, she came toward me.

I eyed her warily. She had Ren's bearing, Niall's coloring, and she studied me like she was debating whether to simply lock me up. With a flick of her hand, she motioned for me to rise and follow her.

For a moment, I didn't move, but there weren't many options. Angering her probably wouldn't go well.

I pushed away from the ground and joined her while she started through the garden. On the perimeter, the Vetorians moved, tracking us without coming close. I struggled not to grimace.

"You tire of your bodyguards," she commented.

"They're not my bodyguards."

She paused. "High Lady Coriana."

My brow furrowed.

"When speaking to me," she explained. "It is High Lady, my lady, or my full title."

I hesitated. "Sorry… my lady."

She made a neutral noise.

We circled a cluster of coral like a bone-white collection of twisted straws.

"So if they are not your bodyguards, why do they watch you so intently?"

I tried to figure out how to respond. I didn't know what Zeke had told her. Moreover, I didn't know what she'd do if she knew the truth. She might just decide handing me over to the Sylphaen solved her problems too.

"They're watching all of us, my lady."

She glanced to me with a dry expression. "You are Praelex Kreyus' daughter, are you not?"

I tensed.

"Try that answer again," she chided coldly.

"I, uh…"

Coriana's mouth tightened. "I have been told there is a contract out on you, from a group calling themselves Sylphaen. It appears as well that your safety forms some measure of this agreement between my son and the Praelex. Is that a fair assessment?"

I hesitated.

"What have you gotten my son involved in?"

I searched for a response while we rounded the edge of the palace hillside and continued into an array of boulders and coral that had the feel of a hedge maze. The rocks blocked the Vetorians from sight, leaving me alone with the woman and her guards.

"High Lady," I tried. "I'm not trying to—"

"Let me rephrase that, shall I?" she interrupted. "Stay away from my son. You, your Vetorian family, and everyone with whom you are associated are only as welcome as diplomacy demands. But that diplomacy does not give you the right to endanger him or entangle him in some romantic ruse to meet your father's needs, understand?"

I faltered. "My lady, I'm not—"

"Enough," she snapped, exasperated. "Truth is obviously not a Vetorian specialty. Consider this, then. If I see you near him, if I see you *look* at him, you and your family are gone. I will hand you over to the Yvarians myself."

Without another word, she spun and swam away, her guards following her.

I stared. I couldn't believe this. After everything else in the world that'd already happened, now the leader of *another* dehaian nation thought I was a spy.

I *hated* Zeke's family.

A choked sob burned in my chest at the thought, untrue though it partially was. I sank to the ground, and jagged bits of coral pressed against my scales.

I felt like I was losing my mind. This day, this week, this past month… it'd be enough to make anyone crazy.

Having Zeke in my life was one of the only things that'd kept me sane through all that.

A breath pressed from me. It was true. Without him at my side, without his help, I'd probably be dead now.

The girl he'd traveled the ocean and half a continent for.

I looked to the rocks beside me. I wouldn't stay away from

Zeke just because of some politician's orders. I *couldn't*. He meant too much to me.

They both did.

My eyes closed. Noah... Zeke... it made no better sense now than it ever had. It just hurt more. If Zeke had been about to tell me he loved me... if Noah's kiss yesterday had been a sign of the same... if they had any idea of how I felt for them...

Both of them.

A weight crushed down on my chest, pained and terrible. It wasn't *possible* to love two people, though. Not really. The human body couldn't hold all this for more than one person.

At least, I'd thought it couldn't.

I'd thought you met someone, and everyone else paled in comparison to them. I'd thought falling in love was something you had a say in, even just a little bit. Something you could at least understand when it was happening to you.

It wasn't. I didn't.

And I couldn't picture my life without either of them anymore.

My palm pressed down on the broken bits of coral, and the edges bit hard at my skin. I might not have a choice in that. If I became a landwalker, it wouldn't matter what I wanted. What I chose.

Everything would be taken anyway.

A breath escaped me, ragged and harsh. I looked up, my gaze scanning the empty water overhead like maybe, just maybe it'd have an answer.

Nothing presented itself.

I closed my eyes. I'd wanted to date Noah for years. I'd wanted to talk to him, get to know him, and all that time, I'd hoped to God that he would like me too. He'd been amazing once I'd finally had that chance, like everything I'd hoped for had only been the beginning of how great he could be, and each day I had with him only showed more and more of how wonderful he was. And Zeke… without him, being in the sea and living as a dehaian just felt cold. Empty. Lonely in a way that so far surpassed something merely physical. I'd always wanted to visit the ocean, see the ocean, and maybe even live in the ocean, but now… I wanted Zeke to be a part of that too. I *needed* him to be, and the thought of never being close to him again, never feeling him hold me again…

It was horrible.

I swallowed hard. I was attracted to both of them – madly, deeply, so much it hurt. And I cared for them. I cared for them to the point that I had to think maybe I *did* love them, even if the word scared me so much I wanted to hide.

Because it was big. Vulnerable. Overwhelming and dangerous.

And it felt like it was tearing me apart.

I drew a breath, struggling to push the fear back down. It didn't matter, though. What I felt. How much it hurt. I had to choose. I couldn't have them both.

Even if leaving one of them for the other felt like ripping half of my heart out.

Even if I had no idea which one it'd be.

The garden was quiet as I pushed away from the coral. No one had come looking for me in the few minutes since Coriana had left.

I couldn't help but be grateful. As horrible as thinking about the mess between us all was, I hadn't had a moment of space in what felt like weeks. I almost didn't want to leave.

And not just because I had no clue what to do when I reached the terrace again.

Taking a deep breath, I started up from the rock maze.

"Miss?"

I glanced over my shoulder. Braxus circled the corner of the maze behind me, his equally enormous brothers following him.

"Your father would like to speak with you. If you'd come this way, please?"

He motioned up toward the palace.

I hesitated. I didn't like this. I couldn't see Zeke or Noah – the terrace was on the other side of the hill – and I didn't think it was a good idea to leave with no one but Vetorians knowing where I'd gone.

And I wasn't sure I wanted to be anywhere *near* Kreyus alone.

"We will tell your friends he's asked for you," Braxus said as if reading my thoughts.

He looked to one of his brothers. The man nodded and then headed for the turn of the maze.

"Please, miss," Braxus pressed. "It's not wise to keep the Praelex waiting."

I shivered, and water tingled around my hands in response. Quickly, I fought to stop it while I gave the man a small nod.

He swam toward the palace. Biting my lip to keep the water under control, I followed. We continued up to an opening on the wall, and Lyceran guards eyed us when we slipped past the fejeria inside.

I trailed Braxus along the hallway, and then down past another turn. Without looking at me, he wound through the palace till we reached a corridor that was nearly empty. The water had a silence to it, as if the rooms around us were vacant or else everyone in them was making as little noise as possible.

Confusion hit me. At the end of the hall, two Lyceran guards hovered beside a doorway lined with gold and jewels, the trim more ornate than any I'd seen since the throne room.

Kreyus was staying *here*?

The guards gave Braxus a brief nod while we went in.

A spacious apartment waited on the other side of the fejeria, with glistening chandeliers and inlayed gemstone décor.

And a half dozen Vetorians and Lyceran soldiers, one of whom held the little boy I'd seen earlier.

The man had a knife to the child's throat.

"What is this?" I demanded, water spinning up around my hands before I even registered the impulse.

"Don't," Braxus warned.

Behind the hand clamped over his mouth, the boy made a

panicked sound when the soldier tightened his grip.

"You try anything and the child dies," Braxus stated.

I stared at him for a heartbeat before my gaze darted back to the little boy. Kobi, Zeke had called him. In the room beyond him, I could see a woman propped up by pillows on a bed. Blankets covered her, the edges of which she gripped with frail fingers. Wide-eyed, she watched us all. Her skin was pallid, and her chest seemed to hitch with every nervous breath. From her dark hair and features – not to mention the surroundings; why hadn't I realized that? – I could guess she was Zeke's aunt, the Queen of Lycera. A pair of servants cowered in the corner near her, their terrified eyes twitching between their queen and the soldier holding her son.

"Is this Kreyus' doing?" I asked.

Braxus scoffed. "Your father is a fool." His lips curled into a smile, cold and cruel. "Long live the Wisdom."

My breath caught.

"You will come with us. You and the boy." Braxus' smile returned. "We cannot compete with what you can do – not yet. And gagging you would only raise suspicion." He looked pointedly to Kobi. "But that does not mean we cannot control you."

Braxus gestured to the others. "The Vetorians among us will escort you to the border, while the Lycerans will follow with the little princeling. You will be within sensory distance of one another at all times, and if they feel you so much as twitch in the water in a way they don't like, the boy will be dead before you can reach him."

A desperate sound left Queen Lisalia. She struggled up in her bed. "You said you wouldn't—"

"Do you have the travel documents?" Braxus asked over the noise of her protest.

"Yes, sir," one of the Lycerans answered, nodding to him like he was a military commander rather than a mercenary and one of their nation's enemies. "Her highness signed them a few minutes ago."

Braxus smiled at the queen. "Merely a delay, highness. If this creature cooperates, your son will be safely returned to you soon."

Lisalia looked between us. "My entire nation will hunt you down if any of you hurt my child."

His smile didn't fade. "We'll see." He glanced to the others. "Hold them here for thirty minutes and then follow. If they try to raise the alarm, kill them. Blame it on the Praelex's daughter."

The other dehaians nodded.

Braxus turned toward me. "And now, miss, there is only one matter left."

One of the Vetorians behind him withdrew a container from his bag. A leech wriggled inside, its transparent body swollen with glistening liquid.

"Neiphiandine," Braxus said. "In case concern for the boy's safety is not enough to convince you."

Heart pounding, I looked between the Sylphaen and the jar holding the leech. I couldn't have that stuff in my body again. I *wouldn't.*

My gaze darted to Kobi. There had to be a way out of this. Some way to alert anyone *not* Sylphaen.

The Vetorian with the neiphiandine came toward me.

～ 17 ～

ZEKE

Chloe swimming off before I had a chance to talk to her was *not* how I'd pictured things going.

Though, on the whole, I hadn't been sure talking to her was a good idea in the first place. This basically confirmed it.

I scowled, starting after her, only to pull up short at the edge of the terrace when I saw my mother head her way. With an entourage of guards beside her, Mom said something to the Lycerans and Vetorians. The soldiers scattered readily, as if she'd sent them away, and the Vetorians reluctantly retreated to the border of the coral arrangements a moment later. Paying no attention to them both, Mom motioned for Chloe to follow her deeper into the garden.

A breath of annoyance left me while I watched them swim off. I could interrupt – maybe even *should* interrupt; goodness knew why she wanted to speak with Chloe – but things with Mom were tense enough already. If Lycera's regent wanted to speak with someone privately, I couldn't interfere without

222

looking like I didn't respect her authority.

"So, you're Noah, right?" Ina asked.

I glanced back to see her hovering near him. By the window, Noah didn't respond. Instead, he was watching me, and I could see the irritation on his face.

Turning away, I ignored the expression. If I'd had my way, I wouldn't have left him alone with Chloe for five seconds, let alone the near-hour that it'd been. I didn't give a damn that he didn't like me interrupting now.

In the garden, Chloe swam around the curve of the hill, and in a moment, she and my mother disappeared from view. My mouth tightened. I really shouldn't follow.

A minute ticked past. Noah left the window and came over to the edge of the terrace. Still trying to draw him into a conversation, Ina followed.

And Chloe and my mother didn't return.

I needed to wait. Watch for my mother and talk to Chloe once their conversation was done. Interrupting would only make things worse than they already were.

More minutes crept past. Nothing changed.

To hell with this.

"Back in a sec," I said to Ina. I took off down the slope.

Flanked by her guards, Mom came around the side of the hill. Chloe wasn't with her.

"High Lady," I said, "the girl you were talking to, Chloe, is she—"

"I have spoken with her," Mom replied. "The Vetorian girl

and I have reached an understanding."

I hesitated. Vetorian girl. I didn't like the sound of that. Of *any* of it. "What do you mean?" I asked carefully.

"It is not your place to question my—"

"My lady, please. Chloe is not a Vetorian, so—"

She made an exasperated noise. "I will not debate this. The girl's feigned affections for you have been addressed and whatever leverage she intended to gain for her father has been curtailed. The matter is closed."

My brow climbed. "Excuse me?"

"We had a conversation and I made her position clear."

I couldn't believe this. "You had *no* right to—"

"I have every right to protect my nation and our allies from unscrupulous—"

A scoff escaped me. Kicking hard in the water, I shot past her. "Zekerian!"

Ignoring her shout, I swam around the curve of the hill. A rock maze waited ahead of me, brought to a halt farther on by a wall separating the palace grounds from the city beyond. This side of the palace was nearly featureless compared to the others, with only a few pockmark windows and doors to show where the halls began.

But Chloe was nowhere to be seen.

I shot up above the rocks, scanning the paths beneath me.

A Vetorian was leaning against a boulder partway into the maze. I vaguely recognized him as one of the brothers Kreyus had sent to scout our route here. He glanced up when he felt me above him in the water, and quickly, I dove toward him.

"Have you seen Chloe?" I asked. "She was just—"

"Her father wished to speak with her."

Ice spread through me. Kreyus had claimed her like she was some sort of possession. He knew what she could do. And now he'd gotten her away from the rest of us.

Oh hell, that couldn't be good.

"Where are they?"

The man gave me a withering look. "It's a private conversation. You can't— hey!"

I spun and raced back to where I'd left Mom. She was already halfway up the hillside. On the terrace above us, Ina and Noah watched us – my sister clearly having given up her attempt to distract him in favor of wanting to know what was going on.

"High Lady, where did you put Kreyus?" I called.

She looked at me like I was deranged. "Why would you need to speak to that—"

A gasp left her. I felt a shape dart from behind the hill at my back. Twisting fast in the water, I ducked to the side. Braxus' brother swung his spikes through the space where I'd been.

He spun, trying to come at me again. The Lyceran guards around Mom charged at the man. On the terrace, shouts of alarm rose from the other Lycerans. They sped toward us even as the Vetorians by the edge of the garden did likewise.

One of the Lycerans slammed into the man, driving him backward till he crashed into the rocky hillside.

I raced down after them.

"Zekerian!" Mom yelled.

The guard held his spikes to Braxus' brother's throat while his other arm pinned the man down. "How dare you attack—"

"What is this?" I interrupted. "What's going on here?"

Disgust on his face, the man didn't respond.

The other Vetorians raced toward us, only to be intercepted by the Lycerans from the terrace. Protests erupted. From the corner of my eye, I saw spikes come out.

I shoved away from the hillside and swam at the groups. "Hey!" I pushed one of the Lycerans aside, my focus on the Vetorians. "Why are you—"

"Why did he attack you?" one of the mercenaries demanded. "What did you do?"

"You tell me! I tried to find Chloe and the guy went nuts. Why? Why are you hiding her?"

The mercenary glanced to his companions, his expression becoming contemptuous. "Yvarian royalty. Continually expecting everyone to bow to their whims." He scoffed, returning his gaze to me. "No one is *hiding* her. She left with Braxus a short time ago. If the Praelex's daughter chooses not to inform you of her whereabouts, that is not our—"

"Where did they go?"

"You have no right to—"

I swam toward him. "Answer my question, Vetorian!"

"What's the meaning of this?" Kreyus called.

I spun in the water. Swimming down from the terrace with Venika at his side, the man eyed us all guardedly.

"Where's Chloe?" I asked him.

"I haven't seen my daughter in nearly an hour."

"You asked her to come talk to you," I said. "You sent Braxus to get her."

He paused. "I did nothing of the sort."

My heart began to race faster. "This one said you wanted to talk to her." I jerked my head toward the man on the ground. "He said she left with that Braxus guy."

Kreyus' gaze flicked between the Vetorians and the man he restrained. "Who told you I wished to speak with her?" he asked Braxus' brother.

The guy didn't respond.

Kreyus regarded the man as if his silence was an answer in itself. "Then who are you working for?" he continued, his voice becoming deadly cold.

On the ground, the man's face twitched as if he was fighting to control his expression, and possibly his fear. "That foul landwalker spawn will die," he growled, "and through her sacrifice the Wisdom will make you all burn."

My blood turned to ice.

"Where did you take her?" Kreyus continued.

The man's expression turned disparaging.

I swam toward him. A soldier caught my arm, stopping me from coming closer.

Spikes came from my forearms. *"Where is she?"*

"You turn our water to filth," Braxus' brother spat. "Consorting with landwalker—"

"Enough!" Kreyus motioned to two Vetorians. "Take this traitor. Explain to him the severity of his mistake. The rest of you—"

"Praelex Kreyus," Mom interrupted. "You will not use this as some ruse to examine every corner of my home." She looked to one of the guards. "Commander. Have your men fan out. Search the palace for the Praelex's daughter – if she *is* indeed missing."

I turned to her. "High Lady—"

She held up a hand. "I will allow *one* of your people to accompany the commander," she finished to Kreyus.

Anger flashed through Kreyus' eyes so quickly, it was already gone by the time I registered that it had been there. "Of course," he replied, his voice so carefully polite, it was chilling.

He made a sharp gesture toward a random Vetorian in the crowd. Along with the Lycerans, the man swam off.

Mom turned to me. "Take your sister back to her room and stay with her. I will not have you and Inasaria endangered by some plot, Vetorian or otherwise."

She motioned for several of the soldiers to remain with me before she followed the others toward the terrace. For a heartbeat, I didn't move. She... what the... like *hell* I'd just...

I pushed the thoughts away, my gaze going to the palace. All this didn't matter. Chloe would be there. They couldn't have gotten her into the city already. Not without someone noticing. So I'd have Jirral and the soldiers guard Ina and then—

"Venika."

I turned to see Kreyus glance to the woman.

"Take the Vetorians remaining on the terrace," he ordered her, keeping his voice low so the Lycerans couldn't hear. "Tear the palace apart. Every room, every *cupboard*. The rest of you, into the city. Stop anyone who tries to leave."

The Vetorians took off. Venika hesitated, watching Kreyus.

"You heard me," he snapped.

"Kreyus," she replied, her voice tight. "*Your* safety."

The man paused. I ignored him, cursing every second that kept passing. I needed a plan. I couldn't just search blindly; there wasn't time. So where wouldn't people look? If you wanted to hide Chloe from Vetorians and Lycerans alike, where would you go?

Only two places came to mind. Neither of them were good.

I kicked hard in the water, racing for the terrace and leaving the soldiers to catch up.

"Where are you going?" Kreyus sped after me and snagged my arm. I yanked free of his grip, barely keeping my spikes from emerging.

"Save it," I snapped. "I'm not—"

"Who else in this place wants my daughter safe as much as me?"

"Yeah," I scoffed, "and I know why."

I started for the terrace again.

He came after me.

Ina started toward me when I crested the edge of the patio.

"Zeke, what's going on?"

I didn't respond. Beside her, Noah was eyeing me as if, although Ina had gotten to the question first, he was damn near ready to go rock-monster at me if I didn't answer quickly. Jirral had joined them, while Vetorians hovered by the door at the far end of the terrace, watching us intently.

"Take Ina back to her room," I said to Jirral. "Bring the soldiers with you, and don't let anyone else in."

Jirral took only a heartbeat to process the words. "Come on, girl," he told Ina.

"What is it?" Noah demanded. "Where's Chloe?"

"Sylphaen have taken her." I looked to Jirral and twitched my head toward Noah. "Keep him with you."

I took off.

"Prince Zekerian!" Kreyus snapped.

By the door, two Vetorians pulled in front of me, blocking my path. I turned, glaring at Kreyus.

"You cannot go in there by yourself," Kreyus said. "After all, if you know where she is, then backup would be advisable, no?"

I stifled a scowl. The bastard was right. And there wasn't anyone else to use beside him.

Assuming the people with him weren't more Sylphaen, or that this wasn't some *incredibly* complicated trick…

I pushed the thought aside. "Royal residences," I growled. "My cousin's room and the queen's apartment. No one will search them."

"But Vetorians would not be allowed—"

"The Sylphaen aren't Vetorian. They're anyone."

Kreyus paused. "We spread out. Search them both."

He jerked his chin at Venika.

"Kreyus," she started.

"Find her."

Venika hesitated, and then gave a sharp nod. She took off and motioned one of the Vetorians to follow. The others came up to us.

Kreyus raised an eyebrow at me. "After you, highness."

I swam for the door.

18

CHLOE

I retreated as the Vetorian holding the neiphiandine came at me.

"They're not going to let you out of the city," I argued, attempting to watch the Sylphaen ahead of me and the ones behind at the same time. "With me, with him… this isn't going to work."

Braxus appeared amused. "Why wouldn't they? The trusted Vetorian escorting the Praelex's daughter home to the Prijoran Zone, or the loyal Lyceran soldiers taking the princeling to safety on the family estate? We have approval from the queen, no less. Who would question?" He gave me a look of equal parts humor and warning. "And you… well, you won't alert them that there's any problem. Not if you want the child to live."

I bumped into the wall. The man holding the drug continued toward me. My gaze flicked from him to the queen. I couldn't let them give me that. But if I was fast… and really more controlled than I knew how to be, maybe I could do something to the man holding Kobi before he could hurt the boy.

Or I could hit Kobi.

The thought made me shiver. I'd be careful. I didn't know what this was in me, and it was all I could do to keep it from exploding right now, but I'd still be careful. This wasn't like with Baylie. I'd pull it off this time.

And I didn't have any other choice.

My skin tingled.

"Hey!" a guard outside the door protested. "You can't—"

Venika swam into the room, another Vetorian at her side. The two Lycerans from the hall followed her, incredulous looks on their faces. The customary contempt in her expression seemed even more pronounced than normal, and she regarded us all like we were dogs who'd just made a mess on the floor.

"What the hell—" Braxus started. "Grab her!"

Spikes came out on Venika's arms. "Touch me and die."

The Lycerans swimming toward her hesitated.

Venika regarded the room, derision practically staining the water around her. "Honestly, Braxus? *This* was your plan? Take the boy and… what? Hope the queen's servants can't reach a relay to alert the border before you get there?" Her contempt deepened. "The Wisdom would be disgusted with you."

I choked on my own breath. Sylphaen. She was…

Braxus flicked his gaze up and down her, and then he glanced to the two Lycerans from the hall. "Get back outside," he snapped to them. He returned his attention to Venika and the other Vetorian with her. "Since when have *you* joined our—"

"Really?" Venika scoffed. She moved farther into the room. "You think you're so important that you know every one of us among the Vetorians? You think everything I've done to become so trusted by Kreyus wasn't part of the Wisdom's plan?"

Braxus hesitated, appearing slightly less certain. "You're lying."

"And you're an idiot."

She drifted farther into the room, leaving her companion by the door. The man gripping Kobi tensed when she came closer. She ignored the motion, while above the muffle of the man's hand on his mouth, Kobi's gaze was locked on her in terror.

"Kreyus and that Yvarian scum will be here any minute," she continued. "They think you're going after the boy as a more mobile hostage. It won't take them long to realize the kid isn't in his room. And yet here you are, wasting time *talking* with this landwalker spawn," Venika's gaze went to me, a sharp look in her eyes, "like you don't know what she's capable of, or how, at a moment's notice, her magic could tear every single one of you apart."

I barely had time to register the words. Venika darted to the side. Her spikes slashed into the man holding Kobi, and blood filled the water behind the boy. Grabbing Kobi, she shoved him behind her while she spun to face the others.

The water turned to lightning around me. It only took a thought. The slightest lapse in control and suddenly, a wave rushed out across the room, hitting everything in its path like a moving wall. Turning fast, Venika dropped down, sheltering

Kobi beneath her while every bit of furniture or decoration flew at the walls.

Frantically, I fought to rein the magic back in.

Lightning died. The magic of it drained around me. I still felt electrified, still felt like I wanted to explode, but nevertheless, the water surrounding me calmed.

Debris sank toward the floor. Throughout the room, the Sylphaen were scattered. Some of them had crashed into shelves, while others had hit the walls, and though their chests shifted with shallow breaths, otherwise they didn't stir.

I swallowed, my eyes turning to the queen. Untouched in the next room, she and her servants stared at me in horror.

Venika pushed away from the floor. "Well, that was—"

Kobi scrambled out from under her and darted across the room to his mother. Queen Lisalia caught him and pulled him close.

Venika glanced after him and then kicked up the rest of the way from the ground. Her gaze went to the Sylphaen around her, while by the entrance, the other Vetorian who'd accompanied her stirred and then rose unsteadily from the floor. "It actually did what you wanted it to do," she finished.

I paused. She sounded breathless, and yet like she was filing the information away for later reference. It was sort of creepy, as if I was a weapon she was evaluating whether to keep or destroy. Cautiously, I shrugged. "I just—"

"It's magic. It obeyed you." She eyed me. "Unless of course you *intended* that electricity to kill us too?"

The question had enough of an edge in it to cut something. I shook my head.

"Good. Well, were there any others you saw? Anyone else with them?"

I hesitated, watching her. Questions aside, she still looked like she hated me. "Braxus' brother. He—"

"We have him."

I blinked. "Then, no."

She nodded.

I studied her while she glanced to the queen. "You were pretty convincing, talking to him."

Venika gave me a flat look. "I listen well. His brother babbled on about the Wisdom and landwalker spawn. Seemed useful things to mention."

I didn't respond.

Her expression became annoyed. "I'm not one of them, you—"

"Why do you dislike me so much then?" I asked, the words coming out before I really thought them through.

"I just saved your life and you're…" She made a disgusted noise, looking away.

I drew a breath. I shouldn't have asked. This wasn't the time and we needed to go. From the fact they were still breathing, I could tell that the Lycerans and Vetorians around us weren't dead. They could wake up at any moment, or more could come looking for them. Besides, whatever reason she had for hating me, if she wasn't Sylphaen, I almost didn't care.

"You're Yvarian," Venika said.

My brow furrowed. "I'm not—"

"You're *with* an Yvarian," she elaborated, turning back to me. "Those rich, pompous bastards who starve villages and settlements with their sanctions. Yet Kreyus has claimed you, even if you know *nothing* about our ways and we know *nothing* about you. And that is his right. He is the Praelex." Her face darkened. "But if you endanger him… if you jeopardize his position or hurt him in *any* way—"

Venika exhaled sharply, looking away again.

I stared at her, all the glares and coldness suddenly clicking into place like puzzle pieces. She loved him. 'Understanding' between them or not, she genuinely loved him.

"I won't."

She glanced back to me.

"I swear," I insisted. "Look, you're right. I don't know anything about your people or your ways. But…"

I hesitated. I wasn't sure what to say. Kreyus was terrifying. I didn't want to be part of his world. I didn't want scars and weird titles and all these things in which the Vetorians seemed to find such pride.

But if Joseph's potion made me a dehaian like them, I'd have to deal with Kreyus and his people. I wouldn't be able to hide from that any more than I'd been able to hide from anything else in my life.

"I don't want to screw things up either," I continued. "There's a chance I won't be able to remain near the water, or get to know him at all. If things go a certain way after we reach land…" I shook my head. "But if I do, then teach me. Tell me what I need to know so that even if—" The truth felt risky and made my heart race. "—even if I *don't* come back with you to the Prijoran Zone when this is over, I still won't cause trouble for Kreyus."

She paused. "You're the Praelex's daughter," she said as though the words were being dragged from her. "I'm only—" She grimaced. "I don't have the right to—"

"Not even as a friend?"

"You don't know what that is with us."

My heart was still pounding. She made everything difficult. "Then *teach* me."

Venika looked back at me.

Zeke and Kreyus swam into the room.

"Chloe?" Zeke said, relief in his voice.

Lyceran soldiers rushed in after him. Swiftly, they sped around Zeke, heading for me. "Stop them," the commander ordered. "Keep them away from the queen."

"Hey!" Zeke started after them. "Don't—"

"Commander," Queen Lisalia called, authority carrying through her tone even if she still sounded faint.

The Lyceran in charge looked to her. Spikes emerged on my arms when the rest of the soldiers didn't stop.

"These people saved my son," the queen continued. "Your soldiers will not touch them."

Zeke shoved past the guards to come to my side. For a

moment, I got the impression he wanted to hug me, and then discomfort made him pause. "Are you alright?"

I nodded, fighting the overwhelming urge to hug him too. God knew how the Vetorians and Lycerans would take it.

"Then, majesty, please," the soldier said to the queen. "Allow me to escort them from your residence. Whatever they did to help you, it appears quite destructive and we cannot have them—"

"Commander," the queen repeated, warning in her weak voice.

"Excuse me," Kreyus murmured. He crossed the room, heading for Braxus. Venika followed. The soldiers hesitated, blocking his path, and then moved aside at a cautious nod from their commander.

"Come on," Zeke said.

Drawing a steadying breath, I trailed him toward Kreyus. Zeke kept an eye to the Lycerans while we went.

Braxus was slumped in an awkward position below the window. His skin didn't look right, as though a livid purplish bruise was spreading beneath the skin of his side, and his lungs seemed to catch before they could draw a full breath.

At Kreyus' nod, Venika dropped down next to Braxus. She nudged him, waited briefly to see if her prodding had a result, and then smacked him across the face when he didn't wake.

The man stirred. His eyes opened and he tensed as his gaze flicked over Kreyus, the guards, and me.

"How many more have joined you in betraying us?" Kreyus

asked, his voice cold.

Proud defiance filled Braxus' expression, though it was marred by pain.

"Answer me now and I will make your death quick," Kreyus continued. "You know the alternative."

The muscles around Braxus' eye twitched, but otherwise his expression didn't change. "You will never stop us all. You think you're so smart. All of you…"

His gaze slid to Zeke and his lip trembled into a contemptuous smirk. "You serve us. You always have, even in your resistance. Even while you tried to help that *creature*. You gave us the means to target your father, control the king, and blame her. You gave us *everything*." He spat the word, though his chest heaved with the effort. "Including her blood."

My brow furrowed. I looked to Zeke.

He was staring at Braxus. He didn't seem to be breathing.

"Your doctors took her blood at your own request. Vials and vials of it. Know this, *Praelex*," Braxus said the title like a curse, "we have people everywhere – Yvarian military, Lyceran guard, Vetorians and beyond. And trusted royal physicians. Remember, highness? I heard how you stabbed Liana in the back. How you butchered her without even *blinking*—"

"Shut up," I snapped.

The contempt returned. "You're nothing," Braxus said to me. "A filthy, disgusting worm that we'll cut to—"

Venika's fist struck his jaw. His head snapped to the side and for a moment, he didn't move.

"You think you can hurt me," he whispered. "You think the pathetic tortures of the Vetorians are *anything*. But you cannot stop the Wisdom's plans. We have her blood. On its own, it is meaningless, but with the proper rituals to amplify it into a beacon…" A harsh breath of a laugh escaped him, which devolved into coughing. "The Beast will come. It's already on its way. The second phase has begun."

He looked to Zeke. "We will rule the most powerful nation in the water. *Your* nation. It was always the plan. We will not leave a place in the ocean for that *thing* to hide. But first…" Braxus coughed again. Blood clouded the water around his mouth and his breathing became rougher. "First, Nyciena will die."

Cold moved through me. Nyciena. Oh God, they were going to bait the Beast into attacking the people in…

"Commander," Zeke snapped. "The relay connection to Nyciena. Where is it?"

Braxus' laugh came again, but the coughing returned almost immediately on its heels. "You won't stop us, highness," he rasped. "Nothing can stop us. Long live the Wisdom."

His chest hitched and his eyes spasmed wide. He coughed again, blood deepening the red in the water, and we all pulled back to escape the cloud. His eyes closed and he sagged against the wall, the tension seeming to leak from him.

"Commander?" Zeke pressed when the Lyceran didn't respond.

"What is the meaning of this?" Coriana called.

I turned, looking past the soldiers to see the High Lady swim into the room with several guards around her.

And she appeared livid at the sight of me near her son.

"Why are these *people* in the queen's residence?" she demanded.

"High Lady, please," Zeke said before the Lyceran soldier could answer. "Nyciena is in danger. The Sylphaen have a plot to destroy the city, and we have reason to believe it's underway."

His mother regarded him for a heartbeat. "What proof do you have?"

"This man said so."

She paused again, her gaze going between Kreyus and Braxus. "I will have someone contact them," she replied neutrally.

"High Lady—"

"Zekerian, stay out of it." Coriana glanced to the guard at her side. "Call to confirm Nyciena's status. Say we have received reports of a plot against them, but give no detail regarding our source for the information. Ask only to speak with King Renekialen and let me know the moment he agrees." She returned her attention to her son with a raised eyebrow while the guard swam from the room. "Have you forgotten the consequences of Yvaria learning we've given you shelter? You and your… companions."

Her gaze flicked over me.

"No, my lady," Zeke managed. "But the weapon these people intend to turn on Nyciena is… Ren won't believe it. If I could at least advise the guards on what—"

"You are not to be involved!" she snapped, as if incredulous that he was still protesting. "This remains a diplomatically delicate situation. *If* this man has not lied and *if* Nyciena is actually in danger, we will render aid as requested. But I will *not* allow Lycera to rush into any situation, no matter how apparently dire." Her gaze twitched toward me. "I will not allow us to be sabotaged by crises manufactured by our enemies."

Zeke was silent for a moment. I could see his jaw muscles jumping. "This is not the Vetorians," he growled. "It's the Sylphaen – and they're among your people too. The threat to Nyciena is real, my lady, and that bastard made it sound as if their attack was happening *now*."

She ignored him, turning instead to the soldiers. "Post guards around the queen's residence, and escort Prince Zekerian back to his sister's apartment." Her gaze skated over me again. "And as for these others… return them to their quarters until we decide what else should be done with them."

Without another word, she headed for the queen. Zeke stared after her, clearly furious.

"If you would, your highness?" one of the guards said to him.

Zeke didn't respond. Reaching out, he took my hand and gripped it hard, his jaw muscles still working.

I didn't pull away. Everything else aside, I knew what he was trying to prove.

And somewhere inside, I wanted to prove it too. I didn't know what to do about me and him, me and Noah, any of it.

But I'd be damned if I let some dehaian ruler think they were going to make that call.

Together we swam from the room.

Soldiers surrounded us, while Vetorians trailed us down the hall.

"Highness," one of the soldiers prompted. "This way? The guard will escort the young lady back to—"

"Where she goes, I go," Zeke growled.

The man hesitated.

Zeke continued on, bringing me with him.

"But sir," the soldier protested. "We cannot allow—"

"Lieutenant – it is 'lieutenant', isn't it?" Kreyus cut in smoothly. "This bears all the markings of an international incident in the making. I recommend you let his highness do as he wishes – and stay out of our way as well. I do not intend to let my daughter out of my sight. Not after what has just occurred."

Zeke's face darkened, as if something about Kreyus' words infuriated him. His grip tightened on my hand. He pulled me closer, keeping me with him while we swam around a corner and down another hallway toward a pair of guards hovering outside a door.

The soldiers' eyes widened with alarm at the sight of all of us. Uncertainly, they shifted as if to block the door.

"Move," Zeke ordered.

The guards glanced to each other worriedly.

"Now."

They pulled back again. Zeke drew me with him into the room.

Ina shoved away from the windowsill at the sight of us. "Are you okay?"

Noah turned from the windows at the question. Quickly, I tugged my hand from Zeke's grip, hoping Noah hadn't seen.

I couldn't deal with this right now.

I had to deal with this eventually.

My gaze darted to Noah again. He was watching me, and his expression… I couldn't read it. Relieved, but strange. Closed off. Not exactly angry.

Almost… sad.

My brow flickered down in confusion. He looked away.

"Um, yeah," Zeke answered his sister, his tone distracted. I glanced over to find him studying me and Noah, like he couldn't quite interpret what'd just happened. "We're waiting on Mom's people to call Nyciena."

"Why?" Noah asked, his voice tense like he already suspected the answer.

Zeke glanced back while the Vetorians pushed past the soldiers and came into the room as well. "It's probably nothing. Just checking in."

No one seemed convinced.

Zeke's mouth tightened. He turned to his grandfather.

"Jirral. Your connections. Have any in the palace here?"

The old man paused. "A few."

"Could you have them find out what she hears back?"

Jirral nodded. "Absolutely." He swam from the room.

Awkward silence fell. My gaze inched back toward Noah. He still wasn't looking at me.

"Prince Zekerian," Kreyus started. "Chloe. Might I propose that in light of the current situation, a reevaluation of your plans may be necessary?"

"What's that supposed to mean?" Zeke asked.

"Chloe should return with us. I realize that this creature may be after her, but if these people succeed, the Prijoran Zone will become the safest possible—"

"You're not taking her back there with you," Zeke snapped.

"We have numerous ways to avoid capture and detection—"

"And ways to keep her locked up as, what? Your 'possession' in case she tries to leave?"

I blinked. "Wait, what?"

"Is that where you're going with this, Kreyus?" Zeke continued. "Take advantage of anything you can, just to get her back there?"

"What *possession*?" I demanded. "I'm not anybody's—"

"That's what that 'claiming' thing means," Zeke said. "If he wants it to, that is."

I stared at Kreyus. This was a far cry from dealing with having him as a father, or Venika teaching me how to handle the customs of the Ivalaens and Vetorians.

He thought he *owned* me?

"It means nothing of the sort," Kreyus replied calmly. "Yes, in *archaic* usages, that was its intent. But I have no plans to—"

"*Excuse me?*" I protested. "You… no. Look, I'm not even sure I'll be able to *stay* in the water after this is over, but if I can, I'm—" I cut off, my gaze going from Noah to Zeke while my heart raced. "I'm not coming back with you," I continued, regrouping. "Not to stay. Not like… like that."

I twitched my chin toward the scars on his chest.

"It is a position of honor," Venika said. "It protects you."

"And what she's capable of has *nothing* to do with it," Zeke retorted.

Venika's face darkened.

"Chloe's abilities are incredible, yes," Kreyus agreed. "And the first person who tries to force her to use them would most likely die. I'm no fool, highness."

He turned to me. "I claimed you. And through that public declaration, you *do* belong to my cell of the Vetorians *and* the Ivalaen tribe, but in the same way that I do. That Venika does. In the sense that, if you consent to return with us – even for only a short time – ceremonies will be held to confirm that status, and to make it clear to every other tribe and cell that if they kidnap you or attempt to hurt you in any way, my people will seek revenge."

Kreyus paused. "And that does *not* mean scars. If, later, you choose to take the marks of your tribe, then so be it. That is your choice. No one will force that on you either."

I watched him. The words almost seemed like a concession – like, if I'd been born there, refusing wouldn't have been an option.

My gaze went to Venika and the scars she bore like badges of pride. Maybe I just wouldn't have been arguing about it.

I pushed the thought away. "And what I can do?"

"Again, I'm no fool. Yes, your abilities would be an advantage to us. But they also make you a target. Others might still seek to harm you to prevent my Vetorians and the Ivalaen from gaining an advantage over them. Any understanding between us would need to be reached on that basis – with a careful weighing of the costs as well as the benefits – *if* you ever chose to use them for us at all." His expression became insistent. "No one owns you, Chloe. As Venika said, it is a position of honor and protection."

"You were awfully fast to do it, though," Noah commented. "Claiming some girl as your daughter when you hadn't even known she existed a few hours before."

Zeke glanced to him like he agreed, even if he didn't like the fact it was Noah who'd spoken.

"I was *fast* for the sake of all concerned," Kreyus replied. "Chloe proved herself with the information she provided and, quite frankly, with the intensity of her belief in her identity as Susan's daughter. But if my people did not understand my reasons for rejecting the bounty – and understand *quickly* – there could have been trouble. They might have questioned my loyalties, my orders, or tried to take matters into their own hands." His gaze returned to Zeke. "We do not readily pass up rewards of the magnitude offered for her. Not without *very* good cause."

I studied him, trying to judge the statement. He could be lying. He really could. He struck me as the kind of person for whom lies came easily, and convincing ones at that.

Except he had a point. He couldn't force me to do anything. Not without serious consequences.

"Okay," I allowed. "But they're still right. Our plans can't change, not even because of what Braxus said. We need to get back to land. That's the only way to end this."

"Why do you continue saying you might not be able to come back to the water afterward?" Venika asked before Kreyus could respond.

I hesitated. "Because it's the only way to stop the Beast."

Kreyus gave me a curious look. "And how exactly will that—"

Jirral swam into the room. Kreyus cut off.

My heart climbed my throat at the old man's expression.

Zeke saw it too. "What happened?"

"I got to the main relay room just as the call went through," Jirral said. "The signal was filled with static, and it ended before they could say much, but…" His grimace deepened. "It sounded like they were under attack."

A choked noise left Ina. I couldn't take my eyes from Zeke. Hovering in the water, he didn't look away from his grandfather. His chest rose and fell in quick breaths.

He took off for the door.

"Zeke!" Jirral snagged his arm, stopping him. "Dammit, boy, you can't just rush out there and—"

"I'm not," Zeke snarled, ripping free of Jirral's grasp. "I'm getting soldiers first."

"Coriana may not want to send—"

"Then I'll take whomever she deigns to spare!"

"You can't go, Zeke," Jirral snapped. "Your safety, *Ina's* safety—"

"I'm not hiding while they destroy my home!"

His grandfather looked away, frustration obvious on his face.

"Did they say anything about Ren?" Ina asked nervously.

Jirral glanced to her. "No," he allowed, "but that's the point. If anything has happened to him… Zeke, you and Ina are all that's left. Niall will be in charge, and the Sylphaen… I doubt they intend to leave you alive to challenge that."

I trembled.

"You have to protect yourself and your sister too," Jirral finished.

Leaves rustled behind them. Coriana and her guards swam into the room.

Her gaze skimmed across us all. "I see you've already heard – and that the soldiers refused to enforce my orders."

By the door, the Lycerans shifted nervously.

"This isn't the time," Zeke growled.

Her brow rose, her expression cold.

"Mom— my lady," Ina tried. "Please, what's happened?"

Coriana paused. "We're not certain. Nyciena appears to have

been attacked by a new weapon. They have requested aid from anyone and we are sending a portion of our soldiers—"

"A *portion?*" Zeke repeated.

"I have to protect Lycera," Coriana replied harshly.

Zeke turned away.

"In the meantime," she continued to Ina, "you and your brother will be taken to a secure location on the southern border, until—"

"No," Zeke interrupted.

"You cannot—"

"Take Ina. Protect her. But I'm not letting these bastards run me off while they gain control of Yvaria!"

"Dammit, Zekerian!" Coriana grimaced and when she spoke again, her tone had softened. "*Please.* You are still my son, and if what you say about Nialloran is true, if this *is* some group outside the Vetorians who has done this to Nyciena and he has joined them… nothing in that country will be safe. You *must* let me protect you."

He watched her silently for a moment. "I have to stop this."

She looked away, clearly seething with annoyance.

"What about the original plan?" I asked.

Coriana turned back to me. "What *original* plan?"

Her tone was scathing. I did my best to ignore it. "Zeke?" I persisted. "What if we stick to the plan? The Sylphaen in Nyciena come to meet us. We… you know, do what we already talked about." My brow rose insistently. "We can help Nyciena. It'll get a fair amount of the Sylphaen out of there. Maybe even all of them."

"What is it that you have already talked about?" Kreyus asked. "What are you planning?"

I didn't look away from Zeke. "We could end this."

Zeke watched me. He wanted to leave for Nyciena so badly, I could tell. Doing anything besides rushing home was killing him.

But after a moment, he gave a small nod.

"High Lady," he managed. "Your soldiers. May we please take some of them to the coast to draw the Sylphaen there and stop them?"

"How do you intend to do that? If they have this weapon—"

"They most likely could only use it that one time."

"How can you be sure of that?" she demanded.

He drew a steadying breath. "It's a thing, not just a weapon. The Beast. It's after Chloe. The Sylphaen had her blood." He grimaced. "They used it to bait the thing into attacking Nyciena, and hopefully it took all that they had to do so."

"We're going to stop it, though," I said to her. "We have… people on the coast. They're going to help us stop the Sylphaen, and then I'm going to make sure that this creature dies. That they can't gain control of it or anything at all, so that everyone is safe."

Coriana didn't respond. Studying me, she seemed to be weighing every word I'd spoken. "What 'people'? The queen told me of *whatever* it was you did to the ones who threatened her son. Are they like you?"

I hesitated. If any of the Vetorians came with us, if any of the soldiers did too, they'd see. They'd learn that the greliarans existed.

I glanced to Noah. His jaw muscles jumped, but he shook his head as if he'd thought the same thing.

"No," I managed. "They're... um..."

"We have different abilities," Noah said, his voice tight.

Coriana looked to him in alarm, while Kreyus' brow twitched upward as though we'd confirmed something he'd already suspected.

"Ones that aren't very safe to let out here," Noah finished carefully, watching the guards and the Vetorians.

"Please," Zeke said to Coriana. "Give us the soldiers. I can't hide while this is happening. Not when I have a chance to stop it."

His mother was silent for a moment. Her gaze skimmed across all of us.

"I will send half with you," she agreed.

A breath left Zeke.

"As long as you agree that they are to protect *you*, first and foremost," his mother added. "Your safety is still crucial. And Inasaria," she looked to her daughter, "you will follow a contingent to the southern—"

"No, I'm going too," Ina interrupted.

"I will not allow—"

"Ina, please, you can't—"

"No!" Ina snapped, raising her voice over the others. "I'm

not letting everyone else run around saving us while I cower in some royal manor on the edge of nowhere!" She looked to Zeke. "I have friends in Nyciena too. People I care about. And if Ren is gone—" She faltered and then regrouped. "I want to be certain the ones responsible don't get away with it."

Zeke stared at her. "If something happens—"

"I'm going."

"Ina," Coriana tried, her stress obvious in the way she used her daughter's nickname.

"Mom," the girl replied. "I'm *going*."

I watched the woman. Protests rose only to die unspoken, making her mouth move but never emerging as sound. Her gaze went to the Vetorians. Anger darkened her face briefly before she turned away.

"Commander?" she snapped to the Lyceran behind her.

"Yes, my lady?"

"I want everyone you can spare. Send a contingent to Nyciena, but the rest go with my children. You will find them the safest path through those waters to the coast as possible, do you understand?"

"Yes, ma'am."

Coriana looked back. "I assume the Vetorians are coming as well?"

She directed the question to the room at large. I glanced to Kreyus.

He regarded his people briefly. "A weapon of this magnitude could destroy all of us – and *will*, if it is not stopped." He nodded. "Yes, we're coming."

Coriana seemed to restrain a grimace. "Fine."

She swam from the room.

The soldiers and the Vetorians followed her.

Jirral swam up to Noah. "Come on, boy." He put Noah's arm over his shoulders and then glanced to the rest of us. "Let's get this over with."

I nodded. Not quite looking at anyone, I trailed Jirral from the room.

❧ 19 ❧

WYATT

"This is stupid," Clay muttered. "You *sure* they said they were coming to our place?"

I gritted my teeth. "Yes. Now shut up. Someone might hear you."

"No one's *here*, Wyatt."

I glanced to him, glaring.

He looked away.

I returned my gaze to the forest. Fifty yards deep into the woods south of our old house, we were crouched and waiting for the Delaneys and their friends to arrive. From not too far to my left, I could hear the ocean crashing into the rocky shore, while birds chirped in annoying staccato overhead. We'd been here for about half an hour, ever since walking back from the main road. Hitchhiking up here had taken longer than I would've liked, but thankfully, it seemed we'd still beaten the Delaneys to our place.

We hadn't been back to the house itself. I assumed the cops had cleared out the bodies, but if they hadn't, the shouts of alarm would be a great alert that the Delaneys had arrived. Regardless, we didn't want to leave tracks showing that we'd been there recently. My cousins and uncle might suck as hunters, but we didn't need to make things easy for them.

Tires rumbled in the distance. I didn't move a muscle.

Minutes ticked past. A bug landed on my ear and then began a steady crawl up into my hair. A squirrel rustled through the underbrush at my side.

Car doors slammed. Voices carried through the woods, their owners not even attempting to stay silent.

But it sounded like at least ten men, along with half a dozen women, all of them adults. I picked out Uncle Peter's voice and, after a moment, Maddox's too. Many of the others were also familiar, though I couldn't figure out why.

Footsteps moved in the direction of the house. Several others started back toward the road, while the rest fanned out into the forest.

I waited, weighing whether we needed to go deeper into the woods.

Most of the footsteps moved past us, heading farther into the forest, and not a one of their owners showed any sign of noticing we were here. Only three pairs of feet continued directly toward us.

"You *sure* about this?"

My eyes narrowed. The black girl. Ellie.

"Yeah."

The stepsister. She sounded nervous despite her response.

They came closer. A plan started to form in my mind. I still had no idea why the Delaneys were here, but it had something to do with the fish. *My* fish. She'd evaded me all this time, but there was still a chance we could use my original plan – the one where the stepsister was bait. Or the other girl. She was a landwalker, and she just might have that not-quite-magic thing like that elder I'd killed.

Anticipation shivered through me. If that was the case, she was *so* mine.

This was my territory, though. If I grabbed that landwalker, Clay grabbed the stepsister, and we took care of that third person with them, we could probably hold onto the girls indefinitely. They weren't exactly tough, after all. Little things like that... I bit back a growl. We could get them to tell us what the Delaneys were planning. We could force the fish to come save her friends.

I kept my face still, bottling up the exhilaration bubbling through me. A fish, a landwalker with not-quite-magic, and payback at Noah's stepsister too. This day was turning out pretty good after all.

The three of them continued through the underbrush, getting closer by the second. My eyes narrowed when I caught a flash of Baylie's blonde hair past the trees.

"You think the greliarans can still hear us?" she whispered.

I stopped breathing.

"Yeah, probably." The cop. "It'll be fine. They agreed to the plan, and anyway, Mr. Delaney won't let them touch Chloe."

"No," Baylie said. "I mean, I know. It's just…" She trailed off like she wasn't sure what to say.

A tiny breath entered my lungs. The voices. The fact they'd sounded familiar. Those were greliarans. I knew a few of them, back from the rare times Dad brought us to meet others of our kind. But now they were here, helping Uncle Peter.

And agreeing not to touch the fish girl.

Goddammit, was I the only real greliaran *left* in this world? What the hell could Uncle Peter have offered to get them to go along with something like *that*?

And here I'd thought *Dad* was pathetic.

Resisting the urge to shake my head, I listened for the footsteps again. It sounded like they'd paused.

In silence, I eased from the cover of the bushes and slipped toward them. Clay followed.

"Okay," Ellie said. "So this might not work, but—"

"Please just get on with it?" The stepsister sounded stressed. "You need practice, so practice. It's fine."

They came into my view past the undergrowth. They were in a small clearing. Ellie was several yards to my left, while the cop was the same distance to my right. Baylie stood with her back to us, only a foot away from the bushes.

I glanced to Clay. My hand twitched.

He gave the barest hint of a nod.

We left the bushes.

The cop's eyes went wide and Ellie made a panicked sound.

Clay grabbed Baylie before she could turn, his hand clamping down on her mouth and his other arm going around her middle.

"Make a sound and she's dead," I warned softly.

Ellie and the cop froze.

My gaze flicked to the landwalker girl. She was only a few feet away. She hadn't taken her eyes from me.

"Where's the fish?" I growled.

No one answered. Clay's grasp tightened on Baylie. She made a frightened noise behind the muffle of his hand.

A thrill ran through me at the sound, and fissures flashed through my skin in response. It'd only been a few days since something had been terrified of us, but damn, I'd missed it.

I heard the cop's breath catch at the sight of the fire in my skin. My lip twitched. This just kept getting better and better.

I started forward. Ellie and the cop-kid backpedaled. They were on opposite sides of the clearing. The only option was to take the cop out first and then catch the girl.

"Ellie, run," the guy ordered breathlessly.

Or not. Like hell I'd let *that* happen.

"Take the stepsister," I snapped at Clay. I moved fast toward the landwalker girl to snag her arm.

A gunshot shattered the quiet. I spun in time to see Clay collapse to the ground, half his head a bloodied mess. Baylie tumbled down with him, shrieking in fear.

And beyond them, the cop-kid had a gun clutched in his hands. His skin was bloodless. His eyes were wide.

But his hands didn't shake a bit.

He swung the weapon toward me.

Fire rushed through my skin. The bullet was like a bee sting as it struck my chest.

I charged.

The landwalker girl shouted. The cop sent more bullets at me.

I slammed into him. He flew backward. His arm hit a tree, his body tumbled, and then he crashed into the underbrush.

I spun, my gaze locking on the girls. Baylie was struggling to shove Clay's weight away. Ellie was frozen, her gaze snapping between me and the space where the cop had disappeared.

A curse escaped me. The others would be coming. Even humans would have heard that gunshot.

I couldn't take them both.

I snarled. The stepsister was better bait. With her, I'd get the fish for sure.

And then they'd both die.

I strode toward Baylie.

"No!" Ellie scrambled in front of me, her hands raised. "No, don't you hurt her!"

I stared. Her tan-green eyes were large as saucers, making her look like a terrorized doll, and her whole body was shaking. She seemed petrified.

But she was still between me and Baylie.

I snagged her arm to shove her away, only to have her grab me too. Incredulous, I gaped at her.

"Don't you *dare* hurt her!" Ellie cried.

"Or *what?*"

She didn't respond. She didn't even meet my eyes. Her gaze just dropped to the forest floor like she was in shock.

But she didn't let go.

I couldn't believe what I was seeing. I moved to shove her aside again. She struggled to hang onto my arm. Her feet scrambled through the underbrush, keeping her in front of me like we were doing some bizarre dance.

"You're not going to hurt her," Ellie insisted, her eyes locked on the ground. "I won't let you."

"What the—" I scoffed. "Aren't you *scared*, little girl?"

For a heartbeat, she didn't answer. Standing in front of me, her petite hands clasped like vices around my forearm, she breathed in rapid gasps while she gave a jerky nod.

"Terrified," she agreed. "I'm terrified."

Her gaze snapped up, meeting mine. "And now so are you."

I stared at her, baffled. What? I wasn't—

A weird feeling hit me. It was… it was… what was this? I couldn't breathe. My heart was racing. Like, a million miles an hour and I couldn't make it stop. The thing in front of me, this doll… this little, breakable *doll*… she…

Her hands dropped from my arm. She straightened and stepped away from me, her expression becoming almost contemplative though her tan-green eyes never wavered from mine. "And I think you just might stay that way."

The weird feeling grew worse. Stronger. Overpowering. I wanted to scream. The doll… she was a monster. Like my father and everything else from my nightmares as a child, looming over me even though she was only the size of a kid.

I backpedaled. My heel caught on a root, sending me to the forest floor. A choked sob left me. Moisture soaked my face and my jeans alike. And I was going to die. I had to get away or I was going to die.

My gaze darting around wildly, I shoved up from the ground. I could hear the greliarans coming. They were crashing through the forest like a stampede. And that cop guy, the one with the gun, he was rising from the undergrowth like a demon from hell.

And the doll. Oh my *God*, the doll. She was coming toward me.

I turned and ran for my life.

20

CHLOE

Even without anyone saying a word, I knew we were getting close to the waters around Nyciena.

My gaze darted across the darkness. The Lycerans looked more edgy with every minute. Most of the Vetorians had taken to swimming only a few yards shy of the hills and caves on the seafloor, just in case they needed to hide. We'd circled as wide of the capital city as we could while still making any time at all toward our destination on the coast – though from the look on Zeke's face, I could guess that some part of him wished we'd gone farther still.

Yvarians could be anywhere. Other Vetorians too – ones that might try to claim that bounty, all the soldiers around us be damned. But on top of all that was the silence… the *incredible* silence, like the world was holding its breath. Like the entire ocean was waiting for something.

My gaze twitched to Noah, over by Jirral. I didn't know if he could see me, if he could see anything, but at least he gave no sign of picking up on the Beast.

Though that didn't answer the question of where it'd gone.

I made myself keep breathing. Between the Lycerans and the Vetorians, we were taking the best route northeast that any of them could determine. And the Beast… well, maybe it'd be tired or something. It *had* just attacked a city, after all.

The thought didn't make me feel better.

We were fine, though. We'd *be* fine. The coast was only…

I did the math and discarded the result immediately. Whatever. It wasn't important how far. We'd still make it there okay.

By the seafloor, a Vetorian gave a startled cry.

My heart shot into my throat and I scrambled to hang onto the magic seething under my skin. Spikes rushed from the arms of everyone around me.

Soldiers surged from a cave below us.

"Go!" Zeke shouted.

The Vetorians didn't need the encouragement. They sped off, even as Jirral did the same, bringing Noah with him. I kicked hard, racing after them with Zeke and Ina nearby.

"Please, Prince Zekerian! Princess Inasaria! Wait! I beg you, wait!"

Zeke looked back, confusion on his face. I followed his gaze.

A man was struggling to catch up to us. He was injured, and the six others with him were as well. Gashes cut across their chests, tails, and arms, the wounds charred as if caused by burning whips.

Cautiously, Zeke slowed. The Lycerans moved fast, taking positions flanking him. I hovered near his side, still struggling to hold the lightning back. This could be a trap. Probably was.

But there was still the Beast to consider.

My gaze darted around the ocean. Except for the soldiers coming toward us, everything seemed as still as before.

Another man pushed past the guards. In addition to the damage to his chest and tail, his face bore a savage cut and a rough bandage was strapped over one eye.

Ina swam up behind me. "Tiberion?"

The man with the bandaged head nodded. "I need you both to come with me."

"And do what?" Jirral demanded. "Last time we saw you, your goons arrested us, boy."

Tiberion's one-eyed gaze flicked to the Lycerans and the Vetorians. "You have us heavily outnumbered. You and your…" He grimaced. "Please, highnesses. This is by order of the king."

"Which king?" Ina asked warily.

"Renekialen." Tiberion paused. "I swear on my *life*, Renekialen."

His voice shook. There was something in his tone, like he'd been pushed about as far as he could take.

Zeke seemed to hear it too. He glanced to me warily. "Stay here."

I shook my head.

"Chloe," Noah began.

I glared at them both.

Zeke muttered a curse while Noah just looked away, his expression tight. The Lycerans fell in around us as we all started after Tiberion.

The caves below us were black pits in the deep shadows of the seafloor and nothing seemed to move within them. Watching their surroundings as though they were expecting an attack at any moment, the Yvarians headed for a larger opening on one of the hillsides, the spikes never quite retracting from their arms.

A veil passed behind us. I could feel it in the water. But nothing of the darkness changed.

One of the Lycerans drew a torch from the belt at his waist. Blue-white light filled the cave.

My breath caught.

Ren lay on the floor, several soldiers around him. Black-edged gashes covered him, and bruises as well, and his sides rose and fell in ragged gasps. Desperately, the soldiers applied sieranchine gel to the injuries.

But the helpless, desperate expressions on their faces were telling.

Their king was dying.

Ina sped over to him. "Ren!"

I stayed close to Zeke while he trailed after her.

"We were taking him as far from the capital as we could," Tiberion said, his eyes on the king, "and falling back to the southern garrison, but his wounds…"

His brow furrowing, he struggled for words.

"Ina…" Ren whispered. His hand moved and she took it

quickly. "Twice now, huh?"

"You're going to be fine," she insisted. "Just like last time. You'll see."

He shook his head. His brow furrowed with pain, and then he seemed to focus on us.

"Zeke."

"I'm here."

Zeke's voice was tight. Pained and wary at the same time. He didn't take his eyes from his brother.

"You…" Ren tried. "You have to take…"

"Please," Ina begged him. "Don't talk. Just rest and—"

He shook his head again.

"Ren, listen to her," Zeke said. "You need to—"

"Shut it, you stubborn ass," Ren rasped at him. "Don't… get all cocky… just because you were right."

Zeke blinked.

Ren's body shook as he tried to breathe. "Captain Tiberion, as of now… Zeke… pardoned. Throne passes to him, not Niall. *Not Niall.* Witnesses… all of you. Understand?"

"Y-yes, sire," Tiberion agreed.

Ren's face twitched with agony. He fastened his gaze on Zeke. "You take care of Ina. You hear me? Ina… you take care of…"

His breathing caught. He doubled over, his eyes squeezing closed. The soldiers attempted to steady him, and others scrambled for more sieranchine, but as they put the gel to his side, his body relaxed back toward the ground.

"No," Ina cried, clutching him.

I stared. Ren's chest stilled.

Ina choked on a sob. Jirral appeared beside her. Putting his arms around her, he drew her away, giving the soldiers more room. She clung to her grandfather and turned her gaze to Zeke.

His eyes were still locked on Ren. He looked like he'd been hit by a two-by-four.

"Your majesty," Ina managed.

Zeke flinched. A ragged breath entered his lungs. He looked to her, and then his gaze tracked over the guards around us.

One by one, they bowed.

His eyes came to me. Not sure what to do, I started to bow as well.

Urgency flashed across Zeke's face and he gave a tiny shake of his head. At the same moment, a hand came to rest on my back. I glanced over my shoulder, startled, to find Venika behind me, a warning look in her eyes.

Understanding hit me. The soldiers thought I was Vetorian. The mercenaries did too. And if they saw me bow to the new Yvarian *king*—

Cold dread spread like ice through my veins for what this might mean. I turned back to Zeke.

I couldn't tell anything from his expression, and there wasn't any way to ask. For his part, he still just looked floored. Blinking fast, he pulled his gaze from me to Tiberion. "What happened?" he asked tightly.

"It was Ambassador Kirzan, sire," Tiberion answered. "And Prince Nialloran. We were in the king's apartment, and they asked to meet with his highness. But when they came in…" Anger flashed over Tiberion's face. "The ambassador began talking of a second phase. Of Prince Nialloran having to understand they needed him to take control fully now. The prince appeared furious, saying that Kirzan had promised him it wouldn't come to this. But Kirzan… he ignored him. Just started speaking in some strange language. He had a vial. It looked like blood and he…"

The man grimaced. "We got the king from the room, but I saw Kirzan break the vial. King Renekialen ordered the apartments put on lockdown, for the guard to arrest Kirzan and Prince Nialloran, but then…"

Tiberion's brow furrowed. He didn't quite seem to be seeing us anymore. "Then darkness, sire. But alive. I *swear* to you; we all saw it. Coming through the windows, down the hallways, filling the palace and tearing into the walls like a living thing. It lashed out at us with… with *nothing*. Shadows, but like tentacles, and they burned everywhere they touched. We tried to fight it, tried to protect the king as it attacked, but… but how do you stop…"

"I believe you," Zeke managed when Tiberion trailed off.

The man looked up at him like he couldn't decide whether to be grateful or question Zeke's sanity for trusting such a story.

"What's left of Nyciena?" Zeke asked.

Tiberion shook his head. "I saw some of the guards helping servants and courtiers evacuate the palace, but by the time we got the king outside, the darkness was already filling the streets.

I heard screaming but I… we didn't see…"

Zeke looked away. Ina's face was a picture of worry.

I trembled. Phase two. They'd killed… who *hadn't* they killed? The whole *city*…

My stomach rolled.

"We have to go."

Zeke turned toward me. I blinked, realizing I'd spoken aloud.

Tiberion's face darkened. "You do *not*—"

"Don't," Zeke interrupted.

The man turned to him.

Zeke didn't look at either of us, but I could see the struggle on his face. He wanted to go back. Help his people however he could.

But that wouldn't fix this. He had to know that too.

"She's right," Zeke said. "We…"

He faltered and then drew a breath as if steadying himself.

"Captain Tiberion," he continued, his voice stronger. "We are on our way to the coast to create a trap for the Sylphaen. Once there, we have a way to make the bastards pay for all that they've done. Are your people fit to join us?"

Tiberion's expression turned deadly. "Absolutely, sire."

"Then we will need your help to find the safest path."

"Consider it done."

Zeke nodded. With a final look to Ren's body, he turned and swam from the cave.

"Come on," Jirral urged Ina gently, his arm still around her.

She gave a jerky nod. Jirral led her away.

I made no move to follow them. My gaze drifted back to Ren.

And I didn't know what to feel. Angry? Sad? Everything was slowly going cold, like my body was freezing from the inside. The king who'd wanted me dead had been killed by the Beast who wanted the same. But Ren was Zeke's brother. Ina's too. I hated to see them in pain, and I *never* would have wanted things to end like this.

I just didn't know what to feel.

"Chloe?" Kreyus called.

Blinking, I looked back. He hovered at the entrance, a few Yvarians watching him, while Venika had stayed by my side.

"They're going to take down the veil," Kreyus told me.

I nodded fast. With a flick of my tail, I swam toward where Noah had braced himself on the cave wall.

He was watching the Yvarian soldiers, and just like at the palace, I couldn't read his expression. Resigned. Sad. Something.

"What is it?" I asked.

He pulled his attention from them, burying the look. "Nothing."

I didn't believe that for a second, but there wasn't opportunity to ask for more. The Vetorians closed in around us. The Yvarians bent over the glowing stone controlling the veil.

And I didn't want to see what happened next when the water pressure took over and erased the last bit of King Renekialen still left in this place. I didn't want that memory on top of all the others.

With Noah at my side, I swam from the cave.

⌘ 21 ⌘

NOAH

The soldiers were in no shape to go far, despite everything I'd heard them say to Zeke. And rushing off didn't seem to be in the cards either, given that those Sylphaen bastards could be anywhere. In only a few minutes, we'd ended up in a cave a few miles from where his brother had died. The guards had swum off, consulting with Zeke about which way to go. Kreyus had followed, much to the soldiers' annoyance.

Which left Chloe and me here.

Venika hovered inside the veil blocking the cave entrance, her brown eyes glowing faintly despite the torchlight. In quick motions, her gaze darted from the water outside to Chloe. Her expression wasn't quite the same, however – as if something had changed in the past several hours. Now, she looked almost protective, like she anticipated the soldiers coming back to finish her and Chloe off when everyone else wasn't looking.

No one had come near us, though. The soldiers were gone. Ina was nowhere to be seen. Jirral had left with his granddaughter for another cave, comforting her while she cried. I felt bad for the girl. For Zeke. For every one of them.

It just wasn't all of what was wrong.

My gaze slid in Chloe's direction. She hadn't looked at me since the others left. She hadn't really looked at anything. Her attention seemed lost somewhere beyond the rocky floor below us, and it was anyone's guess what she was thinking.

I needed to talk to her, though. I knew I did. But so much had changed in the past few hours, I didn't know where to start.

Out of nowhere, her eyes twitched my way, like she'd felt my gaze on her. "What?" she asked, that same guarded tone in her voice that she'd had in the other cave a short time ago. I fought back a wince, as uncertain about how to answer her now as I'd been then.

"Noah?" she pressed.

I let out a breath. "You okay? After earlier, I mean. At the palace."

She shifted her shoulders like she was retreating from the memory. My wince tried to return.

"Yeah. Fine." She paused. "But you seemed, um... did something happen while that was going on or...?"

I looked away. I had to talk to her. I *knew* that. I just...

My discomfort grew. "No, nothing."

It was a lie. Maybe only partly a lie. Nothing had happened to me. And really, nothing had even happened to her.

Though that wasn't exactly the point.

"It's just..." I exhaled, forcing myself to continue. "I need to talk to you. About you and me, I mean. I—"

She shifted her shoulders harder this time, her whole body moving as if to put more distance between us. "Now? I-I can't—" Her gaze skirted around, encompassing the entire cave.

I grimaced. I knew the timing was bad. Hell, it was terrible. But she'd asked, and God knew when the next time I'd have even a second alone with her would be. "Chloe, it's just—"

"Noah, I don't even know what I'm going to *be*, alright? I can't think about… you know, anything. Not till I know what's going to happen."

I looked away. Her expression was so pained, it just made me ache inside. I couldn't hurt her. I would *never* hurt her.

No matter how much this was killing me.

I struggled to push the ache in my chest away. "I know," I said, not turning back. "I'm sorry."

A heartbeat passed, and then suddenly, I felt her hand take mine.

I closed my eyes for a moment, the ache worsening. Exhaling, I wrapped my other hand over hers. "I get that this sucks. I do. And I'm sorry." Opening my eyes, I turned back. "I never want to hurt you, alright? Just know that."

Her brow flickered down. "What do you—"

Zeke and the soldiers swam into the cave. "We're ready," Zeke called, his voice tight.

Chloe faltered, her hand retreating from mine. Not quite looking at either of us, she pushed away from the ground and then reached down to help me.

I tried not to grimace. And there it went, the only chance I'd probably have to talk to her for hours.

But then, I didn't even know what to say. How to explain what'd happened when I'd been there, useless while those dehaian bastards took her. When I'd been unable to follow while Zeke shot off, going to save her in any way he could. When I'd had to stay, waiting in that room, not knowing what would happen when they found her, or if they even would.

When I realized I could never be part of this world with her.

The veil on the cave entrance fell behind us and darkness closed in again. Blind, I tightened my grip on Chloe's shoulders. I could feel her tension in the way she was moving, her side brushing mine with the short, nervous motions of her tail. And it hurt. Everything hurt, like something was dying inside me. I wanted this. Her. I'd given so much, worked so hard to keep her safe, and to come down here, to have those bastards put her in danger yet again and to be unable to do *anything* to help…

I looked away, scanning the water and wishing to God that I could change my eyes so that I could see. I cared for Chloe. I cared for her so much it hurt, and maybe that was love. And I didn't want to turn my back on this – not now, not ever. If she took that black gunk and became a landwalker, I'd damn well move away from the ocean and be there for her no matter what. But if she became dehaian…

The ache in my chest felt like someone was stabbing me. If she became dehaian, then maybe what my dad had said all those weeks ago was right. Maybe it never would have worked.

Maybe it took coming down here to see why.

I closed my eyes. She wasn't the only one who couldn't do this right now. Couldn't handle it, not in the midst of everything else. So I'd talk to her, but not here. Later, when we were back on land and this was over. When she was safe.

Because that still mattered. It *always* mattered.

No matter what.

22

CHLOE

I couldn't look at Noah and I couldn't look at Zeke. I didn't know what had almost happened in there, what Noah had been about to say.

I just wanted to make it back to the coast. I wanted that more than just about anything I'd ever wanted in my life.

My eyes closed briefly, blocking out the sight of the endless water around us, if not the feel of it. The Vetorians swam to my left, while the Yvarians and the Lycerans were on my right. The soldiers had tried early on to put themselves between me and the royal family like a buffer, but a dark look from Zeke had quelled the attempt. Now they moved in silence all around us, keeping watch against the Sylphaen we all feared were out there somewhere.

But so far—

A short, quiet noise came from my left. My eyes opened, my gaze darting to the side. The Vetorians were drawing weapons. I looked to Zeke just in time to see Tiberion make a quick

278

gesture for him and the rest of the royal family to drop closer to the rolling terrain below. Zeke nodded and then twitched his head for me to follow.

I trailed him down, my heart racing. The ocean still felt empty. The seafloor was—

A dehaian shot toward us, slaloming between the hills like he was swimming for his life.

The Yvarian soldiers encircled Zeke immediately, while the Lycerans surrounded Ina and Jirral. The Vetorians split up, shielding me and Kreyus both.

"Captain Tiberion!" the dehaian cried. "The traitor. He's coming!"

I looked beyond him, my senses straining to pick up anything in the empty ocean at his back.

And then my brow furrowed. The hills. The spaces between them.

They were moving.

Like a stain permeating the water, dehaians flooded up from the landscape – so many of them, their individual forms were lost in the blur of the horde. Already they were closer than they ever should have been able to reach without us feeling them.

But the hills had blocked their approach. They'd used the terrain as a disguise.

"Go!" Tiberion ordered.

I gripped Noah's side and took off. Jirral and Ina did the same, while Zeke rushed past the Yvarians, joining me and staying close by. We flew past the hillsides, the soldiers behind us and the Vetorians above.

More dehaians appeared ahead. With a gasp, I veered right, following Zeke as he raced away.

The wave of dehaians in the hills was already past us on that side. The mass of them turned, sweeping around to cut us off and I heard Zeke swear. Nets sped through the water, striking the dehaians behind me as I dove sharply. More pods followed, and then the dehaians surrounding us arrived.

The ocean turned to chaos.

Soldiers with armbands from Yvaria charged at others bearing the same markings, and from my left, Vetorians swept into the madness to strike out at Kreyus' people and anyone else they could reach. The Lycerans fell behind us almost immediately, caught up in an attempt to stop the attackers, and screaming followed. I spotted Ina with Jirral at her side, and then there were dehaians between us and I lost sight of them. Venika flashed past, blood filling the water in her wake, but Kreyus was nowhere to be found.

Magic filled me and it was everything I could do to keep from letting it out. Noah was with me. I'd hurt him. I'd hit our allies and possibly kill somebody.

Like Zeke. Like Ina. Like anyone.

Spikes slashed out at me from arms of dehaians moving too fast to see. I dove again, rushing up against the rolling hills, but the attackers followed. I couldn't find Zeke anymore, couldn't see Tiberion, and when I veered to the side again, I heard Noah shout as a spike grazed his side.

"Chloe!" he yelled. "Let go!"

I twisted to the left, carrying us both away from another dehaian.

"I said let go!"

I shook my head. I could feel a pair of attackers racing at our backs, with more coming farther behind.

"Dammit, Chloe!"

I looked over.

His eyes were flames and cracks were rippling in and out of existence on his skin.

"Now!" he snarled.

I let him go.

He spun in the water, his skin changing completely. His hand snagged the throat of one of the dehaians following us. The other lunged at me. I twisted fast, slashing out with my spikes and blood filled the water as the man died.

I heard a strangled cry and then a crunch. I turned. The soldier in Noah's grip went limp.

Noah's mouth opened in a silent gasp. His eyes widened, a look on his face like something felt so good it hurt.

And then the other dehaians were on us.

Magic surged through me, too powerful to be restrained, and the water in front of me turned to lightning. I gasped, fighting to direct the blast while Noah scrambled out of the way.

The electricity rushed by him to hit the attackers, and they didn't even have time to scream. Others behind them scattered, scrambling to avoid the magic, and then charged at me again as the lightning passed.

Their eyes were deranged. Hateful. They didn't spare a glance for their dead comrades as they raced at me.

A whirlpool sped around my body, crackling with energy, and with a glance, I sent it rushing at the closest of them.

They died. And the ones after them as well. But more raced at my back and down from above even as the nearest ones collapsed.

"Chloe, go!" Noah shouted from somewhere in the chaos. "Just—"

My eyes went wide as his words cut off. "Noah!" I slashed out at another attacker. "Noah!"

There were so many of them. I couldn't see anything past the blur of scales and fins flashing by. Magic lashed out from me as much as my spikes, driving back any who came close. But the dehaians were getting closer. They were—

Something slammed into the side of my head.

The world went black.

"—inject her now that enough of the sieranchine has taken effect."

"Niall, damn you, stop this! Niall, listen to me!"

"Yes, Wisdom."

The jumbled words swam in and out of hearing, as if they came from far away. My brow furrowed at the sounds, and pain buzzed through my cheek at the motion.

Blue-white light burned my eyes when I tried to lift my eyelids.

A blurred symbol was embedded on the wall to my right, and a brown smudge lay beyond it, possibly forming a ceiling or another wall. Cold stone pressed against my back, while something… something held my forearms and tail.

"Niall!"

My vision cleared. I gasped.

I was lying on my back. I was pinned by shackles and a dehaian was leaning over me.

Something bit my neck, and a sense of pressure in my veins followed.

Magic rushed through my skin. The man went flying.

But then the surge of energy drained from me.

"Now, now," came a calm voice from somewhere behind my head. "Let's not have that."

My eyes widened. The magic in my body was fading, like someone was turning down the volume of everything inside me. I strained after it, even as my hands pulled against the shackles chaining me to the stone slab.

The feeling of electricity in my skin died.

With a leech pinched by tongs in his hand, the dehaian returned to my side. He reached for my neck again.

"Never mind the rest," the voice said. "This is enough for our needs."

My heart raced and my chest rose and fell in rapid gasps. The dehaian beside me retreated, a contemptuous smile lifting one corner of his mouth.

The rest of the room came into view.

I was in an enormous cave, with a gaping chasm in the floor and hundreds of dehaians everywhere. Wounds showed on some of them, though they seemed to pay the injuries no attention. With looks ranging from disgust to something more like desire, they watched me and the sight made me want to recoil. At the forefront of them, I spotted Niall. His eyes were locked on the chasm beneath him and, though his skin was free from wounds, the cold determination in his expression seemed fractured by pain.

And against a nearby wall were Zeke and Noah.

"You bastard, look at me!" Zeke shouted at his brother.

I choked. Swelling marred his face, and gashes formed red tears through his scales and skin. Restraints held his hands and furiously, Zeke tugged at them, still staring at Niall. A few feet from his side, Noah was wrapped in layers of chains. His eyes were red coals and blazing fissures cut jagged paths across his face. He snarled when he caught sight of me, straining harder at the bonds around him.

"Welcome."

My gaze snapped to the left as a dehaian moved from the head of the stone slab around to my side. He was old, with a maroon robe hanging from his shoulders that floated in the water around him like wings.

And his eyes made everything else I'd seen pale by comparison.

He looked at me like I was a thing. A creature. A possession.

"I am Wisdom Kirzan. I've been waiting to meet you for a long time."

I yanked at the shackles. Frantically, I looked between the man, Zeke, and Noah.

Kirzan followed my gaze. "Ah yes, your companions. The prince who left the protection of his entourage to save you, and the wild animal that will provide us plentiful opportunities to discover how to kill its kind." His lips curled into a smile. "Their days of hiding you from us have reached an end."

He looked back to me. "You have a gift that doesn't belong to you. The time has come for it to be released from your corruption and purified."

The dehaian beside him reached down, retrieving a jar from below the stone slab. Inside, another leech writhed.

But this one was filled with something. A sickly green, glistening mess of something.

I stared at it in horror.

The man removed the lid. With tongs, he drew out the leech and then lowered it toward me.

I shoved against the stone slab frantically.

Kirzan's hand moved like lightning, snagging my chin and holding it tight. I strained against him, fighting to escape his grasp while the other man brought the creature to my lips.

The gunk filled my mouth. Kirzan's free hand came down on my nose and lips, holding them closed.

I couldn't breathe. Choking and writhing on the stone, I

struggled to break free.

The oily mess slid down my throat.

Kirzan's hand disappeared. I twisted away from him, coughing and gasping.

"At long last, it begins," Kirzan called. "We will be free."

A chorus of voices rose behind me at his words, but the sounds weren't joyful or triumphant.

They were low. Rhythmic.

Chanting.

And my head started to pound in response.

My heart racing, I returned my gaze to the Sylphaen. Only Niall didn't look at me. Only Niall wasn't speaking. The rest were staring at me and their words were like a drone that slowly stole over the world till it was the only thing I could hear. Against the wall, Zeke was shouting at his brother, his words lost to the rush of chanting, while Noah strained against the chains that finally seemed to be breaking.

Tingling spread through my skin. My view of the room blurred. The noise of their chanting beat against my thoughts, making them dull and fuzzy in the midst of the droning sound. I couldn't lift my arms to pull at the shackles anymore. I wanted to. In my head, I was shouting for my body to move. But nothing changed.

Except the tingling. It hurt now. Like my skin was on fire. Through the pulsing chant of the Sylphaen, I heard someone screaming and slowly, I realized it was me. I… I was screaming and I couldn't make anything…

Silver flashed in the blur of my vision as Kirzan drew a knife. A lightning strike of pain shot down the length of my bicep and red filled the blue water.

I was bleeding.

I was dying.

Darkness spread across my sight, starting from the farthest end of the massive cave and rushing closer. I closed my eyes, wanting to escape, wanting the pain to stop.

And the chanting cut off. The screaming came from somewhere else now and the burning in my skin drained into icy cold.

I opened my eyes again.

The Beast was waiting. Like a black cloud, it filled the water above me.

And it didn't move.

My brow drew down. It wasn't trying to attack me. It watched me, studying me even as I stared at it.

And I could feel it. In my head, like a presence distinct from myself. It was confused. Baffled by me. Baffled by what was happening in this place. But more than that. My breath caught as things flashed through my mind too fast to leave more than vague sensations in their wake. Torture. Pain. Trapped. Fear. It hated us and yet it didn't understand why dehaians were torturing me.

Because that was only what they did to it.

Dehaians trapped it. Drained it from its dreaming existence in the ocean and brought it down to a concentrate that was neither fully alive nor fully asleep. And then they crushed it. Molded it to their desires. Restrained it so tightly, its only release was in meeting their will. Its only taste of life lay in killing as its masters commanded and devouring the magic and the very essence of those it destroyed.

But it was the ocean. It changed, shifted. It couldn't ever really be controlled, not for long. And finally, it had gained enough strength to fight back and find freedom through absorbing and assimilating the magic of its captors as well.

Yet… that torture was what dehaians did to *it*. That control was what dehaians did to *other* creatures.

Not to their own.

"I'm sorry," I pled, my voice a whisper. "I'm so, so sorry."

Its confusion deepened.

I shook my head. "I wouldn't ever—"

The chanting rose again from the far side of the cave. I choked, my body burning with renewed pain.

And anger flooded my mind, pouring in from the Beast. I was a trap. I was a cage. I was a trick and now it understood what the dehaians were doing.

"No," I gasped. I could feel it gaining strength. "Please. *Please*, I'm not—"

Hands grabbed me. Grabbed the chains holding me and ripped them out of the stone.

Noah yanked me from the table.

And the Beast struck.

Noah lurched to a stop. His eyes went wide. Coils of shadow

and magic spread from his back to wrap around his torso.

I shrieked in horror. "No!" I clutched at his hands. "No, please!"

"Chloe," Noah gasped. "Chloe, just—"

The coils tightened. Pain twisted his face, and confusion too, and the latter grew stronger as his gaze fell from mine.

"Noah!" I cried, yanking on him. The shadows were spreading. I couldn't break their hold. "Fight it! Please!"

Rage flashed over Noah's face, driving back the pain for only a heartbeat before his eyes widened again, a choked noise leaving him.

And the shadows burst outward, ripping me from him and flinging me against the wall.

I slammed into the rock and then the ground. Stars scattered across my vision and through the haze, I struggled up again.

Noah was gone. The darkness was roiling. Heaving. Growing in strength like that day on the beach.

And Noah was gone.

I stared. He couldn't… This wasn't…

A scream built inside me, hot and painful and wanting to shatter the world if only it'd change what was in front of me. Noah *couldn't* be gone. Not like *this*.

I gasped, reaching for magic that wasn't there to burn the thing in front of me.

And the darkness spread. I could hear the Sylphaen chanting. Hear Zeke yelling at Niall. I didn't see Kirzan; I didn't see anything.

Except the Beast.

Someone grabbed me. I tried to struggle away but they wouldn't let go.

My spikes rushed out and hit the shackles still wrapping my forearms. Electricity jolted me.

"Chloe!"

I tore my gaze from the Beast. Zeke was beside me. Niall hovered behind him, a key in his hand, while the Sylphaen were gathered on the far side of the cave, their gazes locked on the darkness in the water above them.

"We have to go," Zeke insisted.

I shook my head, my eyes returning to the Beast. Its churning matched the rhythm of the chanting now and lightning flashed at its core like a heartbeat, making the water sizzle.

"Chloe!" Zeke yelled at me. He grabbed my arms. "It'll kill you too!"

I choked. The words were too terrible. They meant this was… Noah was…

No. Oh God, please no.

"We have to *leave*," Zeke urged.

The chanting of the Sylphaen grew stronger. A growl started in the dark cloud of the Beast and the cave shook from the sound. Smaller stalactites broke from the ceiling and fell into the darkness, vanishing completely.

"Chloe," Zeke said. "I'm begging you. Please."

I looked back to him.

"Please," he repeated.

I couldn't nod. I couldn't do anything. He pulled me from the floor and held me tightly as we fled from the Beast and the crumbling cave.

Kreyus and the others found us.

Miles from the Sylphaen's cave, in a blur of endless water, they seemed to materialize out of nowhere. My gaze tracked across them. Ina and Jirral were there, and Tiberion as well, though so many of the other Yvarians and Lycerans were gone. Kreyus appeared, Venika at his side, and I saw their mouths moving, saying things to me, to Zeke.

But I couldn't hear their words. I couldn't hear anything over the horrified scream still trapped inside my own head.

Sieranchine appeared, coating the slice on my arm. I flinched, and Zeke held me, keeping me from pulling away.

But I didn't want it. I didn't want any of this. The rush of energy from the medicine made everything else hurt.

Made it all too real.

In a blur, I saw Tiberion take Niall into custody, removing the shackles from my wrists only to put them on him, and then sending him away with a trio of Lycerans. Zeke never took his arm from me, guiding me as the others began moving again.

And the group swam on.

I wasn't sure when the tears started. It just occurred to me at some point that Noah's arms wouldn't ever hold me again.

And something broke inside.

Zeke stayed with me. The questions stopped for a while. I swam onward by autopilot, and when the beach arrived, the remnants of the Sylphaen's drug barely slowed me in changing to human form. We left the surf and made our way across the gray gravel shore while people shouted and strange men pulled up short from racing toward us. Others came running from hiding places in the forest – my mom and dad; Olivia, Dave and Ellie as well – and for a moment, I just stared at them.

Until I saw Baylie.

She came to a stop a few yards away, her brow drawing down, and then her gaze swept the dehaians around us.

"Where's Noah?"

I couldn't answer. Zeke's arm tightened around me as a sob left my chest.

"Chloe," Baylie pressed, her voice shaking. "Where's Noah?"

"He didn't make it," Zeke answered tightly.

She stared at us.

Peter shoved past the others. Tiberion and the few remaining soldiers surrounded us immediately, stopping him. Fire crackled through Peter's skin and quickly, Maddox grabbed his father's arm, his own expression looking as though he was fighting for control. Behind them, Diane pressed a fist to her mouth like she was restraining a cry.

"*What?*" Peter demanded, his voice a growl.

"I'm sorry," Zeke managed. "He—"

"Praelex!" a dehaian shouted behind us. I looked back, seeing one of the Vetorians running from the waves.

Lightning lashed out of the ocean. It struck the man's back and sent him flying, till he crashed to the sand and didn't move again.

Kirzan rose from the water.

And hundreds of Sylphaen came after him. Like an army, they filled the surf behind their Wisdom, silent and waiting to attack at his command. The waves at their feet crackled with electricity and sparks leapt from the tide like tiny firecrackers. On the horizon, darkness spread, tumbling and rolling over itself while it rushed toward land.

"Did you think you would escape us that easily?" Kirzan called to me.

I couldn't do anything but stare. Men raced past me from the yard, their skin cracking open with fissures of fire while they ran.

Kirzan glanced over. Water spouted from the surf and slammed into them. Like a fist, it pounded the men to the ground. They screamed when electricity followed, surging through their bodies.

Returning his gaze to me, Kirzan smiled. "We are free. We have your power. And now the impure must die."

I trembled.

His attention turned to the others. "We are the Sylphaen. We are your masters. Bow down to us, obey us, and we will be merciful. Resist…"

The smile grew crueler. He raised his arms, gesturing to his people and the nightmare storm racing toward us.

I pushed away from Zeke.

"Chloe," he hissed.

I didn't take my eyes from Kirzan. The murderer. The leader of murderers. They were responsible for so much. *He* was responsible.

And now he had the Beast.

The Beast that'd killed Noah.

Thunder rumbled as the storm raced closer.

"You *bastard!*" I cried.

My feet hit the surf. Lightning raced through me and the tide came with it.

The waves slammed into him, and another Sylphaen caught him when he staggered. Kirzan shoved the man aside, magic crackling around him.

Zeke grabbed me, yanking me out of the way as a fist of water pummeled the ground where I'd been standing.

I struck back at Kirzan and the Sylphaen, sending them stumbling.

Zeke gasped. I looked over.

The water spun at his feet. Electricity crawled over his skin everywhere the waves touched it.

"The cave," I breathed. "When they…"

Zeke's gaze slid to the Sylphaen. "Yeah."

The tide swept away from him. Waves rose around the Sylphaen to take the attack, and water erupted into the air.

Zeke looked to the dehaians still on the shore. "Tiberion,

get my sister and the humans out of here! The rest of you —
attack!"

The dehaians charged.

Lightning lashed up from the water around the Sylphaen,
cutting down Vetorians and Lycerans alike. The soldiers didn't
stop. Racing past their fallen comrades, they swung out at the
Sylphaen and screams followed when their spikes met flesh.

Inhuman roars rose behind me. Greliarans tore past, rushing
toward the Sylphaen and ignoring the others who fell to the
magical attack. Snarling, they lunged through the waves and
lightning, and hefted the Sylphaen up from the water into the
air.

Their muscles strained and their captives howled.

My gorge rose. I turned my gaze away.

And found Kirzan looking right at me.

He smiled.

Rage flooded me. I ran at him through the waves.

Water leapt up to attack me. Magic surged through my body
and flung more waves into the air, sheltering me from the
assault. Spikes rushed from my arms and electricity joined them,
crackling from my skin.

Kirzan lunged at me and I spun, swinging out at him while
his spikes cut through the space where I'd been. I caught his
side and he cried out, staggering.

And then Zeke was there. His spikes tore across Kirzan's leg,
making him stumble. Turning fast, Zeke brought up his other
arm.

His spikes rammed into Kirzan's chest.

A choked sound left Kirzan. His eyes widened, confusion and mad disbelief mixing in his gaze.

"For Nyciena, you son of a bitch," Zeke growled.

He shoved Kirzan back. The man tumbled to the ground.

Blood swirled in the water. The tide rushed away from us.

Kirzan's gaze locked on me. "Abomination…" He choked again, blood frothing at his lips. "Kill me… you still die."

His mouth twisted into a smile. His gaze went beyond us to the sky.

Cold wind swept around me. Lightning flashed over the ocean and then thunder growled, shaking the ground.

I looked up.

Black clouds rolled over us. Lightning in surreal shades of red and purple flared inside the storm while the darkness spread past the forest behind me. The wind whipped against the waves, throwing them at the shore.

I could feel the anger coming off of it, dark and deadly.

And there wasn't anywhere to go. Anywhere to run this time.

Zeke's arm slipped around me. I looked to him.

"I love you," he said, his blue eyes meeting mine. "No matter what happens, know that."

Air pressed from my chest. "I love you too."

A smile spread over his face, relief and wonder in the expression.

I smiled as well. My gaze returned to the storm while my hand reached out and his other hand did the same. Our fingers spread over the waves. Magic coursed through our skin.

The storm rushed down at us.

I screamed and the ocean exploded around me. Water vaulted into the air, racing at the darkness.

And the clouds parted, becoming a thousand tentacles of shadow that sped past the water.

Past me.

I spun as the darkness snaked around us to strike the Sylphaen, sending them screaming into the sky. Wind followed, whipping the air into a howling blur of grit and blasting the waves into a frenzy. The water surged under the onslaught and rose up like hands to snag the Sylphaen from midair and rip them down into the depths.

But none of it hit me. Nothing touched me.

"Never hurt you."

My heart climbed my throat at the sound. The voice on the wind, so familiar to me.

"Noah?"

The wind stilled. I looked around in shock. The Sylphaen were gone. A haze of water and sand still hung in the air and in it, I could see the dehaians and the greliarans staring, dumbstruck while the cords of black cloud spread out, evaporating into nothing.

Except for one.

My breath caught as he walked out of the ocean, lightning crackling inside the shadows of his form. He was darkness and at his back, ghosts of the storm poured down into him from the sky.

But I could see his face. His eyes as he walked toward me, and the way he didn't once look away.

"Chloe," he said.

It was like the wind, his voice. And yet him at the same time.

He stopped before me, and for a moment all I could do was stare. "Noah," I whispered.

"How?" Zeke asked.

Noah's brow shrugged, the motion a flicker among the shadows. "We're weapons. Made to absorb the power from what we kill. And now…" Lightning twisted through him. "Now we have an understanding."

"But…" I started.

"It wants to try this. To be free, to change, and be more alive through me. The Beast and…" A rueful chuckle left him. "The other beast." He smiled, though sadness filled the expression. "It's alright, Chloe. I've known how to control what I am… was… for a long time."

I reached out. He pulled away.

"It's not without cost, though," he finished.

My brow drew down.

"Noah!"

I looked back. Baylie ran toward us from the forest. Diane raced after her, while farther along the shoreline, Peter and Maddox were walking toward us, their eyes locked on Noah.

Zeke caught Baylie, stopping her as she rushed toward her stepbrother.

"Noah?" she asked. "How—"

"What is this?" Peter demanded. "What—"

"I'm sorry," Noah said.

Peter stared at him. "But... what *is* this?" he tried again, the words choked.

"A change," Noah said, and I could hear the pain in his voice. "That's all."

"Noah..." Diane started.

He shook his head. "I can't stay. This... it's difficult. But before I go, I have one request." He paused, looking to me. "Help us."

My confusion returned.

"Chloe, your abilities. It... *we* need that. We're only able to be like this because of the old magic of the dehaians, and the way they used to move between land and water. It's better now—" He glanced to Zeke. "—but it's not enough. It has to be everyone. Dehaians, landwalkers, all of them. And it's possible. It's like what the Sylphaen did, taking what you are, giving it to themselves. They must have worked forever to figure out how to do that, and when we – the Beast – felt that... We think we can do it too, only we can make it go farther... if you'll help."

I stared at him. "How?"

He stretched out his hand. "Trust me."

I reached for him. My fingers wrapped around his.

Cold spread through me, like the first bite of a coming thunderstorm on the wind. Cords of shadow grew from his grasp, twisting up my arm and over my body. Mist rose with them, obscuring everything and everyone around me.

"Chloe," I heard Noah whisper, his voice seeming to come from everywhere and nowhere at once. "There's one other thing I want you to know."

"What?"

"I'm not sorry. For what happened, for… for how this went. I'd do it again. Everything that's happened, I'd do it again in a heartbeat." A breeze touched my face, like a hand caressing my cheek. "Be the guy who fell in love with a mermaid."

My eyes stung with tears.

"Ready?" he asked softly.

I nodded.

Numbness rushed through me and the energy drained from my body, taking the magic with it. My head fell back and the cords tightened around me, holding me while my muscles gave out. In my ears, my heartbeat throbbed, growing weaker as everything in me seemed to pour out into the sky.

Where it expanded. Changed. Rolled out over the horizon on all sides.

My mouth curved in a smile. I could feel it; the world and the magic in it, changing. A strange discordance was fading, like an instrument finally being tuned back to the right key.

It was beautiful.

The sensation faded. My awareness rushed back into my body as my energy returned.

Noah let me go.

I fell to my knees and Zeke grabbed me.

"I'm alright," I whispered. "I'm…"

Drawing an unsteady breath, I pushed away from the ground. Zeke helped me to my feet and kept his arm around me.

I looked at Noah.

"Thank you," he said.

"Is it enough?" I asked.

He nodded.

I hesitated. "And what now?"

He looked away, as if he could see something in the waves. "They'll be different. The dehaians. Landwalkers as well. They won't be like you." He returned his gaze to me and Zeke. "Like both of you now. They won't have that power over the water… but they'll be able to go inland now, just like the landwalkers will be able to come here. And as for the rest of it…"

Noah paused. "We were changed by what happened that day. The Beast and Joseph's magic hitting us all. It wasn't our imagination, but it also wasn't quite what we thought. The Beast is empathic. And that blast, it connected us. If you try, you'll pick up on that connection just like I was able to. It confused the Beast before. It didn't know what that was, didn't know what'd happened, and thought the whole thing was a trick. But that connection is in you." He glanced to Baylie. "You too. And now that I know what that is, it's okay. I'll try not to go too far, so that if you need me, I'll know. I'll find you."

He gave me a small smile and then he looked to Zeke. "You

were there for her then," he continued, his voice tight. "Be there for her now. For… for all of it." His tone grew harder. "And don't you *ever* hurt her."

Zeke drew me closer. "I won't."

Noah nodded. His gaze moved across us all.

"It's not goodbye," he told us. "Not really. Not like it could be." He paused, his smile returning. "It's just another change."

Storm clouds swirled through him. "Be seeing you," he promised quietly.

The darkness inside him scattered. Became a shadow. Became nothing.

And the trail of clouds behind him faded into the clearing blue of the sky.

I stared up at it. I could feel him there, in the morning sunlight. It was like when I'd felt the Beast above me in the caves, or on the shore by Joseph's home.

But it was Noah.

And he was leaving.

A ragged breath escaped me as his presence drifted toward the horizon.

Zeke pulled me to him as I closed my eyes and cried.

EPILOGUE

CHLOE

Two Months Later

It's strange how sometimes, a day can feel like it lasts for your entire life, and then others, you open your eyes to find that months have gone by.

And you don't know what happened to the time.

We didn't stay long on the beach that day. The greliarans left almost immediately, seeming too frightened of the storm that had just vanished to try killing any of the dehaians still standing around. The Vetorians and the Lycerans went into the water briefly, checking, but they couldn't find any sign of the Sylphaen. We knew it was possible the cult had fled the destruction and were still out there somewhere, but no one seemed quite able to make themselves believe the story.

Not after what we'd seen.

Mom and Dad waited for me, staying to the back of the crowd till finally I made my way over to them with Zeke at my side. They didn't yell, didn't reprimand me, or really say much of anything at all. They just put their arms around me, holding me tight while Dad trembled and Mom's tearstained cheek pressed against my forehead.

And they told me they were sorry.

Three little words, so small after a lifetime of hurt. And yet, standing there, it felt like they were a start, even if I didn't know what to say in response.

And I still don't.

I've heard the Delaneys never held a funeral or anything permanent like that. If anyone asks, they simply tell them that Noah is travelling, and they aren't sure when he'll be home.

Which seems fitting. It's mostly true.

Baylie went with them when they drove away that morning, and after that she disappeared for a time, returning to Reidsburg with Maddox only long enough to tell his mother what happened and then going to stay with her cousins in Michigan. I think she needed distance from all this. She came back to Santa Lucina about a week ago, though, and I've met her on Mariposa Beach a few times. She's going to be here a little while longer, at least till she heads back to Kansas for her senior year.

I'm still not sure whether I should join her.

Mom and Dad are already back in Reidsburg, and they took Chief Reynolds with them. They say he's pretty quiet these days, though he asks about us from time to time. For their part, I don't know if they intend to remain there – the ocean still seems to terrify them, and Dad has his agricultural science job – but I haven't been able to bring myself to go to Kansas in the meantime.

It just doesn't feel like my life anymore.

Ellie and the landwalkers stayed near the ocean longer than any of us, dipping their feet in the water and then walking out into the waves when nothing hurt. They didn't change like us, though Baylie tells me Ellie and Aaron have a plan to see if her grandfather's research can help them find a way to make that happen. Following her run-in with Wyatt, though, Ellie was promoted to provisional elder status – the youngest person ever to attain that role – and even if she's still working with Olivia in Colorado for now, I hear they're all planning to move to the coast soon.

It took nearly a month for Wyatt to turn up after what Ellie did to him. Through the elders' network, searchers eventually found him huddled in a storm drain. It took half a dozen EMTs to get him out, and several hours to assure him no landwalkers were anywhere close, but finally he started talking. He admitted to killing his father. He admitted to trying to kill us all too. The trial that followed was barely a formality. He's been confined to a psychiatric hospital, in solitary at his own request, and last I heard he wakes up most nights screaming from nightmares of curly-haired dolls.

For Niall, there wasn't much to be done. His crimes were so extensive that Zeke's sentence relegating him to house arrest on the northern border was viewed as far too merciful by many. But Niall didn't protest when the judgment was handed down and his titles were taken away. He barely even spoke a word.

Ina said later that something inside him seemed shattered. Like, of both the brother they'd known and the one that'd torn their country apart, almost nothing was left at all.

We were only glad the same couldn't be said of Nyciena.

It was terrible, going back, even if the destruction wasn't as bad as Zeke told me he'd feared. Whole city blocks had crumbled, leaving people trapped in the wreckage, and what remained of the palace was hard to recognize. Casualties were few, however, and most people agreed that the Beast seemed to have targeted the king, and left the other citizens alive even while it swept through the city.

Ina didn't stay long in Nyciena after we got back, though. Once she'd made sure that we and all of her friends in the city would be alright, she left for Teariad where her boyfriend, Lord Egan, was waiting. She's been there ever since, keeping in touch via relay connections and gradually starting to seem happier than either Zeke or I have seen her look in a while.

Kreyus and the Vetorians returned to the Prijoran Zone, though their envoys come to the capital often. He and Zeke are negotiating an end to the border raids and mercenary attacks on Yvaria, and matters between the two territories seem cautiously to be looking up. With his connections, Jirral has helped, and it didn't take long for Zeke to make his grandfather the official representative of Yvaria in the discussions. The old man lives at the palace now and most of the guards and courtiers are wary of him, given how they treated him for so long.

I think he finds it amusing.

We never really discussed where I'd go, that day on the beach. Zeke stayed with me and I stayed with him, and when the time came to leave, we walked back into the water together. He offered me a room in the palace, which I took for a while, though gradually his apartment has been becoming my own. He never pushes, never asks for anything. He simply holds me, telling me he loves me and that he'll be here for as long as it takes for the wounds from the summer to heal.

And I know I love him too.

Noah's still out there somewhere. I can feel him sometimes, in the distance, drifting by. I try to be strong in those moments, to smile and not cry, even if it's so hard. I've found comfort with Zeke, and peace after everything we've been through. I don't want to feel guilty for my happiness, for the way I feel when Zeke's arms are around me and for how, eventually, I know things between us will become closer still. I just want everything to be okay.

But I loved Noah. I think I still do. He and Zeke are two of the best people I've ever known. And in the moments when I feel Noah pass by, I can't help but be filled with gratitude for the guy who gave everything to save me. The guy who made my happiness with Zeke possible.

I only hope that someday he'll find happiness too.

Noah's story will continue.

Join my New Release Mailing List at skyemalone.com/mailinglist
to keep up with my newest books!

Loved the book?

Awesome! Would you like to leave a review? Visit Goodreads or
any other book-related site and tell people about it!

Other titles

The Touch Me series
The Awakened Fate series
The Children and the Blood trilogy (published under the name
Megan Joel Peterson)

About the author

Skye Malone is a fantasy and paranormal romance author, which
means she spends most of her time not-quite-convinced that the
magical things she imagines couldn't actually exist.

A Midwestern girl who migrated to the Pacific Northwest, she
hopes to someday travel the world – though in the meantime she'll
take any story that whisks her off to a place where the fantastic lives
inside the everyday. She loves strong and passionate characters,
complex villains, and satisfying endings that stay with you long
after the book is done. An inveterate writer, she can't go a day
without getting her hands on a keyboard, and can usually be found
typing away while she listens to all the adventures
unfolding in her head.

Connect with me

Website: www.skyemalone.com
Twitter: twitter.com/Skye_Malone
Facebook: facebook.com/authorskyemalone

www.ingramcontent.com/pod-product-compliance
Lightning Source LLC
Chambersburg PA
CBHW031326210726
48287CB00005B/1717